Painted Lady

Also by Harriet Crawley

A Degree of Defiance
The Goddaughter
The Lovers and the Loved

Harriet Crawley

Painted Lady

M

MACMILLAN

LONDON

First published 1994 by Macmillan London Ltd

a division of Pan Macmillan Publishers Limited
Cavaye Place London SW10 9PG
and Basingstoke

Associated companies throughout the world

ISBN 0-333-59581-5

1 3 5 7 9 8 6 4 2

A CIP catalogue record for this book is available from
the British Library

Typeset by CentraCet Limited, Cambridge
Printed by Mackays of Chatham PLC, Chatham, Kent

For Aunt Mary, with love and admiration

ACKNOWLEDGEMENTS

I have been helped by many friends in writing this book but none more so than David Cotton who so cheerfully plundered his rich past, drawing on a detailed knowledge of several professions to guide me in the plotting and the execution of this novel. My debt to him is incalculable. Phillip Saunders, managing director of Trace has been lavish with his time and help; so has James Emson of The Art Loss Register, and Colin Reeves, security advisor to Christie's. I spent many profitable hours with police officers dedicated to the recovery of stolen art, and I am particularly grateful to Detective Sergeant Richard Ellis of New Scotland Yard, Detective Constable Simon Muggleton of Sussex, and Detective Constable James Hill of Thames Valley. I am grateful to Fred Warner, Nicholas Pearson, Alan Bradford, Leslie Du Cane, Sebastian Taylor, Esme Boughey, John Cass, and Joanna Birt, who excelled herself in a blitz of proof-reading and double checking. All remaining errors are, of course, my own and bear no reflection on the expertise of those whom I consulted.

No one has been more encouraging, or more challenging than my editor Jane Wood; this book is her child as well as mine.

Chapter 1

Harry Wardington straightened his bow tie, put a comb through his dishevelled blond hair and, as he looked at himself in the mirror, allowed himself one delicious moment of vanity. He had poetic good looks and he knew it. He glanced at his watch: a quarter to six. The auction started at seven thirty. His picture was lot 8 and he was going to enjoy himself, bidding eleven million pounds for a Renoir.

The girl, Minako Setsu, was on his mind, the porcelain doll with the razor-sharp mind and a smile so soft that he wanted to take her to bed. He wanted very much to take her to bed, but it wasn't the right move at this stage of the game.

Harry took a bottle of Stolichnaya vodka from his deep-freeze, poured himself a short drink, and reflected on what had been an extraordinary twelve hours.

His day had begun with the usual angry mail addressed to 'Harry Wardington Fine Arts'; a red reminder from British Telecom to pay his bill or else; a terse letter from the bank advising him that his overdraft limit had been reached, and could not, repeat *not* be extended. It was death by a thousand cuts in this blasted recession. But at least he had low overheads: no gallery, no secretary, just a second-floor flat in Vigo Street where he lived and worked.

One day he'd strike it rich, have his own flag, his own building. Meanwhile, business was so slack he'd sent his paintings out on consignment, anything to shift them in a stagnant market. The only picture in his office, standing in solitary splendour on an easel, was not for sale.

Harry slipped a hand into his pocket and felt the reassuring crackle of new fifty-pound notes. At least the gambling was going well. At 4 a.m. that morning he was poised to win or lose a fortune at backgammon. Lady luck was on his side and by 4.30 a.m. he was £5000 richer. His old pal Archie Gibbs had stayed with him to the bitter end and by 5 a.m. they had polished off a bottle of Krug by way of celebration.

The telephone rang. It was Sebastian Guthrie, Harry's mole at Shackleton's, the new auction house which had sent shivers down the spine of the art establishment. This bizarre conglomerate was backed by Bavarians and Chinese with an unlimited supply of German marks and Hong Kong dollars. To the alarm of Christie's, Sotheby's, Phillips and Bonham's, the graph on their profit sheet was going straight up.

'Harry, I've got a pigeon for you,' Sebastian said. 'A Japanese girl, Minako Setsu. Very pretty. She's been viewing our Impressionist sale for her boss – won't say who he is but he must be big because this girl talks megabucks. She wants to check out the art market and I've told her you're the answer to all her prayers, best dealer in town, all that crap. So make a good impression, and remember our arrangement. I get ten per cent of anything you sell.'

'All this dealing on the side is strictly *verboten*, Sebs.'

'What do you expect me to live on? The lousy salary they pay me?'

Harry just had time to straighten his desk, wash the coffee cups and throw out the dead irises when the doorbell rang and he found himself face to face with a young woman barely five feet tall with huge dark eyes and the sleekest black hair he had ever seen. She bowed and handed over an engraved visiting card.

'Miss Setsu, please come in,' Harry said.

'Most gracious.'

The voice was almost a whisper and the hand she held out was so small and light Harry could hardly feel it.

'Have a seat,' he said.

'Most kind, thank you.' Minako looked at him with a solemnity that was impenetrable. She was immaculate, with tiny wrists, delicate hands, long red fingernails and very expensive French clothes.

'I am assistant to a Japanese businessman who buys Impressionists, Post-Impressionists and Expressionists. Also Marie Laurencin. You know Marie Laurencin?'

'Yes, yes, I do,' Harry said, thinking how much he loathed her pallid, sugary pictures. The Japanese girl surveyed the empty walls and her eye lit on the easel.

'You show only one painting at a time. That is very Japanese. Please, what is this picture?'

'A marriage portrait by a Flemish painter called Mabuse. His real name was Jan Gossaert and he painted this around 1510. I'm sorry to say it's not for sale. It's a family picture.'

'I have seen very few Flemish paintings,' the girl said hesitantly, 'but in Japan such a picture would cause great offence.'

'Offence? It's the most innocent picture I've ever seen!'

'Yes, but the lady is smiling. In Japan the correct way to paint a portrait is without expression.'

'What, just a blank face?'

'A blank face. Anything else would be impolite. The human being has so many moods, we believe it is not right to paint just one expression. Better to leave the face empty; the onlooker can fill it with whatever mood he wishes; happy, sad, whatever.'

She turned away from the painting and faced Harry, appealing to him apologetically, 'So you see it is very hard for me to judge Western representative art.'

'Impossible.'

3

'No, Mr Wardington, not impossible. I am learning. It is my wish to understand, and my employer is allowing me time to study and to look. He is interested in Old Masters. He says they are undervalued.'

'He's right.'

'You have other paintings?'

'I do, but not here. But don't worry, Miss Setsu, I can find you pictures that will make your boss very happy.'

Like what? he asked himself, thinking of his own stock; the Arcimboldo? Hardly. The Wootton of Lord Derby's favourite thoroughbred? Never. The Samuel Palmer of Rome? No way. As he racked his brains, Minako Setsu stared at her hands and in her softest voice said, 'Sebastian Guthrie at Shackleton's has told me that your father, Sir William Wardington, is a very famous man. He is related to Her Majesty the Queen?'

'Miss Setsu, you're getting carried away. He's not related to the Queen, he works for her. He's Director of the Royal Collection.'

'Ah, so,' she said, 'a very important position, I think.'

'It sounds good but as far as I can see it's rather dreary, nothing but exhibitions and cataloguing. Pa never sets foot in a saleroom. You see, the Queen isn't a big buyer of paintings. Horses are more her line.'

'But your Queen has so many wonderful paintings . . .' Minako stopped. Her black eyes were anxious. She seemed to be hesitating.

Harry leant forward and said, 'Is there anything I can do for you, Miss Setsu?'

'My employer has asked me to bid in the Shackleton sale today. He wants to buy lot number eight.'

Harry picked up the Shackleton catalogue and leafed through, stopping at the illustration of a girl in a blue velvet dress with white-gold hair holding a wooden hoop.

'Miss Setsu, lot eight is a Renoir estimated at between eight to ten million pounds.'

'I am instructed to go up to eleven million.'

'So what's your problem?'

'I have never bid at an auction. I am frightened that I will make a terrible mistake.'

'I'll come with you and hold your hand, if that's what you want.'

'I want you to do the bidding, Mr Wardington, if you please.'

Harry took a deep breath, plunged his hands into his pockets and paced the room. The girl watched him with pleading eyes.

'Who is your employer?'

'Seiji Hakomoto.'

The name meant nothing to Harry.

'Surely Mr Hakomoto has a London dealer who bids for him?'

The Japanese girl lowered her eyes. 'I am not permitted to discuss Mr Hakomoto's affairs.'

'All right, but I shall need to talk to Mr Hakomoto on the telephone, to receive his instructions personally.'

'We can ring him now, with your permission. He is in Geneva.'

'How good is his English?' Harry asked.

'He studied at the London School of Economics.'

Minako dialled a Geneva number. The flow of Japanese lasted for several minutes, punctuated every few seconds by 'Hai'. At last she handed over the receiver.

'Good morning, Mr Wardington.'

'Mr Hakomoto, Miss Setsu tells me that you want to bid for the Renoir, lot eight, *Portrait of a girl with a hoop* in the sale at Shackleton's tonight. Is that correct?'

'Quite correct.'

'And Miss Setsu has asked if I would bid on your behalf up to a limit of eleven million pounds. You realize there will be a ten per cent buyer's premium on top of that?'

'I know all about the buyer's premium, Mr Wardington.'

The Japanese spoke impeccable English, Harry conceded.

'The eleven million ceiling. Is it final, or can I go higher? Within reason, of course.'

'It's final.'

'And if we are successful, do you wish to remain anonymous?'

'Definitely. I'm a very private man. I dislike all publicity.'

'You place great trust in me, Mr Hakomoto, considering we haven't met.'

'Miss Setsu has my complete confidence.'

'I'll need an official letter requesting me to bid on your behalf. And bank references. Can you fax these to me at once? My fax number is 071-439 8123.'

'My secretary will do it immediately.'

Harry was hesitating. Should he ask about his commission? If ever he needed to earn a fee it was on a sale like this, but his instinct told him to say nothing. Who needs to talk about money? You're Harry Wardington, son of a baronet.

'Thank you, Mr Hakomoto. I think that's everything.'

'There is the small matter of your commission.'

Harry managed just the right tone of polished diffidence: 'What do you suggest?'

'If we get the painting, a hundred thousand pounds. If we don't, nothing.'

Harry drew a sharp breath. 'I accept.'

'Thank you, Mr Wardington. I am most grateful for your assistance. Goodbye.'

Harry found himself staring at the Japanese girl. 'Why don't I give you lunch?'

Minako shook her head and lowered her eyes.

'Well,' Harry said, reverting to his professional voice, 'meet me in the saleroom at Shackleton's at a quarter to seven. And after the auction I'll take you to dinner.'

'You are most kind but I think —'

'Miss Setsu, you've got to have dinner with me tonight. It's part of the deal.'

'Of course,' she murmured, 'most honoured.'

Chapter 2

Archie Gibbs never thought he would miss Northern Ireland but certain things stuck in his mind: the smell of heather in the Sperrin Mountains; wind tasting of salt as he stood by the cliffs on the Antrim coast; violent shafts of light bursting through dark skies before they ripped across the glens. He tried to forget the dead bodies, or what was left of them. It was the poetic things that stayed with him.

And where is the poetry now? he asked himself as he sat in his cramped office in High Holborn looking through a window smeared with city grime on to the polluting, honking, shuddering traffic. The clampers were already at it, descending like locusts on the helpless cars. Archie looked at his watch: soon it would be time to feed the meter. He felt in his pocket for pound coins, realized he had none and anger rose in his throat. Was his life reduced to this? Fussing and fretting over pound coins?

Cool it, he told himself; these are teething pains. You haven't been in business a year. The brass plaque on the door downstairs is shiny new, 'Archie Gibbs, Fine Art Security Consultant'. Anyway, what did you expect? Civvy street's a jungle, you knew that before you left the army. And business has been good, until now.

Archie glanced round the dingy office with its threadbare carpet, broken armchairs and cheap wooden desks where, in glorious contrast, stood a row of sleek new computers; no shortage of high-tech equipment here. Archie cursed his apocalyptic sense of timing. He'd spent every last penny of seed capital to buy the latest office gear just in time to see the art market collapse and security jobs evaporate. There was no market in second-hand computer hardware, he thought bitterly, glancing at the colour laser printer, the pocket-size portable telephone, and the desktop PC with its 100MHz P5 processor and 17-inch SVGA monitor on which was running the latest version of Windows NT. What more could a man want? With his electronic mail and on-line fax, Archie was plugged into the world. The screen should be alive with messages; instead it was blank.

Branch out, look for new markets, was that the answer? Casually he flicked through a brochure which had arrived that morning: 'Pickford International, Commercial Investigators and Security Consultants. Specialists in fraud, surveillance, asset recovery, security, tracing.*' What the hell was tracing? Archie wondered, and he read the footnote: 'Everything from elusive debtors to tracking down natural parents.' God almighty, he muttered to himself.

He lit a Dunhill International and took a long, satisfying drag. Perhaps, after all, he should have stayed in the priesthood of the army, in the brotherhood of the Green Jackets, where a pension beckons at fifty-five. Instead he had taken the offer of 'seed capital' with no strings attached from Harold Barton, his old tutor and now President of Magdalen College, Oxford, and started his own business. Sir Harold was very rich and very trusting; he'd told Archie to come back in five years and report. After five years of spiralling downwards he would not be a pretty sight, thought Archie, blowing a perfect smoke ring.

Suddenly, through the window smeared with rivulets of dusty rain, he saw a traffic warden standing beside his car. He rushed down the stairs into the street only to find he was too late; stuffed under the windscreen wiper was a parking ticket. The traffic warden, a pretty woman – which annoyed him even more – had moved on to her next victim, a Porsche. Archie marched up to her. 'How much over was I?' he asked belligerently. 'Go on, tell me!'

'Two minutes,' she said, without looking up from her black book. He stood for a moment on the pavement watching a sheet of newspaper eddy in the sudden gust of wind; light pinpricks of rain fell on his face. It was early September and the end of a long, wet summer. The smell of sausage and chips drifted from some cheap café; a bus belched a murky cloud of carbon monoxide. A man knocked into him, snarled angrily and stumbled on without apology.

He was in enemy territory, he could feel it. The city was against him, breathing hate. Would he make it? He was thirty-five, jack-of-all-trades and master of none except the art of survival. He found himself staring into a discount travel agency with posters of Paris in the window and he thought of Madeleine. Do yourself a favour, Gibbs, forget about her. It's too difficult, too complicated.

Slowly he walked up the five flights of stairs, pushed open the door of his office and slumped into the sagging armchair. He noticed the light flashing on his answering machine and pressed the play-back button.

'This is Margaret Bourne, secretary to Sir William Wardington, Director of the Royal Collection. Sir William would be most grateful if Mr Gibbs could meet him in the Print Room at Windsor Castle at three o'clock this afternoon. Perhaps he could ring me on 0753 223456. Sir William apologizes for the short notice and hopes very much that Mr Gibbs can make it.'

Archie punched the air. 'You bet I can make it.'

Chapter 3

In the Print Room at Windsor Castle, Sir William Wardington was drumming his fingers on the green baize table which filled the centre of the room. He was surrounded by the finest Old Master drawings collection in the world, housed in gleaming mahogany bookcases which lined the walls. Through the glass fronts he could see the custom-made boxes neatly piled and meticulously labelled: Leonardo, Michelangelo, Raphael.

Gibbs was late. Sir William went over to the mullioned window, threw it open and inhaled the damp September air; it had been a day of relentless drizzle. Below, a steady stream of tourists trod the well-worn path from St George's Chapel past the Keep towards the State Apartments. They were still coming in their droves to gape at the damage from the fire, to plague the weary police with questions, to press against the barriers for a closer look at the massive web of scaffolding and acres of plastic sheeting which completely covered the north-east wing.

Thank God they hadn't lost more paintings in the fire, Sir William thought; only an indifferent portrait of George III by Sir William Beechey. And thank God the fire hadn't spread to the Print Room! He could picture it all too clearly, flames devouring the Old Master drawings. It would have been a national disaster and a tragic end to his career, which, if he said so himself, had been hugely successful. At heart he was a scholar steeped in the history and appreciation of art, and his books on Rubens and the Carracci brothers were classics, but after the death of his wife of thirty years he had turned his hand to administration, taken the Royal Collection by the throat and introduced optical computers. For this triumph of modernization he'd been awarded the GCVO, the Queen's own decoration given to those who render signal and personal service to the Monarch.

Soon it would be time for him to retire but first he must put his mind at rest. Was he worrying unnecessarily? He glanced once again through the mullioned window and caught sight of the guardsman on sentry duty, marching like a toy soldier in front of the entrance to the West Gate.

Poor chap, Archie thought, as he stood outside St George's Chapel watching the guardsman marching up and down his beat, his SA rifle held rigidly at the slope. It reminded Archie of his own days on the drill square at Sandhurst, hours of square bashing in the rain. The soldier did a polished about-turn, his hob-nailed boots crashing on the cobbles. A crowd of Japanese were giggling, ogling, poking cameras in his face, but he took no notice. Staring through the fringe of fur on his bearskin the soldier marched on regardless.

Archie hurried up the hill past the Keep, merging for a moment into the stream of tourists huddled beneath black umbrellas before he turned sharp left and made for a medieval portico discreetly marked 'Side Door'. He gave his name to the policeman on duty and moments later a buxom woman in her fifties appeared, blue-eyed and smiling, and introduced herself as Margaret Bourne. Archie followed her up the spiral staircase, his footsteps echoing on the fourteenth-century stone, and wondered what on earth William Wardington could want with him after all these years.

They found the Director of the Royal Collection in the Print

Room hunched over the green baize table, examining a drawing, his hands sheathed in white gauze gloves.

'Dear boy, how good of you to come at such short notice. Have a look at this: Annibale Carracci. You see the pencil strokes? Sharp, angled, tick, tack and there we are – the agony of Christ on the cross. It's so modern it could be Cezanne.'

A fine web of laughter lines fanned out from Sir William's small bright eyes. He was an older, greyer man, Archie decided, but otherwise this was the same William Wardington, the courteous, erudite father of his friend Harry, a fellow undergraduate at Magdalen. Archie had often been to stay at the Wardington home near Burford in the Cotswolds, where Sir William had introduced him to good wine and to the finer points of Renaissance art. Archie was persuaded to take History of Art as his special subject. He got an Alpha; more important, he learnt to look at pictures.

'Let me see,' Sir William said, putting the Carracci to one side, 'it must be at least five years since we last met.'

'Nearer ten, Sir William.'

'Ten years! Is it really? I must say you don't look a day older. Green Jackets kept you on your toes, did they? Tell me, why did you leave? Money? Boredom?'

'A bit of both, I suppose. The cold war is over, the Soviet Union no longer exists. There's only Northern Ireland, the Gulf and former Yugoslavia, not enough to keep me interested, so I decided to take the gratuity and run.'

'I wish Harry had gone into the army instead of frittering away ten years of his life with all that hippy nonsense.'

'These days he's a respectable art dealer, at least that's what he tells me.'

'He doesn't know much but he has a good eye,' Sir William said with a slow, clever smile, 'and he's cunning as a fox when it comes to getting money out of his old father. The boy's always broke because he gambles. I've told him a thousand times, backgammon and business don't mix. But I must get to the point. I've been checking up on you, Archie. They all say you're very thorough.'

'Who is "they"?'

'The army, the *friends*, the police, Lloyds, and of course my good friend Harold Barton, who I understand has backed you in your security business. Don't worry, he has every confidence you will succeed. So have I. What matters to me is your experience. You're positively vetted and highly trained in the close protection of prominent people and their belongings. You're tactful and discreet, essential qualities for the work I have in mind.'

'Which is – ?'

'Let's talk about it next door. I'm afraid I don't have an office at Windsor, so I am forced to make do with a cubby-hole. Margaret will bring us tea.'

In a cramped room just big enough for a desk and three chairs, Sir William stood by the lattice window looking out over the Great Park with its twisted, gnarled oaks, some of them a thousand years old and recorded in William the Conqueror's 'Domesday Book'.

'Next year I shall retire,' he said. 'But before I leave I am planning a most original exhibition, my swansong.' He turned to face Archie, his eyes glowing. 'The Louvre is putting on one of its extravaganzas. It's all part of this European spirit they want to promote. The theme of the exhibition is "The Europe of Louis XIII". Everyone's taking part, lending pictures, that sort of thing. Well, about six months ago they sent me a draft catalogue and it was transparently clear that this exhibition isn't about Europe at all, it's about France! France in all its glory, fount of all wisdom, cradle of civilization. The British hardly get a look in.'

14

'That sounds fairly typical,' Archie murmured.

'Yes, but I didn't see why we should take this lying down so I discussed the whole matter with the Queen's Private Secretary and the Foreign Office and we decided that *of course* we must show willing, and all of that, but there was nothing to stop us blowing our trumpet by putting on a modest little exhibition of our own at the British Embassy. The theme of *our* exhibition will be King Charles I and his court. It all fits together very nicely. After all, Charles I was the brother-in-law of Louis XIII, married to his sister Henrietta Maria, and Charles was, as you know, the most cultivated and civilized monarch in Europe with superb taste in pictures. We can put on a stunning show.'

Margaret arrived with the tea.

'As I told our Ambassador,' Sir William went on, 'it is our intention to complement the Louvre.'

'To upstage the Louvre by the sound of it.'

'I must confess the idea has crossed my mind. Fortunately, the Prime Minister sees no ulterior motive. He's keen to promote what he calls "joint ventures". And the Queen has agreed to open the exhibition. In fact, it suits her rather well. The day before she's got a horse running at Longchamp.'

Archie sipped his tea and wondered where all this was leading.

Sir William went on, 'Everything's in hand thanks to this marvellous girl, Flora Fenton, the Cataloguer and Exhibitions Clerk. She's got every sort of degree from Cambridge and the Courtauld and she's written a superb catalogue.'

'Sir William,' Archie said, controlling his impatience. 'This is all very interesting but I really don't see where I fit in.'

'I'm coming to that, but first you need to understand the background. The exhibition opens on the eleventh of October, in four weeks' time. It's travelling by road from Windsor to Paris by what is euphemistically known as the Royal Baggage Train.'

'The Royal Baggage Train? I thought that relic had been axed along with all the other army cuts.'

'Not at all. It's in constant use, but as you can imagine security is a nightmare. I have a file six inches thick on all the different stages of the operation. I'm getting too old for this amount of paperwork. I need help, Archie.'

'You'll get all the help you need from Special Branch and the Royal Protection Group.'

'I mean outside help. The Queen's Private Secretary, the Lord Chamberlain and I have discussed this at some length and in detail. We have decided to take on an outside security consultant who will co-ordinate the entire operation. Her Majesty has been informed.'

Archie smiled to himself: from his close protection days in Northern Ireland it was all coming back, the courtly jargon of the Royal Household designed to protect the Queen's private opinions and distance her from any controversy. It was a language of code. 'Her Majesty has been informed' meant she had agreed.

'The police won't like it,' Archie said.

'Given the evidence of the past few weeks, they are on fairly weak ground.' Sir William paused. A thin smile slid across his face. 'An employee walks out of Buckingham Palace with a picture under his arm. A burglar breaks into Prince Charles's private apartments at St James's Palace, rifles through his letters and walks off with family heirlooms right under the noses of the Royal Protection Group. A parachutist sails effortlessly on to the roof of Buckingham Palace in broad daylight. And it wasn't so very long ago a man got into the Queen's bedroom and sat on the end of her bed; thank God he only wanted to chat.'

'They're never going to live that one down,' Archie murmured.

'As for Special Branch, their terrorist conference was a

shambles. In spite of all the sniffer dogs and extra security, someone managed to plant a bomb inside the lectern which, had it not been discovered in the nick of time, would have blown up a cabinet minister or the Chief Commissioner. I tell you, Archie, there have been too many cock-ups. Everyone's confidence is badly shaken, especially mine.'

Sir William folded his long hands on the table and focused his blue eyes on Archie. 'I hope you don't think me some sort of crackpot, but I do worry. I can't help it. The tide's against us, don't you see? Sooner or later someone is bound to have a go.'

'A go at what?'

'At robbing the Queen. She's the ultimate challenge. Every-day one reads in the papers about yet another robbery of quite extraordinary daring. I tell you, Archie, it's only a matter of time, but I'm damned if it's going to happen under *my* director-ship. That's why I'm asking you to take this job. This is my last exhibition and I don't want anything to go wrong.'

Archie thought for a moment: it was a bit of a dead-end job. If things went right, the police would get all the glory, and if things went wrong he would be up to his neck in mire. On the other hand, he wasn't feeling too flush and there would be at least one free trip to Paris.

'I owe you one, Sir William. I'll do it.'

Sir William leaned across the table and shook Archie warmly by the hand. 'I'm delighted. I'll get on to the police straight away. I've taken the liberty of fixing up a meeting for you at the Foreign Office at nine thirty tomorrow morning, if that suits.'

The wily old bird, Archie thought; he was so sure I'd accept he's got everything lined up. 'Nine thirty tomorrow is fine.'

'Excellent. Now then, shall we go and have a look at your precious cargo?'

Chapter 4

The damp air bit into Archie's face as he walked briskly alongside Sir William, past the cannon and the ramparts. Immediately below he could see Eton College with its playing fields and Gothic chapel and the green expanse of the Home Park leading to the Great Park, fenced in by a cityscape of tower blocks and warehouses and thirty miles of London suburbs. Every few minutes the sky was torn apart by the ear-splitting whine of a jet.

'We're on the direct flight path to Heathrow,' Sir William shouted. 'And when you think, Henry VIII came to Windsor to hunt deer.'

They climbed the steps of the State Apartments, shrouded in scaffolding and plastic sheeting. Sir William nodded to a footman in the dark-blue Windsor livery, ignoring the 'No Entry' signs.

'The repairs are going to take five years,' Sir William said. 'Not all the rooms were damaged, thank God, and the restoration has been superb. You'll see.'

Archie had forgotten the magnificence of it all: walls hung in red, blue and yellow damask; chandeliers cascading like fountains from the high ceilings picked out in gold leaf; Sèvres porcelain, Ming vases and bowls, French ornamental clocks and Louis XVI furniture, Persian silk carpets, Flemish tapestries, and world-famous Old Masters.

They passed through one more splendid room after another – the King's State Bedchamber, the King's Drawing Room, the Queen's Ballroom – with Sir William delivering a commentary in his slow, lilting voice. 'The Royal Collection is scattered throughout the Royal houses. The Landseers are at Balmoral, the Victorians and moderns at Buckingham Palace, the Mantegnas at Hampton Court. At St James's Palace we've got most of the Winterhalters, at Holyrood some fine Jacobean paintings. Here at Windsor we've got the Old Master drawings and the best of the pictures. Like this one.'

Sir William crossed the Mogul silk carpet which covered the floor of the King's Dressing Room to admire the painting above the fireplace.

'This is the jewel of the Paris exhibition, the *pièce de résistance*, Van Dyck's triple portrait of Charles I.'

Archie stared at the three faces of the King, front view, three-quarters and profile. There was courage, resolution and above all doom in the fine aristocratic features, the long hair, the heavy lidded eyes.

'What can you tell me about this painting?' Sir William asked with a charming smile, but there was cool appraisal in the pale blue eyes. Archie was on trial and he knew it.

'Van Dyck was asked to paint the King in three different poses so that Bernini, who was sitting in Rome, could use it, much in the same way we would use a photograph, to make a marble bust of the King, which he did, but unfortunately the original is lost and only a copy survives.'

Sir William chuckled with satisfaction. 'Correct in every detail. So much for the painting. What about the man?'

'Charles I was the greatest of all the Royal collectors; he bought only the best. By 1635 the Royal Collection was the finest in Europe, with fifteen hundred superb paintings, five hundred drawings and several hundred Renaissance bronzes. After his exeuction in 1649 almost everything was sold at auction on the orders of Oliver Cromwell.'

'When I think of what we lost!' Sir William said, throwing

up his hands. 'Raphael's *La Perla* – now in the Prado. Leonardo's *St John* in the Louvre, Giorgione's *Judith* in the Hermitage. As for the Titians, there were nine, all scattered to the winds, including a superb portrait of Mary Queen of Scots painted in 1560 when she was only eighteen.'

'Where did that end up?'

'Who knows? It's one of the great mysteries. Unlike the other Titians, this particular painting wasn't sold by Cromwell. The last time anyone heard of it was in 1635, when it was listed as one of the works of art in Holyroodhouse. After that it disappeared. The only consolation is that we have Titian's preparatory drawing, which came to light just the other day, identified by Flora, clever girl. It's going to Paris for obvious reasons.' Sir William paused and looked at Archie with a quizzical smile.

'Sorry,' said Archie. 'Pass.'

'Mary Queen of Scots was Charles I's grandmother. She was also Queen of France, married, at the tender age of seventeen, to that weakling Francis II. The French are fascinated by her.'

On the Adam mantelpiece a Louis XV ormolu clock tinkled four.

'Dear me,' said Sir William. 'We'll have to finish this another time, I'm afraid. I've asked Flora to meet us in the Print Room.'

The wind had dropped and a shaft of sunlight burst across the flagstones of the courtyard. They were hurrying past a massive cannon, a relic from the Crimea, when suddenly Sir William stopped and stroked the smooth iron surface with his hand.

'I don't want you to think I've got robbery on the brain,' he said slowly, 'but there is something that's always puzzled me. When a great painting is stolen, something of the quality we've just seen, what do the thieves *do* with it? I mean, they can't sell it.'

'Why not?'

'But to whom?'

'To crooks who want to launder hot money, to people who don't give a toss about provenance, who buy stolen art for the perverted pleasure of owning it.'

'But if the picture was a world famous Old Master you couldn't enjoy it. You couldn't hang it on your dining-room wall.'

'Depends who you are and where you are. Criminals can be very powerful.'

'You mean drug barons in South America, that sort of thing?'

'Or bankers in Switzerland. Or commodity dealers in Japan.'

'Where *is* Flora?' Sir William said, drumming his fingers impatiently on the green baize table of the Print Room. Suddenly, the sound of a heated argument came from the reference library next door and in walked a middle-aged man and a young woman. The man looked extraordinary in a three-piece suit complete with watch-chain and a cape; his eyes were bright and malicious and he wore a Van Dyck beard. He dangled pigskin gloves from a manicured hand. Instinctively, Archie disliked him. But the girl was lovely. She had the looks of an Irish beauty, white skin peppered with freckles, green eyes and dark lashes and a mass of auburn hair tied back with a ribbon. The tight-fitting black sweater and skirt showed off one hell of a figure.

'I know it doesn't bear a signature,' the girl was saying, 'but it's in the 1710 Scottish inventory as a Honthorst.'

'Where, I ask you, is the Royal cypher or cataloguer's number on the stretcher?'

'Most likely they were stamped on a label and the label's fallen off.'

'You're being ridiculously stubborn. The picture isn't right and it will not be included in the Paris exhibition —'

'Stafford,' Sir William interrupted, 'may I introduce Archie Gibbs, our new security advisor for the Paris exhibition. Archie, this is Stafford Hardinge, Surveyor of the Queen's Pictures.'

Hardinge gave Archie the briefest nod and continued, 'Flora's great discovery is a copy and a bad one at that. I shall delete the entry from the catalogue.'

'In my view —' the girl began, the anger rising in her voice.

'In *your* view?' Hardinge hissed.

'And this is Flora Fenton,' Sir William went on in his most soothing voice. 'Cataloguer and Exhibitions Clerk.'

She stared blankly at Archie and turned to Sir William. 'I *know* it's right.'

'We need something more substantial than your intuition,' Hardinge said tartly.

'Don't forget, Stafford, she's been right before.'

Hardinge slapped a pigskin glove against the palm of his hand. 'It seems her luck has run out. As far as I'm concerned the matter is closed. Unless, of course,' he added sarcastically, 'you find a signature.'

Moments later he was gone. Sir William put an arm round Flora's shoulders. 'Don't let him get you down. Courtesy has never been Stafford's strong point.'

'The picture is right and I will prove it,' the girl said defiantly.

'Let it go,' Sir William urged. 'One Honthorst more or less doesn't really matter. Flora dear, I want you to look after Archie, show him the ropes. I've got to run. There's a dinner at the Royal Academy.'

Through murky rain-clouds a shaft of yellow sunlight filtered through the lattice windows of the Print Room. Archie sat next to Flora at the green baize table; he was close enough to smell her scent, subtle and expensive.

'Is he always like that?' Archie said. 'The Surveyor, I mean.'

'I hate him.'

'He doesn't seem crazy about you, either.'

Flora stared at Archie. 'I rubbed him up the wrong way right from the start. I did the worst thing I could have done – I proved that he was wrong.'

'That *was* tactful.'

'I'm not here to massage male egos, I'm here to advance art scholarship, which is exactly what I did.'

Flora went over to the mahogany bookcases and took a box from one of the shelves, opened it, put on her white gauze gloves and brought over an exquisite drawing of a young woman in pencil highlighted in red chalk. The face was a perfect oval, with wide-apart eyes, a soft smile and a mass of red-gold hair which fell loose around her shoulders.

'Can you guess?' Flora said.

'No idea. But I'll give her dinner any time.'

'This is Mary Queen of Scots at eighteen, drawn by Titian, the sketch for an oil painting, at least that's what I was able to prove. Hardinge was against me from the start; he'd catalogued the drawing as "school of Titian, drawing of a noblewoman, Spanish possibly French".'

'But you weren't convinced?'

'There's an aura about her. She's too beautiful, too regal. The signet ring on her right hand gave me the first real clue. If you look closely you'll see the letter "F". I had a brainwave – "F" for Francis II, King of France, first husband of Mary Queen of Scots. The Bibliothèque Nationale came up with the proof, a letter written by Francis II to his young bride saying how delighted he is with Titian's sketch of her and he hopes the artist will complete the oil painting as soon as possible. In the same letter, Francis says he's sending Mary a signet ring.

'I couldn't believe my luck. Everything fell into place. This wasn't school of Titian, it *was* Titian. It wasn't an unknown lady, it was Mary Queen of Scots, or Marie Stuart as the French called her.'

'A right and left,' Archie said.

'Yes. Sir William was delighted. But Stafford Hardinge was furious. Titian is his period and he wouldn't speak to me for weeks.'

'Wonderful hair,' Archie murmured, staring at the drawing.

'The colour of burnished gold. That's what people said. Titian's picture of her must have been ravishing. But it's lost.'

'I know. Sir William gave me the potted history.'

From the far side of the Print Room, Margaret called out, 'Flora! They've arrived at last. The proofs of the Paris catalogue. A messenger has just delivered them.'

Flora's eyes lit up. 'You must see the catalogue. I've written every entry except two. You know this is Sir William's last exhibition? I want everything to be perfect.'

Margaret brought over a large brown package. Flora tore open the paper wrapping and turned the pages eagerly, her eyes darting from one picture to another.

'Look at the colour printing, it's really very beautiful. And I chose the typeface with great care, not too small, and very clear . . .' As she leafed through the pages her voice trailed off. She snapped the catalogue shut and turned to Margaret. 'I don't believe it! My name isn't mentioned. I don't get a single credit.'

'There must be some mistake, dear,' Margaret said soothingly.

'There's no mistake. My name was here, below the introduction.' With her finger she stabbed at the place. 'Stafford Hardinge corrected the last set of proofs. He crossed me out, that's all.'

24

'You have a word with Sir William,' Margaret said, 'he'll put things right.'

Flora stared at Margaret, her face tense with anger. 'It's such a fight,' she muttered, 'every bloody step of the way.'

Margaret bit her lip. 'Will you see to the lights?' she said, and left.

Flora sat twisting her fingers in her lap, her head bowed.

Archie put a hand on her shoulder. 'Chin up. Here's my card. Ring me if you need anything. Remember, you're younger and prettier and I daresay a whole lot cleverer than Stafford Hardinge.'

Chapter 5

For a long while, Flora stood by the mullioned window staring across the Great Park to the distant lights of London, listening to the stillness which she found soothing. A rainbow spanned the evening sky and the last rays of a dying sun tinged the dark clouds gold. Suddenly she longed for her lover to take her in his arms and kiss her softly and make everything all right. Her daydream was shattered by the night-duty policeman standing beside her.

'Take my advice, Miss. Pack it in for today.'

'There's a picture I want to look at in the storeroom,' Flora said wearily.

The red-faced, kindly policeman reminded Flora of her father, John Fenton. He too was a kind man, full of laughter and energy until he had gone bust in the recession. His Birmingham trucking company was in receivership and these days he drove a mini-cab. But he wasn't bitter and he didn't complain, and he was so proud of his clever daughter who had landed such a grand job with the Royal Household.

'I won't be long.' Flora sighed. She picked up her restorer's bag, a large tapestry hold-all, and climbed the stone stairs to the picture store at the top of the West Tower. In the circular room, beneath the neon glare of strip lights, Flora pulled out the aluminium rack, which moved easily on its metal runners, and lifted out the Honthorst. It was one of those forgotten paintings in the Royal Collection which she had found quite by chance the week before at Holyroodhouse.

It had been a typical Edinburgh day, with a blustery wind

blowing off the Firth and rain slashing down from grey-black storm clouds. The windows rattled on the top floor of Holyroodhouse and Flora shuddered in the draughts which came from all angles. It was a gloomy, ghostly place, and Flora kept thinking of the proud Mary Queen of Scots and her tragic life in this house where she had lived as a prisoner for two years; where the bleeding body of her dead husband Darnley was laid at her feet, and where her infant son James was snatched from her arms by her enemies, to be brought up a Protestant.

Flora had been wandering in the labyrinth of small rooms beneath the roof, among huge Landseer prints of stags at bay, when she found herself face to face with the portrait of a seventeenth-century nobleman. She recognized at once the intelligent, mocking stare of George Villiers, Duke of Buckingham. Then and there she decided to take the picture with her to Windsor.

Flora peered at the Duke through a magnifying glass; how proud he looks, she thought, this sybarite with exquisite taste, favourite of James I and Charles I. Lover to the father, mentor to the son, inspired the young Prince to collect art, taking him off to Spain to meet Rubens.

Flora felt in her bones the picture was by Honthorst. If only she could prove it . . . Crouching over the painting and working with a dowel wrapped in cotton wool and soaked in solvent, she removed centuries of dirt and to her delight found a swirling signature in the lower right-hand corner. She would make Hardinge eat his words, she thought gleefully. But, she asked herself, had Honthorst signed plain 'Honthorst', or, as he sometimes did, 'G. V. Honthorst'? And if so, the initials must be out of sight, on that part of the canvas wrapped round the stretcher.

Flora decided to take the painting out of its frame. She laid it face down on the floor and examined the stretcher at the back. Carved into the wood was a date, 1560. That's odd, she thought. The Duke of Buckingham wasn't alive in 1560. She removed the crossbars and eased the canvas from its original seventeenth-century frame and turned it round, but instead of staring once again at the Duke of Buckingham she was confronted by a blackened canvas covered in a thick film of dirty brown. The Duke was still inside the frame. So what was she holding in her hand? A second canvas, hidden behind the first; two canvases inside one frame, and the frame was so deep it didn't show. What or who, Flora asked herself, was hiding beneath all the grime?

It took half an hour of patient work rolling the dowel over the murky surface before the varnish softened and a rich golden yellow began to come through. She cleaned another small circle in the centre of the painting, and eventually she could see the outline of folded hands and on the index finger of the left hand a ring; she rolled the dowel exactly over this spot and the letter 'F' appeared. Flora gasped; her mouth was dry and a coldness crept over her. Could this be Titian's portrait of Mary Queen of Scots?

Her hand was shaking; she dropped the dowel, reached down and noticed a letter which must have fallen on the floor when she had separated the pictures. Carefully she opened the brittle yellow paper. It was in Latin and her Latin was not good; she would need a dictionary. She folded the letter and placed it inside her restorer's bag.

She thought she heard footsteps and quickly slotted the brown canvas back inside the frame, securing the crossbars. She turned the picture round and faced the Duke of Buckingham; there was a smirk on his face, as if to say, 'So, you've discovered my secret. But it won't do you any good.'

Oh yes, it will, thought Flora. This is the discovery of a

lifetime! The heavy wooden door heaved open and in the doorway stood the night-duty policeman.

'Are you all right, Miss?' he said. 'You look as if you've seen a ghost.'

Archie climbed the two flights of stairs to Harry's flat in Vigo Street.

'Come in,' Harry said. 'I'm just on my way to the Shackleton auction but we've got time for a wee dram. By the way, thanks for the moral support last night. You brought me luck.'

Archie took the neat whisky that was offered. Theirs was an unlikely friendship, Harry Wardington, the Old Etonian son of a baronet, and Archie Gibbs, the grammar-school boy, son of a minor official in local government. A trust paid Harry's tuition fees at Oxford while Archie was sponsored by the army, who signed him up at eighteen as an officer graduate entrant.

'About this job with your dad,' Archie muttered. 'You didn't set me up?'

Harry burst out laughing. 'You must be mad if you think I have any influence with my father. I didn't know anything about it. But congratulations!' He raised his glass.

Archie looked at his friend. Over the past decade the devil-may-care Harry had blasted through life; there had been girl-friends galore, mescalin and cocaine, unpublished novels, treks in the Andes, a spell in a Hungarian jail trying to smuggle out a pretty ballerina, and a thousand apocryphal adventure stories. And now, at long last, the wrinkles of middle age were begin-ning to show, and something else, a new apprehension in his eyes, and a touch of melancholy in his brilliant smile.

'Nice picture,' Archie said, looking at the Mabuse.

'It's worth a fortune. I'm joint owner with my Aunt Margaret, but the old battleaxe won't sell, damn her. It makes me sick to think of all that money locked up in a single frame. But there's nothing I can do about it, at least nothing legal.'

'You wouldn't defraud your own aunt,' Archie joked.

'It would serve her bloody well right. OK, let's hit the road,' Harry said abruptly, and he lifted the Mabuse off the easel. 'I'll just put this lovely lady to bed.'

'What sort of safe do you have?'

'No safe. But she'll be as safe as houses.'

Harry came back seconds later and tossed Archie a bunch of keys. 'The empty offices upstairs,' Harry said, draining his glass. 'Check them out. If you ask me, they're just what you need. You've got to have a good address, especially now you're working for Her Nibs. Holborn's a dump, full of accountants and clapped-out lawyers. Bond Street beckons!'

Harry poured two smaller whiskies. 'One more for the road. I could do with a bit of Dutch courage.'

'What are you bidding on?'

'Come along and see.'

Chapter 6

A royal-blue flag with the Shackleton name in gold fluttered outside 6 Albemarle Street. Inside the main saleroom the computer operators were sitting before their screens to the left of the rostrum while the chairman's assistant, Louise Toynbee, a pretty blonde in a white silk shirt, was testing the electronic monitor which hung from the ceiling. Once the auction started the bids would flash on to the screen simultaneously in dollars, Swiss francs, Deutschmarks and yen. Harry wondered how many yen were in eleven million pounds; a lot, he decided, and went off to register with the sales clerk.

By the time Archie arrived, the saleroom was packed and the room buzzed with pre-auction fever. The atmosphere was conspiratorial, even furtive, with everyone looking at everyone else, hiding behind catalogues and whispering. Several men wore dinner jackets and women showed off expensive cocktail dresses and even more expensive jewellery which glinted in the overhead lights.

But Archie wasn't interested in the diamond ear-rings or the couture clothes. He was making a mental note of the more invisible crowd: the private dick from the Inland Revenue, who always turned up at important sales to check if anyone was spending money they said they didn't have; the man from the Customs and Excise who took such an interest in the payment of VAT; and Archie's old friend Chief Inspector Hewitt, head of the Art Squad at the Met, who stood hesitantly at the entrance of the saleroom, incognito, wearing a pin-stripe suit.

As Archie ambled over to greet the policeman, the Shackleton security officer said, 'Evening, Chief Inspector.'

'Not tonight, Josephine,' Hewitt snapped. The security officer mumbled an apology.

'Tut, tut. Is your cover blown?' Archie said, leading Hewitt to a corner of the saleroom where they wouldn't be overheard.

Hewitt growled, 'That bloke is ex-Scotland Yard. Of course he knows me.'

'Very smart,' Archie said, nodding at the Indian-silk handkerchief carefully arranged in Hewitt's breast pocket.

Hewitt looked at Archie warily; he wasn't sure if he was being sarcastic.

'By the way, Paul, I've got a new job. Working for quite a celebrity.'

'Who?'

'The Queen.'

'Pull the other one.'

'I'm serious. And I'm going to need your help. But right now tell me who the big players are tonight.'

'It's quite a glittering occasion,' Hewitt said. 'See the bald man, third row from the back, second left, he's drugs – heroin, cocaine and the odd ton of crack. On the far right, same row, the bloke with the beard, he's a merchant of death. Sells all types of weapons, anything to anyone. Oh, and look who's just arrived, the fat man in the front row, that's Kretzner. Made a fortune selling chemicals to Saddam Hussein. But nowadays he's pure as the driven snow. Sends his daughter to St Mary's, Ascot, and buys art. Sweet, isn't it?'

'Any Japanese?'

'Only the respectable crowd. The curator of the Suntory museum is here. So's the man from Yasuda Life; they bought van Gogh's *Sunflowers*. But most private Japanese collectors wouldn't be seen dead at a public auction. They bid by telephone or use a London dealer. Funny, I was just talking about the Japs this morning, with Madeleine Husson.'

'Madeleine Husson is in London?'

'She's a guest speaker at the International Conference on Art and Architectural Theft. Her English is superb. I don't know how she keeps it up; I mean, it's years since she did her two-year attachment with the City of London Police, Fraud Squad.' Hewitt paused and added, 'Pretty woman.'

A very pretty woman, the security officer decided as he glanced at the card he had been handed: *Commissaire Madeleine Husson, Office Centrale pour la répression du vol d'œuvres et d'objets d'art.* He'd read about her in the latest issue of *Hello!*; she was head of the French Art Squad and the most powerful police-woman in France. But the photographs didn't do her justice; she was a knockout.

Archie watched as the security officer led Madeleine to a seat near the back of the saleroom. She always wore black; everything about her was dark – her clothes, her hair, her eyes. But it was the smell of her skin he remembered and the sight of her at the dressing table wearing an old-fashioned silk slip, combing her hair and smiling at him in the mirror.

'*Salut*,' Archie said, sitting down next to her.

Madeleine looked at him in astonishment and then smiled, beautifully. 'Archie, I've been in a conference all day. I rang but you were out. I left a message on your machine.'

'I believe you.'

'No, no, I did. Truly. You'll find it when you get back.'

'I'm not going back. I'm taking you out to dinner.'

'Archie, I can't. I'm here with my colleague from the Gendarmerie Nationale, Lucien Rocard. You're sitting in his seat.'

'Get rid of him.'

'I can't.'

'Then I will.'

Archie left his seat and a few moments later it was taken by a tall Frenchman wearing a camel-hair coat. Archie joined Hewitt at the back of the room.

'You didn't tell me you were old friends,' the Chief Inspector said.

'We were on a job together. Gaddafi sent a shipful of arms to Ireland, do you remember? In the hold there were several crates of stolen pictures, some of them French. Madeleine came over. That's how we met.'

'You've got the luck of the devil. I've been trying to work with her for years but she's so sodding efficient I can never come up with an excuse to go to Paris. The bloke she's with, Rocard, deputy head of the Gendarmerie Nationale, is appalling. It's France this and France that. Makes you bloody sick. I can't stand him.'

'Yes, you can, Paul. What's more, you're giving him dinner tonight. Keep him out late and get him drunk.'

'I wouldn't have dinner with that man —'

'You owe me one.'

'I do?'

'That little cock-up in Londonderry . . .'

'I owe you one,' the Chief Inspector said wearily. He looked his friend in the eye. 'She's married, Archie.'

'I know.'

By now there was standing room only. Harry was at the front being briefed by Sebastian Guthrie.

'Thyssen is going to bid but the word is he won't go beyond eight million. It's a three-horse race. There's a rival Japanese, Tatsuo Nagashima, second row, fifth to the right. He's bidding for the Yasuda Life, they're mega-rich but they've just spent an awful lot of money on a Gauguin in New York, which should take the edge off their bidding. The dark horse is the American, Henry Linklater III.'

'Lots of lovely insider information. How did you get it?'

'Pillow talk with Louise,' Sebastian said, grinning. 'Now your main advantage is that no one knows who you're acting for, so they've no idea how far you're prepared to go. Surprise is the key factor in winning any battle, and you've got it, Harry. Good luck!'

As Sebastian strolled over to the rostrum to talk to Louise Archie made his way to the front of the saleroom and sat down next to Harry. 'I've got a big favour to ask. Can I stay in your flat, just for tonight?'

'Of course you can. There's a sofa-bed in my office.'

'I wasn't thinking of the sofa-bed.'

'Archie, I *am* impressed. Someone you've picked up in the saleroom? An Argentinian millionairess with plastic boobs?'

'Yes or no?'

'Of course you can, you fool. I can stay with my cousin, Dave the Rave, but I'll need to go back to my flat and get a few things, and switch off the alarm. Give me till ten o'clock and after that the place is yours. By the way, I splurged some of my backgammon winnings on champagne only this morning. Help yourself.'

Archie thanked Harry and made his way to the back of the saleroom. He couldn't take Madeleine to his grotty little bed-sitter above the office in Holborn, and there was no way she'd let him into her hotel. Neutral territory, that was the answer, and what better than Harry's flat?

Harry was looking round anxiously for Minako Setsu. Suddenly he saw her near the entrance, dwarfed by the taller European women. The Japanese girl stood out in her low-key Valentino evening suit in dark-red silk; the black hair was sleeker than ever. She looked bewildered as she scanned the crowded room; he waved his catalogue and she saw him, smiled and pushed her way through the crowd.

'I am so sorry,' she whispered. 'There was no taxi. I came by foot.'

Suddenly the room went quiet. The Chairman of Shackleton's, Andrew Charlton, had stepped on to the rostrum and looked out at the crowded room from beneath his bushy eyebrows. He was flanked by assistants, among them Sebastian, who positioned themselves at strategic points ready to spot the bids. Meanwhile, Charlton, impeccably dressed in a dinner jacket edged with braid, scanned the front four rows. So far so good, he thought; the big players had turned up. He wished everyone a good evening, and called the room's attention to lot 1, a Sisley, which at that moment was placed on an easel by two porters. The auction had begun.

The bidding was sluggish. After the first seven lots Charlton turned to the chief sales clerk, who sat immediately on his right and muttered, 'How are we doing?'

'Three million so far, Mr Charlton.'

His target – he never took an auction without a target in mind – was thirteen million pounds. It all depended on lot 8.

'Here we go, Jim,' he whispered, and in his most commanding voice he announced lot 8, 'a stunning Renoir of a young girl, formerly in the Henry McIlhenny collection, and one of the artist's greatest portraits.'

How innocent she looks, Harry thought as he stared at the portrait of a girl no more than ten years old with bright blue eyes and a whimsical smile; she thinks we're all mad, and she's right, paying this sort of money for her picture.

The bidding opened at five million and moved up in leaps of two hundred and fifty thousand. The Japanese from Yasuda came in at three million but dropped out at five. Henry Linklater III moved in to fight it out with Thyssen, who was bidding on the telephone. Harry sat back and waited; he was going in at the last possible moment.

'The bid is in the front of the room,' Andrew Charlton said without emotion, glancing at the American who sat in the second row, 'nine million pounds', and the numbers flashed on the large screen in the different currencies.

'I am bid nine million pounds for this very great Renoir,' he repeated, and turned to Louise, who was taking the telephone bid from Thyssen. She shook her head; the Baron had dropped out. A ripple of excitement ran through the saleroom. Andrew Charlton turned back to Henry Linklater III.

'The bid is with you, sir, at nine million pounds. Nine million pounds. Am I bid any more?' Andrew Charlton said, his hammer poised. Harry raised a finger.

'You're bidding, sir?'

Harry nodded and there was another ripple of excitement as people tried to get a glimpse of the new bidder. Who was Wardington's client? Charlton wondered.

'The bid is on my right, at nine million two hundred and fifty thousand pounds.'

Charlton stared hard at the American, willing him to go on. Henry Linklater III nodded his head.

'Nine million five hundred thousand pounds,' Charlton said with quiet satisfaction. He was rooting for the American; after all, Shackleton's had agreed to lend Linklater ten million pounds against his Chicago real estate which would bring in a tidy sum in interest payments on top of the buyer's premium. Once again Harry held up a finger.

'Nine million seven hundred and fifty thousand.' Charlton's voice was cool. 'The bid is on my right at nine million seven hundred and fifty thousand pounds.'

Once again Charlton stared at the American and once again Henry Linklater III nodded his head.

'Ten million pounds, the bid is on my left at ten million pounds. Is there any raise on ten million?'

Harry kept going and so did the American. An excited buzz of voices filled the saleroom as Charlton, glancing at Henry Linklater III, announced, 'The bid is at the front, eleven million pounds.'

Minako stared down at her catalogue. They had lost. She had prayed for victory; the Englishman was full of laughter and so very fine looking. But they had lost, and she would never see him again. Hakomotosan did not tolerate failure.

Andrew Charlton fixed his gaze on Harry. The ivory hammer was poised; the saleroom held its breath.

'Is there any raise on eleven million pounds?' Charlton said, scanning the room, his fingers tightened on his ivory hammer.

Through the forest of heads Harry could see the American in profile, a large nose, bushy eyebrows and a twitching mouth. There was something tentative about the American's last bid which told Harry he was losing his nerve. Henry Linklater III was tired and this was his last shot; he wanted out. Harry raised his finger. Minako gasped.

'Eleven million two hundred and fifty thousand pounds,' said Andrew Charlton. The American shook his head.

'For the last time are there any more bids? The bid is on my right at eleven million two hundred and fifty thousand pounds . . .'

The ivory hammer came down, and Harry sat back and hoped to God Hakomoto would cough up.

Chapter 7

Harry and Minako were besieged by journalists but Harry refused to give any interviews and headed for the stairs. Suddenly there was a hand on his shoulder.

'Well done, Harry, quite a *coup*.'

The Earl of Sulgrave stood there, urbane and smiling.

'Thanks, Dicky,' said Harry. 'I enjoyed myself.'

He didn't know Sulgrave well but he liked the affable well-dressed Earl and they both had their suits made by Duggie Hayward and bought fashionably camp ties from Hackett. Sulgrave was one of London's top art dealers and he came to all the big sales, but he didn't often bring his wife, who, Harry recalled, was a bit of a lush. Cordelia Sulgrave stood nervously behind her husband, holding a bone cigarette-holder.

'What are you doing for dinner?' Dicky said genially. 'I'll take you out, you and your charming companion, we'll celebrate . . .'

'Thanks, Dicky, but I'm taking Miss Setsu to Annabel's. It's part of her English education.'

'Have a good evening.' Dicky smiled and took his wife by her thin arm and led her down the main staircase of Shackleton's.

At the foot of the stairs a girl darted out and in a low, urgent voice said, 'We must talk.'

Dicky turned to his wife. 'Darling, have you met Flora Fenton? She works for William Wardington at the Royal Collection. She's an expert on Old Master drawings. It's good to see you, Flora. Send William my best.'

Dicky let his wife pass first through the revolving door and muttered to Flora, 'Later.'

'She's pretty,' Cordelia said as they stood on the pavement of Albemarle Street waiting for the chauffeur. 'Are you sleeping with her?'

'Don't start that again, Cordelia, it's so boring.'

'Although I can't see you with a blue-stocking. Blonde and brainless, that's more your type. Where's Ken? Why the hell can't he be on time?'

A Jaguar pulled up and a chauffeur jumped out and opened the door for Cordelia. Dicky sat back in the seat and closed his eyes. The recession had bitten deep into his art-dealing profits and worse, he had been ruined by Lloyds. They had taken over a million pounds off him and the cash calls were still coming in. Dicky turned his head and looked at his wife. It was all hers, the car, the chauffeur, the house in the country, the flat in London, everything belonged to her and when she felt like it she handed him out money in the same way she gave her dog, Nelson, a biscuit. It was degrading.

He looked at Cordelia and found it hard to believe that when they'd first met she was a beautiful woman who moved with the grace of a panther, and whose dark eyes shone like lamps. But after ten years of drink and no children – in his mind the two went together – she was a wreck. Her physical presence had become revolting to him. He stopped the car and told the chauffeur, 'It's all right, Ken. I'll walk.'

'Where are you going? I've booked a table at the Savoy Grill.'

'I've got to have dinner with a client. Didn't I tell you? I'm so sorry.'

He slammed the car door.

*

'Let's call Mr Hakomoto and tell him the glad tidings,' Harry said to Minako, heading down Albemarle Street towards his office.

'Mr Wardington, I do not know how you can joke when things are so serious. Mr Hakomoto instructed you to bid up to eleven million pounds. You ignored his instructions and went over the limit. He is not obliged to pay, and if he refuses . . .'

'He won't. And do stop calling me Mr Wardington. My name is Harry.'

'Harry . . . Harrysan . . .'

From Harry's office they made the call to Geneva. Minako's hand trembled as she held the receiver and in a fearful voice punctuated by '*Hai*' broke the news to Hakomoto. Harry held his breath; was it yes or no? He didn't have a leg to stand on. The instructions had been confirmed by fax that afternoon; eleven million was the absolute limit. Hakomoto had every right to refuse to pay and if he did, Harry was finished as a dealer, and there would be a nasty lawsuit to boot. Eventually, Minako passed the receiver over to Harry.

'Mr Hakomoto,' Harry said. 'I'm afraid I took a slight liberty with your instructions.'

'A liberty of two hundred and fifty thousand pounds.'

'Yes.'

'Why?'

'It was a matter of judgement. I felt sure Linklater had set himself the same limit as you yourself, eleven million, and if we went just one bid higher, the picture was ours. I didn't want to lose it, Mr Hakomoto, not for just two hundred and fifty thousand.'

'You're a gambling man, Mr Wardington, but so am I. Tell Shackleton's I will transfer the money by interbank transfer tomorrow. I will settle your commission when I see you. I shall

41

be in London in the next few days, when I look forward to meeting you. Goodbye, Mr Wardington.'

Harry put down the telephone and punched the air with his fist. 'The man's a player and I'm one hundred thousand pounds richer!'

He kissed Minako on the cheek; her skin was ice-cool. Quickly he packed an overnight bag, checked the alarm was off and took Minako to dinner at Annabel's. Nothing much had changed since he brought girls here from Oxford: candles still flickered on stiff, starched tablecloths and nineteenth-century portraits of dogs and beautiful women still covered the walls. Only the fires were different; in the old days coal glowed in the grates, now it was gas. They sat at Harry's favourite table in the far corner beneath a meticulous orientalist painting of a harem; the voice of Nat King Cole drifted from the dance floor.

'Mr Hakomoto likes you,' the Japanese girl said.

'And how much does he like you, Minako?'

Minako lowered her eyes and whispered, 'Mr Hakomoto has been very kind.'

'Let's have a dance,' Harry said abruptly, and led her on to the floor. He held her very close but her body was stiff, unyielding, and her eyes were wary.

That evening, as he made love to Flora Fenton, Dicky Sulgrave no longer felt middle-aged. The vision of Cordelia, glaring at him through the car window, receded; he felt purged of all domestic troubles.

It amused him to see Flora, this smooth-skinned cerebral creature, so aroused, so eager for the act of love. Kneeling over him, her thighs wide apart, she lowered herself on to him, tossing back her mane of red hair, pushing her breasts forward, moaning with pleasure. She was the mermaid on a ship's prow, confident, assertive, taking him, not he taking her. Ah well, Dicky thought, such is the modern woman! Afterwards, breathing heavily, she clung to him.

'Do you love me, Dicky?'

'Flora, my sweet.'

'Say the words, Dicky. Why don't you say the words?'

'Of course I love you.'

Enough to marry her? he asked himself. Perhaps. She was young and sensuous and ripe as a peach. Marriage to Flora was a distinct possibility, but all in good time. First he must make a fortune.

'I love you but you must behave sensibly. Rushing up to me at Shackleton's just now was rather silly.'

'I have something to tell you,' she said quietly.

Dicky stroked Flora's breast and listened as she told him how she had discovered a lost masterpiece, Titian's portrait of Mary Queen of Scots, hidden for three hundred and fifty years behind a Honthorst of the Duke of Buckingham.

'What makes you so sure this painting is a Titian?'

'I cleaned some of the face. I saw the hair. It's gold. Burnished gold. The ring on her finger has a letter on it. "F" for Francis II, the King of France.'

'Even so . . .'

'That's not all. There's a letter.'

'A letter?'

'It's in Latin. I've just finished translating it and it proves beyond a shadow of doubt that this is the lost Titian.'

'That's quite a discovery, my sweet. You've told William Wardington?'

'Not yet.'

'Why not?'

'Because I know what will happen. Stafford Hardinge will make it *his* find, *his* discovery. He is, after all, one of the top

43

Titian experts and he'll push me aside, just as he's trying to do with the Paris exhibition.'

'We can't have that,' Dicky murmured, holding her close.

'I need your help, Dicky.'

'And you shall have it, my sweet. For the time being you must do nothing at all. I'll think of something, I promise.'

By the time Dicky got back to his flat in Rutland Gate it was 2 a.m. The drawing room was in darkness and at first he didn't notice Cordelia until her silhouette crossed the beam of light from the streetlamp outside; she was wearing her white silk dressing-gown, holding a glass of Cognac and staring at the darkness outside. She swivelled round.

'Been with your mistress?'

'What are you talking about?'

'I'm talking about the girl who came running up to you at Shackleton's auction. Flora something. You've been with her, haven't you?'

Dicky stared at his wife with unadulterated scorn. 'Yes, as a matter of fact I have.'

Chapter 8

One of the last people to leave Shackleton's that evening was Madeleine Husson. She stood on the pavement of Albemarle Street waiting for Archie. She didn't believe for one moment that Rocard had urgent business with Hewitt; it was obviously a ploy of Archie's, but she was flattered. Their affair in Northern Ireland had been short and passionate. When she got back to Paris she told herself it was over, but she knew it wasn't.

Five years ago her marriage to a brilliant young lawyer had fallen apart partly because she didn't want to have children; her ex-husband went on to marry a rich bourgeoise from the 16*ième arrondissement* who produced four babies in five years, while Madeleine worked an eighteen-hour day and climbed to the top of her profession. Now and then the ache of loneliness was hard to bear but the anguish passed and, invariably, Commissaire Husson got on with her job.

Wearily, with the feeling that she might have lived it all differently, Madeleine felt pinpricks of rain and opened her umbrella. A car drew up alongside her and Archie opened the door.

'Dinner,' he said.

In Berkeley Square he parked the car beneath the plane trees and took her face in his hands and kissed her eyelids, her forehead, her cheeks, her neck and eventually her lips.

'You don't know how much I've been wanting to do that,' he said.

They had dinner at Mortimer's. Madeleine seemed nervous

and talked shop. Art theft had reached epidemic proportions, she told Archie, especially in Italy, France and Britain; the police were on a hiding to nothing with no European Community law on ownership and a thousand and one crooked dealers ready to handle stolen art. All this and more was going into her speech to the conference.

Archie leant across the table, took Madeleine's hand and said, 'Don't you ever switch off?'

Madeleine stared at him with her blue-black eyes. 'I've missed you, Archie.'

They drove in silence; Archie held on to Madeleine's hand, keeping the other on the wheel, a sentimental gesture which Madeleine found touching.

'Where are we?' Madeleine said, climbing the two flights of stairs to Harry's flat.

'A friend of mine lives here, an art dealer called Harry Wardington. He's away.'

'The man who bid for the Renoir?'

'You never miss a trick, do you?'

'What's wrong with your flat?'

'Everything.'

What could he say? It was a dump, a place for work but not for loving, and especially not for loving Madeleine. He wanted to go on as he had begun, with an affair that was never ordinary or mundane. They had first kissed in the driving rain on a bleak moor above Armagh and for three days they had hidden in a bed-and-breakfast farmhouse and had hardly got out of bed except to drink Irish whiskey in the local pub and clamber over heather to stand in the arc of a double rainbow. There must be no damp Holborn flats with peeling wallpaper and grimy windows and second-hand furniture.

Archie led the way into Harry's flat and felt at home with the bright curtains, the comfortable sofa and the magnificent blow-up photographs of Pacific atolls, green islands rimmed with white sand floating in a translucent aquamarine sea. He found the promised bottle of champagne in the fridge and poured two glasses.

He put his hand to her face and felt the strong jawbone, the smooth plane of her cheek. He touched her arched eyebrow. She was staring at him intently, her face solemn, when suddenly she smiled, edged closer and with her finger traced the outline of his mouth. They kissed, tentatively at first, it had been a long time, then more eagerly. His hand slipped down her neck to her breast and gently he massaged her nipples, first one then the other.

'Bed,' he whispered, and they moved into the next room. There was no zip to her dress; it was Lycra. On the bed, Madeleine took off underpants and tights, then she stood up, took the hem of her black dress and in one elegant movement peeled it off to stand before him naked. He smiled at her beautiful body, and sucked the nipples of her full, round breasts. She laughed and shivered with pleasure and felt her own desire growing by the second as he slid his smooth palm over her flat stomach down between her thighs. She stroked his back, neck and muscular thighs, and kissed his chest, closing her fingers round his hardness as if she were discovering him all over again.

Later, as they lay together naked in the dark bedroom, the streetlight casting a shaft of yellow light across their bodies, Archie stroked her jet-black hair and said, 'I'll come and see you in Paris.'

'No, not in Paris. Please.'

'Are you telling me I'm bad for your image? Can't have a flighty police chief, is that it?'

'We must be discreet, Archie, especially when it's on my home ground,' she said. 'I haven't got where I am without making enemies, especially among my male colleagues. There are those who don't think a woman should have my job and they'd like nothing better than to see me out on my ear.'

'You're paranoid. For Christ's sake, we're unmarried; I'm not a terrorist or an Islamic fundamentalist. I don't have Aids. I'm English, is that the problem? In Paris you can only fuck a Frenchman, is that it?'

Madeleine laughed with her eyes, and pressed her nakedness against the length of his body and felt his cool skin and the light scratch of his hair; they wanted each other, again. They were sliding into sleep when there was a crash as the umbrella stand in the hall toppled over. Archie hurled back the bedclothes, grabbed the dressing-gown from the chair and hid behind the door.

'Bloody fool,' he heard someone say. 'Can't you watch where you're going?'

'Sorry, Fred, I didn't see it. Where do we start? This room or that?'

The bedroom door creaked open and the beam from a torch fell on Madeleine's face.

'Shit, there's a woman in here!' the intruder hissed, and bolted. Archie lurched after him but he was too late. The two burglars jumped down the stairs three at a time and seconds later the downstairs door slammed shut. Archie examined Harry's front door, watched by Madeleine wrapped in a towel.

'They've jemmied the door. It's not reinforced and this lock is fairly ancient,' Archie said. 'And of course the alarm was switched off. But they didn't know that. Those two jokers had to assume the alarm was on, in which case either they were expecting to set it off and reckoned they had enough time to grab what they wanted and get out, or else – ' Archie paused and stared at Madeleine, 'they had the code.'

'What were they after?'

'I don't know, but whatever it was they didn't get it. So let's celebrate with a bottle of champagne. Man cannot live by love alone.'

'I know exactly what they were looking for,' Harry told Archie the next morning, and he led the way into his bedroom. Madeleine's scent lingered in the air; she had left the flat at seven that morning, promising to meet Archie later. Harry crouched down and pulled out the Mabuse from under the double bed.

'Who else knew the Mabuse was here, in your flat?' Archie asked urgently.

'God, Archie, hundreds of people. It's been in the office for days. Johnny van Haeften dropped by on Monday. On Tuesday I met Michael Goedhuis and Dicky Sulgrave at Whites. We all got rather drunk, not Michael, he doesn't drink, and I brought them back here to look at the Mabuse. Well, it's not often you can flaunt a sixteenth-century Old Master, is it? But they're both old friends, part of the art dealers' fellowship, you scratch my back, I scratch yours, that sort of thing. Who else? The Japanese girl, she saw it. That's about it. Not counting Aunt Margaret herself, who's the biggest gossip in London.'

'What's your insurance cover on this?'

'I'm covered for any art on these premises. I've got the right sort of window locks and the place is alarmed.'

'The alarm didn't go off last night, Harry.'

'Of course it didn't, because it wasn't switched on. I never put the alarm on when there's someone in the flat.'

'But the burglars couldn't have known that. They had to

assume – ' Archie stopped himself and changed tack. 'Even without the alarm on, you're still covered at night, in the event of theft?'

'I told you, Archie,' Harry said, getting irritated, 'I'm covered.'

Harry carried the Mabuse back into the office, set it on the easel and surveyed the seductive blonde face. 'Frankly, dear lady, I wish you'd got nicked.'

Was Harry playing games? Archie wondered. Stealing the Mabuse could have been his idea. He was up to his eyes in debt and a clever insurance fraud would solve a lot of problems. Harry a crook? The idea was ludicrous, Archie told himself; but he couldn't shake it off.

Chapter 9

Archie walked from Vigo Street to the Foreign Office, where he spent two hours negotiating with the contracts officer, a pompous civil servant with a patronizing air; but in the end he got what he wanted, a thousand pounds a week and expenses, not bad for a one-off security job.

The police didn't like it. That afternoon Archie was summoned to the cramped office at Windsor Castle, where he found Sir William Wardington and a grim-faced Detective Inspector Burns. Sir William was explaining with consummate tact, why he felt it necessary to recruit 'a new pair of hands'.

'I can't see what he's going to do,' said Burns, a big, powerful man who for the past two years had been on special attachment to the Royal Protection Group.

'Co-ordinate things, Detective Inspector,' said Sir William.

'Too many cooks spoil the broth.'

'Detective Inspector Burns, this exhibition is a complex business.'

'Nothing we can't handle.'

'In France, we're in the hands of the French police. Mr Gibbs will co-ordinate things. He is particularly well qualified, having worked with the French before, in the Lebanon, where he provided close protection for our Ambassador in difficult circumstances.'

The understatement of the year, Archie thought grimly.

'We've all had experience working with the French,' Burns snapped.

Sir William adopted a more peremptory tone: 'This decision has been reached at the highest level. Mr Gibbs will be reporting to me and I count on you to give him every assistance.'

'Yes, sir.'

Of all the men in Special Branch it had to be Burns. They'd clashed in Northern Ireland over security for the Princess Royal when she had opened a new hospital in Belfast. Burns had objected to everything, changed nothing, and yet when the whole operation passed off without a hitch, he took the credit.

'Long time no see,' Archie said to Burns as they followed Sir William into the Print Room.

'Not long enough,' Burns growled, and left.

Flora had a book in her hands but she wasn't turning the pages. Her mass of auburn hair caught the sun and glowed gold; a Pre-Raphaelite muse, Archie thought. She was so pretty, so desirable, she must have a lover. Who? A research assistant at the British Museum? The manager of a rock band? A social worker? An oversexed don?

At that moment a tall, distinguished man with silver hair came into the Print Room. 'There you are, William. I've been looking for you everywhere.'

'Ronald,' said Sir William, 'I'd like to introduce Archie Gibbs. Archie, may I introduce Sir Ronald Butt, the Queen's Private Secretary.'

'I'm delighted to hear you've accepted our proposal,' Sir Ronald said, holding out a hand. 'If I can be of any help, let me know. And, Flora, may I congratulate you on your recent discovery? William tells me it's a magnificent Honthorst. Honestly, the things that turn up in the attics of Royal houses!'

'We'll send the picture over to Alan Bradford for a quick clean,' Sir William said, 'then off it goes to Paris.'

'No need for that, Sir William,' Flora said, getting up from her desk. 'It only needs a surface clean, which I can do myself.'

'Of course you can,' Sir William said, smiling; he always forgot she had a Courtauld degree in restoration.

Sir Ronald turned to Wardington. 'Now, William, if I could trespass on a moment of your time. Just when I'd finished the placement for tonight's banquet, the Japanese have produced an extra princess. She's reading art at Cambridge. It didn't occur to me she should be included but the Crown Prince has dropped a large hint, so now I have to find someone to partner her. Any ideas?'

'It's rather short notice,' Sir William muttered. 'What about Dicky Sulgrave? He knows about art, and he's got the right background and all of that.'

Flora looked up from her book.

'The Earl of Sulgrave,' Sir Ronald said with a touch of irony. 'That's a very good idea. And because it's by Royal Command and at the last minute we won't have to ask his not very sober wife. I shall ring him right now.'

As Sir Ronald turned to leave he put a friendly hand on Sir William's arm. 'Don't forget to wear your decorations and for God's sake have the cross and ribbon of the GCVO properly adjusted. The Monarch notices these things.'

The Monarch. How quaint the word sounded, Archie thought. 'Monarch' was still used among senior courtiers who ranked as equals; otherwise the sovereign was referred to as 'The Queen'. The arcane complexity of it all, Archie mused.

'If you'll excuse me,' Sir William said to Archie, 'I have a meeting with the Keeper of the Privy Purse. Flora will fill you in. She knows the form better than I do!'

Sir William put on his Burberry raincoat and left the Print Room. Flora placed a thick file on the green baize. 'In two weeks' time the Royal Baggage Train will transport all exhibits to the packers for boxing and crating.'

'But that barely gives the packers a week—'

'They don't need more. Everything's been measured up and the boxes and cases are ready and waiting.'

'Very efficient,' Archie murmured.

'I try to be methodical,' Flora said, smiling for the first time. 'Once the exhibits are crated up they are loaded on to the Royal Baggage Train and driven to Dover. The drivers, all soldiers in the Royal Logistic Corps, will be armed and we'll have our usual escort from the Royal Protection Group up to Dover, and again in Paris at the British Embassy. What happens between Dover and Paris, I'm not quite sure. That's your department, you and the French.'

The Royal Baggage Train, there was a relic from the Middle Ages, Archie thought; not a train as you might expect but a special squadron of dark-blue vans polished to a shine and bearing the Royal cypher. Part of the Royal Logistic Corps, it was commanded by the Queen's 'Baggage Master', who never referred to the vans as anything other than 'wagons'.

Gloriously archaic, the Royal Baggage Train was used to carry the Queen's personal belongings, anything from jewellery to Malvern water. The Queen always took her own linen and quite often her own china, and if she was giving a reception in a house that was underequipped, like Holyrood, she would bring her own silver in the medieval manner of a peripatetic monarch.

'For our purposes,' Flora went on, 'I've had the wagons fitted with special picture racks so nothing gets damaged.'

'Flora, you should run a government department. I hope they're paying you properly. I'd say you're worth your weight in gold.'

'Would you?' she said bitterly. 'Well, *they* don't think so. Not Sir William, he's wonderful, or Sir Ronald, but the others, they ignore me. You see, I don't belong. The ladies-in-waiting keep mistaking me for the secretary. Sometimes I think they do it on purpose. I don't even eat with the Royal Household. I eat with the staff in the canteen. That's how snobbish and petty it is. I'm not even in the Green Book. Can you believe it?'

'What in God's name is the Green Book?'

'The internal directory of the Royal Household,' Flora said, opening a desk drawer and pulling out a slim green volume. You won't find my name in there even though I've worked here for three years. You'll find all sorts of entries for Lady This and Lady That but not one column inch for the Cataloguer and Exhibitions Clerk.'

Archie could have said: 'You're an outsider, like me. You haven't been to the same school as the others, because your parents couldn't afford the fees. You didn't have holidays abroad or weekends in country houses. What's more, you're a woman in a male establishment, out of place, out of class. It's tough on people like you and me. I know.'

Archie could have told her all of this but instead he said, 'Chin up.'

That evening, after Archie had left, Flora sat alone in the Print Room listening to the ticking of the grandfather clock in the corner, thinking about Dicky. What would Sir William Wardington say if he knew they were lovers, and that Dicky had taken her on trips to Venice, Prague and St Petersburg, and laid a whole new world at her feet? She had been spoilt rotten and she liked it, and she was never going back to Chester Close, Birmingham.

She pictured Dicky in his white tie, having dinner with the Crown Prince of Japan; he knew everyone, went everywhere, but she was never asked to these glittering court functions; she wasn't grand enough. Suddenly Flora longed to hear the soothing sound of Dicky's voice. She picked up the receiver and dialled his home number. A woman answered; she sounded slightly drunk and aggressive.

'Yes? Who is it?'

Flora put the telephone down.

Chapter 10

And what are they giving the Crown Prince of Japan to eat? Archie wondered as he sat in the back row of a drab classroom at the Cundy Street Adult Education Centre. He was hungry; he had come straight from Windsor and there hadn't been time even for a snack. His mouth watered as he imagined the wholesome English food favoured by the Queen, the home-made tomato soup, the sole, the beef (pink not red) with spring vegetables, and the lemon mousse with Jersey cream.

Archie's gastronomic dream was shattered by the girl in front who was filing her long red fingernails with an emery-board. She turned round and said, 'Are you a cop?'

'No,' Archie said, 'why?'

'Dunno, thought you might be. We don't get many men for history of art. It's not a macho subject, is it?'

Chief Inspector Paul Hewitt shifted uncomfortably in the seat next to Archie. In the men's room on the seventeenth floor at Scotland Yard he had taken a lot of trouble to dress as little like a policeman as possible. His denims were frayed and his black leather jacket was twenty years old, an essential part of Hewitt's undercover kit. As for Archie, he was wearing the ex-army officer's proverbial faded jeans with a tweed jacket.

'I don't know why you're looking so worried,' Archie said. 'It was me she took for a cop, not you.'

'What are we doing here?' Hewitt growled.

'Now wait a minute, Paul, you were dead keen. Couldn't wait to enrol. I'm just here for moral support, remember?'

Hewitt rocked back on the canvas chair; there was no getting away from it, he was here of his own free will. No one had twisted his arm. One evening over a pint he had poured out his heart to Archie, 'I'm head of the Art and Antiques Squad and I don't know a bloody thing about art.'

'Go to evening class,' Archie had said, as a joke. And here they were, in a drab schoolroom, curtains torn, paint peeling from the walls, waiting for the lecturer to turn up and talk about the Renaissance.

Archie and Hewitt had been in the army together, in 'S' company, a little-known anti-terrorist squad. They had spent a year together in Northern Ireland but in the end the killing got to Hewitt and he joined the police. As a copper the hours were unsociable, but at least you got overtime and were less likely to get shot.

'Paul,' Archie said, leaning across, 'something happened last night which I think you ought to know about.'

Briefly he told Hewitt about the bungled attempt to steal a Mabuse from Harry Wardington's flat. Hewitt, who had been rocking back on his chair, sat up. 'Mabuse. Never heard of him.'

'Sixteenth-century Flemish.'

'Never mind the date. A wedding portrait of a young bride, you say. What colour was her hair?'

'Blonde.'

Hewitt looked up sharply. 'And why didn't you call the police?'

'I wasn't alone.'

Hewitt sat back in his chair and smiled. 'Caught red-handed with the beautiful Commissaire Husson in your little love nest. You were over a barrel, mate. Bloody funny if you ask me.'

'I didn't.'

'Take my advice, Archie. Keep your mind on Her Majesty's property. You've got a big job there, lad. A lot can go wrong, especially when you're flying high. And it's a long way to fall.'

Eventually the teacher arrived. She spoke loudly and passionately about Piero della Francesca. In the middle of her peroration, Hewitt's bleeper went off and he hurried out of the room, his portable telephone pressed to his ear. The girl in front turned round and winked at Archie.

'The Blond Maniac strikes again,' Hewitt said to Archie as he switched off his telephone and hurried down the school stairs. 'I need a lift,' Hewitt muttered.

'Where to?'

'Rutland Gate.'

It had just stopped raining and the old-fashioned streetlights on Constitution Hill glimmered in puddles on the wet road. Hewitt briefed Archie. Some joker was going round London nicking oil paintings of blondes, all shapes and sizes, eighteenth century, twentieth century, it didn't seem to matter. They'd had three robberies in a week, and now a fourth, and perhaps the bungling attempt in Harry's flat was also his handiwork. Each time it was the same story, the villain didn't take anything else, no silver, no porcelain, no Persian rugs, not even a fur coat. Just the blondes.

'Stealing to order.'

'That's what it looks like,' said Hewitt. 'Edgar is busy imagining all sorts of weird and wonderful things. You haven't met my number two, have you? Eager Edgar. He wants to change the world. I keep telling him he should be an evangelist.'

'Who's been done this time?'

'The Countess of Sulgrave. Her husband's an art dealer, the Earl of Sulgrave.'

Archie pulled up outside 4 Rutland Gate and waited for Hewitt to get out. He did not expect to be invited in.

'Get a move on,' Hewitt said. 'Park the car, and come on

in. But don't say anything until I introduce you. We must play this one by the book.'

As they climbed the stairs to the first-floor flat, Hewitt muttered, 'You might even get the lady as a client, you never know.'

Everything about the flat had an opulent feel to it. The heavy chintz curtains were draped in carefully arranged folds on the floor; large bunches of arum lilies and yellow roses stood in blue and white Chinese vases; sofas were smothered in cushions and the ottoman in the middle of the room was covered in the latest fashionable magazines. On the walls Archie noted a curious mixture of art: a Persian saddle rug in a frame, a Japanese screen of mauve wisteria, an Edward Lear watercolour of Greece. Above the fireplace was a large empty space and a picture hook.

Cordelia Sulgrave stood warming herself by the coal fire, holding a neat vodka in one hand and a cigarette in the other. She had long beautiful hands and her nails were painted bright red. She was tall and much too thin but there was an elegance about her, and a self-assurance. Her eyes were almost too large, and set far apart. Perhaps because of this she had a haunted look.

Detective Sergeant Edgar Quinn was taking notes when Archie and the Chief Inspector arrived. He jumped to his feet; Hewitt introduced himself and Cordelia Sulgrave offered a limp hand.

'Thank you for coming,' she said, and turned to Archie. 'And you are – ?'

'Mr Gibbs is an expert on security,' the Chief Inspector said quickly, 'I asked him to come along. If you have any objection. . . .'

'I don't.' Cordelia stared at Archie. 'Do you have a card?'

From his breast pocket Archie pulled out a business card.

'Thank you,' she said. 'I should have thought about security before. There isn't any. No alarms, nothing. Dicky keeps a few things in his office in Mount Street where he has a safe but this flat is unprotected; on the other hand it's very seldom empty. We have a Portuguese couple who live in, but they're in Lisbon for their son's wedding.'

She swallowed one large gulp of the vodka.

'Have a drink, Chief Inspector. You can't be on duty, not dressed like that, surely. Help yourself.'

'We don't wear uniforms in our line of work,' Hewitt said as he poured himself and Archie a good measure of malt whisky.

'That picture was the only thing I cared about,' Cordelia Sulgrave said with a sudden burst of passion. 'I don't give a damn about anything else in this flat, the dreary Edward Lears, that vulgar Japanese screen. But that picture, I loved it.'

Detective Sergeant Quinn turned back a few pages of his notebook, and spoke in a clipped, efficient voice: 'At ten p.m. this evening Lady Sulgrave came home from a reception at the Spanish Embassy, number twenty-four Belgrave Square, and she noticed that the painting which had previously hung above the fireplace was missing. The painting in question is a portrait of her mother by Augustus John. A photograph of the painting is available; it was shown last year in an exhibition at the Royal Academy.'

'Could I see a photograph?' the Chief Inspector asked gently.

'The catalogue is there on the desk. Page forty-six.'

Hewitt turned to page 46 and found himself staring at a proud, flirtatious face, with large blue eyes and abundant blonde hair.

'She was his mistress for a while,' Cordelia said. 'That's why he painted her with so much affection. She was so beautiful, and she went on being beautiful even when she was old. Some women improve with age, have you noticed?'

'Yes,' said Hewitt. 'I have.'

Doggedly, Detective Sergeant Quinn went on, 'Last night Lady Sulgrave was at a Shackleton's auction and she is quite certain the painting was above the fireplace. This morning she drove to her house in the country, the Lodge, Yattendon, near Newbury. She returned to London this evening, arriving at number four Rutland Gate at seven fifteen p.m.'

'And the picture was here?' asked the Chief Inspector.

'I don't know. I didn't turn the lights on. I helped myself to a drink—'

'In the dark?' said Hewitt.

'There was plenty of light from the hall. Anyway, I was in a hurry. The reception at the Spanish Embassy was at eight. My husband's secretary rang me in the country to say he couldn't make it and I was to go on alone. Dicky's always doing that, chucking when he gets a better invitation.'

She tipped the glass back and drank the last drops of vodka.

'I shouldn't really have bothered you. I mean, it's not as if you can do anything. There's not a chance in hell that I shall ever get the picture back, is there now, Chief Inspector?'

Archie noted the sarcasm in her voice. The drink is getting to her, he thought.

'I read an article about the Art and Antiques Squad, just the other day. It sounds so frightfully glamorous, doesn't it? Art and Antiques Squad! One thinks of an army of detectives, lean supersleuths. And then I discovered there are only three of you. Three police-officers for all the art robberies in London. Is that true, Chief Inspector?'

'Yes, it's true,' Hewitt said coolly. 'There are three dedicated officers, Detective Sergeant Quinn, myself and a detective constable.'

'A Mickey Mouse organization, that's what they say.' Cordelia Sulgrave murmured as she crossed the room to the drinks tray and helped herself to another vodka on the rocks. 'Have another drink, Chief Inspector. What's the recovery rate? Five per cent, or is it three?'

She's getting nasty, Archie thought, and he wondered how much more Hewitt would take. A lot, by the look of it; Hewitt was helping himself to a generous glass of the twenty-year-old malt.

'Recovering stolen property isn't a top priority,' Hewitt said testily. 'And that's not our decision. It's the politicians and the public who decide what police priorities should be and chasing stolen art and antiques comes a long way down the list. But if you want to see a bigger Art and Antiques Squad here in London, I suggest you write to your MP.'

She probably doesn't know the name of her MP, Archie thought. All the same, it was a good dig, just this side of civility.

Hewitt turned to Edgar. 'Right, Edgar, point of entry?'

'That isn't clear, sir.'

'What do you mean, it isn't clear?'

'Well, sir, nothing's been forced. At least not that I can see.'

'What's the market rate for Augustus John?' Cordelia Sulgrave interjected. 'Twenty thousand? Fifty thousand? I have no idea.'

'Your husband could tell you that,' the Chief Inspector said.

'My husband doesn't tell me anything.'

'Is anything else missing?' Hewitt asked. 'Silver, jewellery?'

'My jewellery is in the bank.'

'No open drawers. No mess?'

'Just Dicky's suit in his dressing room. He came here to change before going to a banquet at Windsor Castle. It's just his sort of evening, sucking up to royalty.' Cordelia pressed a new cigarette to the glowing butt end of the one she was smoking.

'Excuse me, Lady Sulgrave,' Hewitt said, 'but I'd like to have a word with my colleague.' He led Quinn over to the window.

'Edgar, this doesn't look to me like a robbery. When the lady sobers up, she'll remember that she sent the painting off to be cleaned, or took it down to the country. She's plastered, and frankly, I've had a bellyful.'

'Someone's nicked her painting. She's sure of it. And it's a blonde, Chief. Another blonde.'

'Eager Edgar!' the Chief Inspector said with sarcasm. He turned back to Cordelia Sulgrave. 'I don't think there's anything more we can do this evening,' he said. 'We shall be contacting your husband in the morning.'

'Well, you won't get him. He's going to Geneva, I don't know for how long. He always stays at the Richemond, if that's any help. Well, talk of the devil.'

The Earl of Sulgrave stood in the doorway, in his white tie, his blond hair swept straight back off his forehead, flashing a gold cuff-link engraved with the family crest.

'Cordelia, who are these people? What's going on?'

Hewitt stepped forward. 'Chief Inspector Paul Hewitt. Your wife called the police to report the theft of the Augustus John painting of her mother.'

'There's been no theft, Chief Inspector. The painting was taken by me to be photographed for insurance purposes. I've got it right here.'

Dicky Sulgrave disappeared into the hall, and returned with a picture wrapped in bubble paper.

'Excuse me, Lord Sulgrave,' Hewitt said, 'but your wife says you came back to change earlier this evening. Why didn't you bring the painting back then?'

'Because I forgot. It's been sitting in the boot of my car all evening. I daresay it was a Freudian slip. I don't really like Augustus John. Darling,' he said to his wife as he ripped off the bubble paper, 'I told you I was taking your mother to be photographed and would bring her back this evening. Don't you remember?'

'You didn't tell me anything.'

'But, darling, we spoke only this morning, on the telephone.' With a long-suffering smile he turned to the Chief Inspector. 'Now and then my wife is a little forgetful. I'm so sorry you've been troubled for nothing.'

Dicky Sulgrave hung the painting above the fireplace, stood back and said, 'There. Back where it belongs.'

'All's well that ends well,' the Chief Inspector said, and shot an angry look at Detective Sergeant Quinn, who snapped his notebook shut. Cordelia drained her glass and stared at the picture.

'Let me show you out,' said the Earl. 'I'm so sorry you've had a wasted evening.'

'That's all right, Lord Sulgrave,' Hewitt said. 'It goes with the job.'

'We thought this might be part of a pattern,' Quinn blurted out.

'Really?'

'We've had a series of burglaries in central London over the past week, and in each case the villains have stolen a portrait of a blonde woman: a Gainsborough, a Modigliani, an Elizabethan lady in a ruff.'

'And you thought my mother-in-law was the next on the list?'

'She's a platinum blonde,' Quinn said portentously.

'Well, happily for all of us, she's safe and sound above the fireplace. But it is worrying, this stealing to order. Good-night, gentlemen. And once again, I apologize on behalf of my wife for wasting your time.'

Archie followed the police downstairs.

Edgar said, 'When she said Mickey Mouse organization, I had to laugh, Chief.'

'Did you?' Hewitt said in a deadpan voice. 'Tell it to the Home Office. I've got work to do.' He was tired; he longed to be at home with his wife, Debbie, sipping a cup of tea in front of the fire in their semi-detached house in Kentish Town, the kids asleep in bed, the front door firmly shut, keeping out this whole twisted miserable world of drunk rich women who call in the police because they're lonely. Brusquely he said good-night and disappeared into the sharp September evening.

From his drawing-room window Dicky watched the unmarked police Rover drive slowly down the street. He turned to face his wife, who was staring at the picture of her mother. That was a very stupid thing to do. What possessed you to call in the police? Three of them!'

'Only two were policemen. The one with brown hair was a security expert.'

'Oh, really. Which firm?'

'I don't know.'

'Well, who was he, for God's sake? I don't like strangers in my house.'

'My house, Dicky darling, my house. Don't get cross. I didn't catch his name. By the way, your girlfriend rang. Around six thirty. As soon as she heard my voice she hung up. Do tell her it's very common to hang up. Common and cowardly.'

'You're drunk,' Dicky said.

From Rutland Gate Archie drove back to Holborn and climbed the damp staircase to his flat, inhaling the smell of curry from the second- or possibly third-floor flat, counting the days until he would move to the salubrious air of Vigo Street. The top landing was badly lit and Archie fumbled for the right key in the half-light. Suddenly he froze; someone was behind him in the shadows. He swivelled round to face Madeleine, who was smiling and holding a cigarette in her hand.

'Got a light?'

Chapter 11

At 9 a.m. the next morning, Archie and Chief Inspector Paul Hewitt stood on the steps of 15 Grosvenor Place, facing the high spiked wall of Buckingham Palace.

'Last year,' Hewitt said, 'eight women put a ladder up against that wall in broad daylight and climbed into the grounds of Buckingham Palace. Incredible, when you think about it.'

'Who dares wins,' Archie muttered, wondering where the hell Madeleine was. At six that morning they'd been woken by the high-pitched bleep of her portable telephone. When Archie asked for the mobile number she told him only three people knew it and one of them was the President of France.

Now we are four, Archie thought to himself. He could still feel her soft skin against his, her cool hand on his face, her lips kissing him, wanting him. She had left in a hurry, giving nothing away, standing impatiently on the pavement of High Holborn waiting for a taxi against a murky London dawn.

'It's very unlike Commissaire Husson to be late. You wouldn't know what's keeping her?' Hewitt said mischievously.

'Search me.'

'By the way,' Hewitt said, rocking back on his heels. 'I've been checking up on your pal Harry Wardington. He's in a spot of financial bother. I'm the sort of bloke who always thinks the worst and it strikes me that that little burglary at his place might have been a put-up job. Your proverbial insurance fraud.'

Archie glanced at Hewitt warily and murmured, 'Everything's possible.'

'Of course, things are looking up for your friend since he

68

earned himself a fat commission bidding for the Renoir on behalf of his Japanese client.'

'How do you know his client is Japanese?'

'There's an informer at Shackleton's who'll do anything for money.' Hewitt remembered the eager expression on Sebastian Guthrie's baby face as he counted the three hundred pounds.

'So who is this Japanese?' Archie asked.

'Seiji Hakomoto. A construction king. He bought some office space in Docklands and he's got an office in Leadenhall Street, but he's hardly ever in London. Keeps a very low profile. In the last few years he's bought some very expensive paintings.'

'And the girl?'

'Minako Setsu, his assistant, at least that's the cover. She's new to the art world.'

'Thanks, Paul.'

'You scratch my back . . .' Hewitt smiled and Archie knew that next time it would be his turn to give away a little free information.

At 9.15 a.m. Hewitt decided not to wait any longer. The lift was out of order so they climbed the five flights of carpeted stairs to the roof-top offices of the Art Loss Register. At each landing Hewitt caught his breath and briefed Archie on the essential details. This was the largest database of stolen art in the country and a useful tool for the police. Of course, Hewitt argued, it was ludicrous the Met didn't have its own inter-national database of stolen art; God knows they'd been asking for it for well over ten years but the Home Office always pleaded poverty. Meanwhile, private enterprise had filled the gap. The man in charge of the Art Loss Register was Mark Toynbee, an ex-army troubleshooter with a bluff exterior, manic energy and a razor-sharp mind.

They looked like any modern offices, open-plan with computers on desks. Toynbee, a trim, good-looking man in his fifties, bounded towards them, exuding cordiality.

'Welcome, Chief Inspector. And Mr Gibbs, delighted to see you. We need more customers in the security world. Coffee? Tea? But where's Commissaire Husson?'

Hewitt muttered she was on her way and settled down beside the chief of operations, Sarah Willis, a shrewd, attractive blonde who sat behind her Canon computer and knew her technology.

'We operate two Canon RE552 video visualizers here in London, and two in New York,' she began, glancing at Archie with a cool smile.

'I'm not here for the patter, love,' Hewitt said, opening his briefcase. 'I've got work to do. There's a villain going round London stealing pictures of blondes; it must be some sort of fetish. I call him the Blond Maniac. His haul so far is a Gainsborough of Miss Grenville in her riding habit – he took that one from the boot of Sir Hugh Lynton's car – he was a former Ambassador at the UN. A week later our villain helped himself to Baroness Brechin's Elizabethan ancestor while she was banging on about pornography in the House of Lords. Lastly, there's Mary Marchant, daughter of the sculptor Hugh Marchant. Her father was given a Modigliani nude by the artist – they were friends – and she kept it in her cottage in Devon, and hey presto when she got down last Friday the picture was gone.'

Hewitt handed over the photographs to Sarah Willis, who placed each one carefully beneath the Canon scanner and moments later a perfect image appeared on the screen. She said, 'That picture is now in the memory bank of the Art Loss Register for ever. All I need now is a verbal description plus details of size, provenance, all of that and then we can complete the log.'

Hewitt handed her a neatly typed sheet of paper. Archie

stood behind Sarah as she fed the computer the data on stolen art.

'Interesting,' Archie murmured, and took Hewitt to one side. 'These pictures have something in common.'

'I've told you, he's a Blond Maniac.'

'It's not that, Paul. It's the provenance. They've always been in the same family, owned by the same people. Take Baroness Brechin's Elizabethan portrait. It's hung above the fireplace in Brechin Hall since it was painted. And the Modigliani was a present to Mary Marchant's father from the artist; and Sir Hugh Lynton's Gainsborough came to him through his brother who had no children. Not one of these pictures has ever been sold.'

'Coincidence?' queried Hewitt.

'Perhaps. Or perhaps the man or woman behind this stealing to order is sophisticated and wants paintings untainted by the auction house. Interesting idea.'

'Too abstract for me,' Hewitt grumbled.

Suddenly Mark Toynbee cried out, '*La voilà!*'

Madeleine walked into the office, demure and professional in yet another black suit. Archie was irked to find not a flicker of intimacy in her dark eyes; her handshake was indifferent and she greeted everyone with the same charming smile.

'Forgive me for being so late but this morning I had bad news. The Musée Municipal de Tours was robbed last night and a picture I loved as a child has been stolen.'

From her briefcase she produced a photograph which had been faxed from Paris that morning and handed it to Sarah.

'Monet, from the Haystack series,' Sarah said. 'Can't tell which time of day until I get a good quality colour photograph.'

'Sunset,' Madeleine said quietly. 'The colours in the haystack are extraordinary, purple and mauve and green and blue and brown. I'll get a colour photograph to you by tomorrow. Then perhaps you could log it on your computer?'

'No trouble at all,' Mark Toynbee said enthusiastically.

'Of course there are many others,' Madeleine went on, producing a thick wadge of photographs. 'Here's a cross-section of the paintings stolen from our provincial museums over the past few years – Pissarro, Renoir, Manet, Monet, Sisley, Degas.'

She tossed the photographs on to the table. Archie picked them up and thumbed through.

'We'll log the lot,' Toynbee announced. 'It's a good way to show you the finer points of the Art Loss Register. Afterwards, perhaps I can give you a spot of lunch? The Cavalry Club's just over the road and their Bloody Marys blow your head off.'

Archie and Hewitt left Madeleine in Toynbee's eager hands. As he was leaving, Archie glanced back at Madeleine hoping to catch her eye but she was hunched over the computer.

Harry walked through the revolving doors of the Connaught precisely at twelve noon, punctual to the minute. Seiji Hakomoto and Minako were sitting at a table by the window.

'Mr Hakomoto, may I please introduce Mr Wardington,' Minako said, jumping to her feet.

'Mr Hakomoto, I am delighted to meet you,' Harry said, holding out his hand. The Japanese had an iron grip.

'May I offer you a drink? Waiter!'

A waiter fluttered around the table and took their orders.

Hakomoto turned his black eyes on Harry. 'You're a gambling man, Mr Wardington.'

'Win some lose some, that's my motto. But these days I seem to be on a lucky streak.'

Minako smiled at Harry. Seiji Hakomoto noticed and frowned leaving Minako staring nervously at her hands. After several moments of silence Hakomoto said, 'Your commission – would you like cash or a cheque?'

'Half and half, if I may.'

Hakomoto spoke in Japanese to Minako, who listened attentively, chanted '*Hai*', and left.

'Mr Wardington. I understand that your father is the Director of the Royal Collection. You are an art dealer and I am an art collector. We can do business together.'

'I'm very flattered but I find it hard to believe you don't already have a man in London, Mr Hakomoto.'

'I never put all my eggs in one basket, Mr Wardington.'

Minako returned with a small black Gucci attaché case which she handed over to Harry, her eyes lowered, deliberately avoiding his. She then handed Hakomoto a cheque which he signed and passed to Harry. In her softest voice, still avoiding Harry's eyes, Minako said, 'Fifty thousand pounds in fifty-pound notes, and a cheque for fifty thousand. That is correct, I think?'

'Quite correct, thank you.'

'Keep in touch,' Hakomoto said, getting to his feet and holding out his hand. 'I'm interested in only the best. Any period. Any artist.'

Harry shook hands first with Seiji Hakomoto and then with Minako. Her hand was limp.

On the way out Harry lingered at the porter's desk, where he bought the first edition of the *Evening Standard*. As he scanned the racing pages he muttered to the hall porter, 'Laurie, tell me something. The Japanese girl, Minako Setsu, is she sharing a room with Seiji Hakomoto?'

'Different rooms, different floors.'

'If he pushes off to Japan and leaves her behind, let me know, will you. Now let's have a good tip for the two thirty this Saturday at Ascot.'

*

'Flora?'

'Yes, my love.'

Flora was sitting on the sofa next to Dicky, sipping champagne; outside the September sun was setting blood-red.

'The other night I had a talk with my old friend William Wardington. Stafford Hardinge is applying for a visiting professorship at Yale which he's almost certain to get. And that means he'll be leaving for America in January. So all you have to do is wait. Once Hardinge is out of the country you can reveal to the world your amazing discovery, and the glory will be yours and yours alone, as you deserve. What's the matter? You don't seem very pleased.'

'Dicky, I'm worried about the Honthorst going to Paris. The Honthorst and the Titian.'

'What can happen to the Honthorst in the British Embassy? Don't forget, my sweet,' Dicky said, stroking Flora's hair, 'no one knows about the Titian except you and now me. And we must keep things that way. Can you keep a secret, Flora? If you're discreet our little ploy is sure to succeed. And don't worry about Paris. As far as the rest of the world is concerned, this painting is a boring old Honthorst.'

Dicky pulled Flora towards him and kissed her, and ferreted in her mouth with his tongue. Later that evening Flora lay beside Dicky, her long smooth legs pressed against his thigh. He slept while she admired his aristocratic profile and asked herself for the hundredth time, does he love me? The question was tormenting her. He was a married man and she was his mistress, his bit on the side, as her father would say. If John Fenton knew his daughter was having an affair with a married man he'd be furious; but he'd never know, Flora reassured herself, and she mustn't spoil things by being difficult or demanding.

'Love you,' Dicky murmured as he woke.

Flora held Dicky's face in her hands; he was the most handsome, civilized man she'd ever met. He bought her clothes in Paris, took her to the private viewings of art exhibitions where everyone was a celebrity, talked to her about politics and art, made love to her with the vigour of a twenty-year-old. To hell with the future! Flora thought as she kissed Dicky softly on the lips. Anything might happen. Dicky might even divorce his wife.

Chapter 12

Archie ran the Entente Cordiale operation, as he code-named it, from his new offices in Vigo Street, but he spent a good part of the week in the Print Room at Windsor Castle where he was allocated a desk next to Flora Fenton. They worked together long hours checking lists, visiting the packers near Maidstone, holding meetings with the police and the Royal Logistic Corps.

Archie spent five days in Paris finalizing arrangements with the Gendarmerie and the Paris police. Madeleine refused to see him except formally, in her office in the Ministry of the Interior with her assistant, Lamartine, by her side. An ambitious little snake, was Archie's instant appraisal. Were they lovers? Unlikely, Archie decided. Madeleine was too professional for in-house affairs.

The final briefing was held in Sir William Wardington's office at St James's Palace on 30 September, eight days before the off. Archie sat in a deep armchair and looked out through the elegant Georgian window at flowerbeds filled with dahlias, Michaelmas daisies and nerine lilies, which reminded him of Madeleine. On his last day in Paris he had sent her a dozen white lilies, more as a protest than a sign of love.

'Good of you to come,' Sir William said, getting to his feet while his secretary, Margaret, distributed cups of coffee. Flora sat directly in front of him, clipboard in hand. Stafford Hardinge struck an elegant pose, leaning on his gold-tipped cane next to a Chinese Chippendale mirror which reflected the Canaletto of Carlton House Terrace hanging above Sir William's desk. Detective Inspector Burns sat in a high-backed leather armchair beneath a grandfather clock which chimed prettily on the hour. Next to him, leaning on a side table perilously close to a Sèvres vase, was Mr Phillipps, Warrant Officer Class 1 of the Royal Logistic Corps and Acting Royal Baggage Master.

Sir William said, 'I'm going to hand over to our special security advisor, Archie Gibbs. He's just back from Paris, where he's been putting the finishing touches to our security arrangements. Archie.'

Archie got to his feet and began: 'First, I would like to thank you all for being so co-operative.' Except for you, Burns, he thought. You don't know the meaning of the word, you obstructive bastard. But in the end you couldn't stop me, could you? 'And I would like to pay special tribute to Flora Fenton, who has been unstinting in her help.'

Flora blushed and was clearly pleased at the compliment; she looked beautiful that morning in a brown dress which set off her green eyes. Archie held up a document printed on pink paper.

'You should all have your copy of the Pink,' he said.

The Pink! The word stuck in his throat. Who in God's name had decided to print Royal timetables, these blow-by-blow, minute-by-minute accounts of who does what and when, on pink paper? Some poncing courtier in green velvet breeches, no doubt. There was a Pink for everything, for each garden party at Buckingham Palace, for State visits, Trooping the Colour, for the opening of hospitals and schools. The Royal Family didn't move without a Pink.

'I'm sorry we couldn't get it to you earlier,' Archie muttered, privately cursing Burns, who had held up the Pink as long as possible, questioning every one of Archie's proposals.

'It's fairly straightforward,' Archie went on, 'and you will have time to familiarize yourselves with the order of events. All the same, it might be helpful if I summarize. We kick off next Saturday.'

Burns had wanted Friday, but as Archie pointed out, driving to Paris on a Friday would be hell with the usual massive traffic jams on the *périphérique*.

'Next Saturday, the eighth of October at six thirty a.m. the exhibition crates will be loaded into the three Royal Baggage Train wagons. Departure is at eight thirty a.m., arriving Dover at nine forty-five. The hovercraft leaves at ten thirty a.m. There will be a police escort. I am still waiting for details from Detective Inspector Burns.'

'Royal Protection Group,' Burns snapped, staring grimly at his notebook. 'With myself in charge.'

Getting off his ass, at bloody last, Archie thought, and went on: 'Each wagon in the Royal Baggage Train will be driven by a driver of the Royal Logistic Corps. Mr Phillipps, representing the Queen's Baggage Master, will be in the rear wagon. These men are hand-picked, experienced in driving and guarding the Royal Baggage Train. There is one civilian passenger, myself, in the front wagon.'

Burns had done his best to veto it but he had been over-ruled, blown away in an avalanche of tact and charm by Sir William.

'The Royal Protection Group under Detective Inspector Burns will escort us to Dover and see us on to the hovercraft. On disembarkation at Calais we'll be met by a motor-cycle escort from the Calais police. The details are on page seven. The deputy head of the Gendarmerie Nationale, Commissaire Lucien Rocard, requests that our men are not armed.'

'Has he the right to make that request?' Sir William said anxiously.

'He has. And if the position were reversed, British police would do the same; we would not accept armed French soldiers on British soil. The Calais police will escort us to the beginning of the autoroute to Paris, where at the *péage* another motor-bike escort from the Gendarmerie will take over. We'll drive non-stop to Paris at a steady sixty miles – one hundred kilometres – per hour. As far as Arras there is very little traffic. At Arras we merge with the A1 from Lille and the autoroute gets busy, so keep closed up. There's an autoroute map on page eight. At exit five just before Paris the Gendarmerie will hand us over to the protection of the Paris police. Is that clear so far?'

Heads nodded in silent assent.

Archie continued: 'The Paris police will escort us through the city and into the courtyard of the British Embassy. Flora Fenton will be there to supervise the unloading, and to hang the exhibition. The props, the exhibition walls, lighting, stands, etc. get to Paris by truck the Wednesday before, giving the exhibition contractors plenty of time to have everything ready and waiting by the time we arrive on Saturday afternoon. The exhibition will be opened on Tuesday evening by Her Majesty the Queen. There will be a reception that evening at the British Embassy, hosted by the Ambassador, attended by the President of France as the Queen's guest. If there are any questions I am here to answer them.'

Archie sat down, his eyes sweeping the room, lingering for a moment on Burns.

'The pictures are currently at the packers, being crated up, if I understand right,' said Phillipps. 'And security there is OK?'

'It's better than it was,' said Archie, remembering the hours he had spent in the warehouses of Ellis and Sons, surrounded by the deafening noise of fork-lift trucks screeching forwards and backwards loading the crates on to vans, carpenters drilling and hammering, packers knee-deep in polystyrene chips wrapping priceless oil paintings in yards of bubble paper.

'I arranged for the Royal Collection to be kept in a separate storeroom with a twenty-four-hour guard. I've electronically tagged each crate so nothing can move without setting off an alarm. And I've doubled the security, two men on four-hour shifts around the clock.'

There were no further questions.

Sir William Wardington got to his feet and murmured, 'Admirable, Archie, admirable.'

'Yes, well, that's all very interesting,' Stafford Hardinge said, 'but transport and security are nothing to do with me. If you'll excuse me, William, I really am very busy.'

'The security of the Royal Collection concerns us all, surely,' Sir William objected, but Stafford Hardinge wasn't listening; he turned to Flora.

'You've finished those corrections to my index?'

'No . . . no, I'm afraid I haven't.'

'And why not?'

'Because she's been working flat out for me,' Sir William said, the anger rising in his voice.

'Then I shall have to bring in outside help. My index is overdue.'

Stafford Hardinge stalked out of the room and the meeting broke up. Archie went over to Flora, who was sorting papers on her knee; he noticed her hands were shaking.

'Hardinge really has it in for you, doesn't he?'

'I don't care. Not any more!'

'Oh?'

Flora turned to Archie, her green eyes blazing. 'The last laugh will be mine, you'll see.'

Flora couldn't take her eyes off the Princess of Wales. It was the first time she had seen Princess Di in the flesh and she was mesmerized by her creamy skin, her piercing blue eyes and her shy, seductive smile. She seemed to Flora unbelievably glamorous in her short, tight-fitting black dress and pearl choker.

The Daily Telegraph annual dinner was, Flora admitted, a glittering occasion, hosted by the newspaper's Canadian proprietor Conrad Black in Spencer House for a hundred and forty guests including half the Cabinet. At the last minute the Countess of Sulgrave had dropped out; officially she had a migraine, unofficially it was a blinding hangover. Conrad Black's secretary, who had spent days finalizing the placement, was only too pleased when Dicky offered to bring a replacement, one of William Wardington's protégés.

Flora was in a mood to celebrate. The final briefing that morning had gone so well, and Archie's handsome tribute was ringing in her ears. To hell with Stafford Hardinge and his carping; tonight she was going to enjoy herself.

She had lost Dicky in the crowd, but she was happy sipping champagne, waiting for dinner to be announced, wandering from one gilded room to another, admiring the massive Venetian chandeliers reflected in the huge Chippendale mirrors; looking at the vast battle scenes which covered the dark-red damask walls. Suddenly an upper-class voice drawled, 'Flora Fenton, what on earth are *you* doing here?'

Flora turned to face Lady Venetia Stubbs, lady-in-waiting to Princess Michael. 'Enjoying myself,' Flora said, forcing a smile, at the same time cursing the snobbish fool with the long, horsey face.

But Lady Venetia was curious. 'Who brought you?'

'A friend,' Flora said tersely. How dare the condescending old bat talk to her like that? Who was she, anyway, Lady Venetia Stubbs? Had anyone ever heard of her outside the claustrophobic circles of the Royal Household? Of course not. But pretty soon the whole world would hear of Flora Fenton.

Dinner was announced and Flora found herself sitting at the

head table opposite the Princess of Wales while Lady Venetia had been shunted off to another room. Serves her right, Flora thought with satisfaction. How elegant everyone looked in their dinner jackets and long dresses! Jewels glittered and beautiful women smiled and there was a low, conspiratorial buzz of conversation. Her neighbour, a Belgian banker, told her she was beautiful and tried to get her telephone number.

I belong here, she told herself, and what's more I shall carve a place for myself in this rich and beautiful world. The ivory place card in front of her said 'Countess of Sulgrave'. It was, Flora decided, a good omen.

'The Princess of Wales is lovely,' Flora said to Dicky in the taxi home.

'She's too thin,' Dicky murmured, kissing Flora on the neck, 'and her nose is too big. You're much prettier. I shall miss you terribly when you go to Paris. When is it you leave, my sweet?'

'A week tomorrow. But you are coming to the opening, Dicky, aren't you, by yourself, without Cordelia? And you will take me to dinner at the Tour d'Argent?'

Dicky kissed Flora on the mouth. The taxi drew up outside 18 St Maur Road, and Flora led Dicky into her flat, where she took a bottle of champagne from the fridge and poured two glasses. They sat together on the sofa, drinking and kissing; slowly Dicky unzipped her dress. He stopped to pick up a pink document which was lying on the coffee table.

'Flora, my sweet, this is marked "HIGHLY CONFIDENTIAL". You shouldn't leave it lying around.'

'It's not lying around. It's in my flat and nobody comes here except you, my darling Dicky.'

Flora's dress slipped from her shoulders.

*

Archie stood in the card room of the Clermont Club, watching Harry locked in a duel with a doe-eyed Egyptian; both men were hunched over the backgammon board rolling dice. Archie wasn't following the game, instead he was going over in his mind for the hundredth time the security arrangements for the following day. He had closed every loophole, checked and double-checked every phase of the operation and he knew that he was as ready as he would ever be. And yet, for some reason, he was uneasy. He wondered if the root of his malaise was not the Royal Collection, nor the Paris exhibition but Harry and the sneaking suspicion that his old pal might be a crook.

The game was over; Harry looked satisfied.

'He wouldn't take the last double,' Harry said. 'Still, I made six hundred quid. I want to play a really big game with someone who isn't afraid.'

They were sitting at the bar drinking when a voice with a clipped enunciation said, 'Your luck seems to be holding, Mr Wardington.'

Harry turned to face Seiji Hakomoto and Minako.

'What a surprise!' Harry said with a grin. 'I didn't expect to meet you in this den of vice. May I introduce my old friend, Archie Gibbs. Archie, meet Mr Seiji Hakomoto and Miss Setsu.'

Be discreet, Harry told himself. Don't reveal that you know her name is Minako and her hands are soft as velvet; and don't say a word about his art collecting, he won't like it.

'I am told your game is backgammon,' Hakomoto said to Harry. 'Shall we play?'

In the eighteenth-century gaming room beneath cornices picked out in gold leaf and walls hung with sober ancestral portraits the two men faced each other across the backgammon board.

'What shall we play for?' said Hakomoto.

'A thousand bucks a point,' said Harry. The Japanese stared at Harry and smiled.

Hakomoto got off to a better start and doubled aggressively until the doubling dice stood at 16. Harry took the dice cup and blew on his hands; there were sixteen thousand pounds riding on the one throw. He got a useless 2 and a 1. Hakomoto smiled and turned the dice to 32. The Japanese threw an unhelpful 4 and a 1. Harry's next throw was good, a 6 and a 5. The Japanese turned the dice to 64. Sixty-four thousand pounds win or lose.

Harry took the dice cup and whispered, 'Come on, baby, double sixes, that's what I need. Give me double sixes.'

He got it. At first he couldn't believe it and he stared at the board incredulously; then he punched the air with his fist and moved his pieces. After that it was a race to the finish and Harry won.

Minako, who was standing behind Hakomoto, smiled, but only for a second. By the time Hakomoto got to his feet she was staring demurely at the ground.

'A lucky man indeed,' said Hakomoto, holding out his long, tapered hand. He muttered something in Japanese to Minako, who disappeared up the William Kent staircase. Hakomoto turned to Archie. 'And what do you do, Mr Gibbs?'

'I secure art.'

'Can it be done?'

'With luck.'

'Everything seems to depend on luck!'

Minako returned with a white envelope which she handed to Harry.

'Count it, please,' Hakomoto said.

'I'm quite sure there's no need,' Harry said, taking the money. 'Can I give you dinner?'

'No thank you. We have an early flight tomorrow.'

'Back to Japan?' Harry said casually.

'I go to Geneva. Miss Setsu goes to Paris. She's enrolled in a History of Art course at the Louvre.'

'I'm off to Paris myself tomorrow. Perhaps I can give Miss Setsu lunch?'

Minako stared at her hands and whispered, 'I shall be working very hard, Mr Wardington. You see, my French is poor.'

'Of course,' Harry said.

The receptionist arrived with Hakomoto's coat and while he thumbed through a wadge of bank notes looking for five pounds, Minako whispered to Harry, 'Hotel Plaza Athénée.'

Moments later Hakomoto and Minako stepped into the black limousine waiting outside and were gone. Harry threw back his head and laughed. It was the same infectious laugh which Archie had heard so often, echoing down the cloister at Magdalen, and it reminded him of the old Harry, bold as brass and generous to a fault. Archie scrutinized his friend and found in his brown eyes nothing but good humour and candour.

'Come on, let's have a slap-up dinner,' Harry said, clapping Archie on the back. 'Life is looking up.' Insurance fraud, Archie decided, was not Harry's style.

By the time he got back to his new offices in Vigo Street the Asprey clock in Bond Street was chiming twelve midnight. In less than nine hours the Royal Baggage Train would be on the move, Archie thought, and he lit a Monte Cristo number 3. With a glass of brandy in one hand, the cigar in the other, he swung his feet on to one of the unopened packing cases which cluttered the floor. On the pristine walls he'd hung his own watercolours of the Sperrin Mountains from his Northern Ireland years. He was no Turner but they weren't too bad, he decided. The room smelt of fresh paint. He needed curtains and a carpet but there was no time to think about that now. October 8th had begun.

At 12.05 a.m. Archie's telephone rang. It was Madeleine.

'Archie, I rang earlier but you were out. Thank you for those beautiful lilies and I'm so sorry I couldn't have dinner with you. I really wanted to.'

'Did you?'

'Archie, don't take offence. Please.'

'Have dinner with me tomorrow night. You can always say it's business.'

Madeleine hesitated then said, '*À demain*,' and hung up. Archie took a long warm sip of brandy, inhaled deeply on the Havana cigar and wondered why he had this bad taste in his mouth. Everything about operation Entente Cordiale had gone smoothly. Too smoothly, he thought.

Chapter 13

It took exactly one hour and twenty-three minutes to load the Royal Baggage Train. The three dark-blue Bedford vans known as wagons arrived at Ellis's on schedule at 6.15 a.m. At 6.30 a.m. loading began in a small yard out of view from the main warehouse.

In the sharp autumn air with dawn spreading across a misty Kent sky, Archie and Flora worked fast. As a precaution against substitution Archie activated the electronic tagging on each crate and the moment she heard the high-pitched sound Flora ticked off the coded number on her clipboard and the crate was cleared for loading. The rear wagon carried the silver, made up of plates, candlesticks, tureens, salvers and a Charles I wine-cooler big enough to bath a baby in, and the only one in England which had not been melted down in the Civil War. The middle wagon carried drawings, books, manuscripts, royal seals and Renaissance bronzes. The front wagon carried the Old Master paintings in special racks to allow the pictures to travel upright.

By the time the Acting Baggage Master, Warrant Officer Phillipps, had locked the last wagon door a murky sun glimmered in the October sky. The Royal Logistic Corps drivers who had helped with the loading took their places behind the wheel while Phillipps climbed into the passenger seat of the rear wagon.

'See you in Paris,' Archie said to Flora as he climbed into the front wagon. The Royal Protection Group was out in force, two brand-new Rover police cars, three men in each and two motor-cycle escorts both armed, nothing flash, just a gentle bulge at the waistline. Detective Inspector Burns, who had watched the loading operation from the front of his police Rover, now glanced at his watch. It was exactly 8.30 a.m.; they were punctual to the minute.

'Move it,' he said to his driver. The convoy moved out. Archie glanced in his side mirror and saw the solitary figure of Flora staring at the Royal Baggage Train as it left the packer's yard.

The convoy joined the M20 at junction 5 and travelled at a steady sixty m.p.h., the speed limit for commercial vehicles. At Folkestone they took the A20 to Dover Hoverport. Warrant Officer Phillipps handled the paperwork. There were no complications and the Royal Baggage Train drove on to the hovercraft watched by Royal Protection Group officers who remained at the embarkation dock until the hovercraft took off; their job was over.

During the crossing the soldiers had permission from the Home Office and Hoverspeed to stay in their driving seats. This had taken hours of delicate negotiation on Archie's part but he didn't want the vehicles unattended at any time.

With his back to the Channel, Archie watched as the three Bedford vans, dark-blue and polished to a shine, rumbled off the *Princess Anne* hovercraft on to the tarmac at Calais. The Royal cypher, a discreet red crown on the side of each wagon, passed unnoticed, and none of the passengers, including a chattering party of schoolchildren, had the slightest idea that inside these ordinary-looking vans was over a hundred million pounds worth of art.

Archie wasn't looking forward to the drive; it was autoroute all the way through the killing fields of the First World War. Archie's grandfather had drowned in mud at the battle of the Somme in 1916 on his twenty-fifth birthday. This was a graveyard, calcium-rich from crushed bones.

As the wind whipped up sand on the dunes, Archie searched

the horizon for the fourteenth-century red-brick town hall of Calais with its odd-shaped campanile, but all he could see was a cloud of smog belching from the *Parc Industriel* on the coast.

Customs was a formality: the wagons had been cleared at the highest level. The Warrant Officer was asked if his men were armed; he replied they were not. All the same, the soldiers were frisked for weapons, an indignity they bore in silence.

'Everything is in order,' the chief customs officer announced. At that moment, six BMW 750 motor-bikes roared ostentatiously into the customs hangar followed by two dark-grey Safranes, *banalisées*, as the French call their unmarked police cars. A door opened. Out stepped Captain Bertin, head of the Calais Gendarmerie, in his military uniform, dark-blue and red with knee-high black leather boots. He hurried towards Archie. '*Bienvenu*, Monsieur Gibbs,' he said, holding out his hand.

Archie liked Bertin and had spent an evening at his home eating a delicious supper cooked by his pretty wife who was looking forward to moving to Provence when her husband retired. Warrant Officer Phillipps gave Bertin a formal salute and moments later they were underway.

The convoy left the customs hangar at 12.34 a.m. local time; France was an hour ahead of England. Bertin in his grey Safrane led the way. The three Bedford vans were flanked by the six *motards* mounted on their BMWs and dressed in their space-age uniforms: dark-blue leather trousers, black boots, white gauntlets that reached to the elbow and gleaming white helmets with black visors. A second grey Safrane brought up the rear.

The road sliced through the soft white sand-dunes tufted in coarse grass, a few hundred metres from the grey-blue waters of the Channel. The *motards* were carrying a lot of hardware, MAB 1949 sub-machine-guns as well as the usual 9mm automatic pistols. Archie was reassured: they were getting the VIP treatment.

Four kilometres outside Calais the convoy swung on to the A26 to Paris, and settled down at a steady one hundred kilometres per hour along the flat and empty motorway. Archie's calculation had been right; it was Saturday morning so there was only a trickle of heavy-goods vehicles from the ferries. For the first time Archie began to relax. It was twenty-six kilometres to the *péage*, then three hours of motorway through a dull, flat landscape.

Archie paid no attention to the distant cloud of dust thrown up by the wheels of a Renault station-wagon as it pounded down a dirt track parallel to the motorway, a few hundred yards to the right. The Renault headed for the steel gates of a disused works exit which had been padlocked for over two years. That morning they stood open.

Ahead an articulated lorry was rumbling along the slow lane of the autoroute. It was slowing down and Archie assumed the driver was having engine trouble. Either way, it wasn't a problem, he decided. The convoy, keeping rigorously to the middle lane, would simply overtake.

And then the nightmare began.

The lorry swung across the autoroute blocking all three lanes. Bertin, who sat in the front police car, grabbed the handset of his car radio and barked an order at his driver, 'The hard shoulder, and keep going. Whatever you do don't stop.'

The Safrane swerved to the right while Bertin stabbed at the buttons on his radio telephone, spitting out the words: 'Call sign three to control. Hold-up on the A26. Articulated lorry is blocking the road. Send reinforcements immediately—'

'Jesus,' Archie muttered, and told his driver to make for the hard shoulder but the hard shoulder was blocked by a blue Renault station-wagon. By the front wheel a masked gunman was kneeling, balancing a Russian RPG7 anti-tank rocket launcher on his shoulder. In front of the lorry three other men, all masked, were crouched on the road holding Heckler and Koch 9mm sub-machine-guns.

The door of the Safrane flew open and Bertin dived to the ground, pistol in hand.

'The bloody fool!' Archie said, and watched helpless as Bertin was ripped apart by a burst of sub-machine-gun fire. The outriders hurled themselves to the ground and fired back with their sub-machine-guns. Suddenly there was a flash, followed by a massive explosion; the gunmen had fired the rocket launcher blowing Bertin's Safrane apart and roasting the driver alive. The *motards* stopped firing and everything went quiet.

'Throw down your weapons, all of you, now!' the tallest of the gunmen shouted in French, his sub-machine-gun trained on another of the outriders crouched behind his BMW. The six *motards* exchanged glances: with Bertin's dead body sprawled on the asphalt and the charred body of his driver still sitting in an upright position in the blazing Safrane there was no choice. The sub-machine-guns clattered as they hit the ground.

'Get out,' the man yelled at Archie, banging his sub-machine-gun against the bullet-proof glass. The wagons had no handles on the outside and all doors were locked. Archie didn't move.

A short, thickset gunman walked over to a *motard*, pulled him to his feet, slammed a Smith and Wesson .357 Magnum revolver across his face breaking his nose, which spurted blood, and stuck the pistol to his head. In a thick accent he shouted in English, 'Get out or I will kill him.'

'Do what he says,' Archie said to his driver, pressing the release button to unlock the doors. Warrant Officer Phillipps and the Royal Logistic Corps drivers followed suit, climbing out of their wagons, hands in the air. Everyone was spread-eagled – Archie, the British soldiers, the *motards* and the two gendarmes in the second Safrane who had been forced out of their car by the fourth member of the gang, a masked gunman in a black Peugeot who had been tailing them for several kilometres.

As Archie lay on the asphalt, the ground hard against his cheek, he could almost touch Bertin's dead hand, and he remembered the pretty wife and the dream of retirement in Provence. He watched as a rivulet of blood meandered over the smooth surface of the autoroute.

The gunmen didn't waste time. With bursts of machine-gun fire they blasted the radios on the motor-bikes, inside the Safranes and the second and third Royal Baggage Train wagons, but Archie's wagon was left untouched. Another burst of fire ripped holes in the tyres of the Safranes, the motor-bikes and two of the three wagons; again the front wagon was left untouched.

One gunman loaded the RPG7 rocket launcher into the back of the Renault, another picked up the MAB sub-machine-guns and the automatic pistols and slung them in the boot. Both men then jumped into the station wagon. Meanwhile, the tallest of the gunmen climbed into the front wagon of the Royal Baggage Train, jerked it into gear and veered off the motorway down the muddy slip road of the disused works exit. The Renault station-wagon and the black Peugeot followed. The convoy lumbered through the open steel gates down the dirt track, leaving behind a mocking trail of dust.

Archie grappled with the enormity of the theft: thirty-five priceless Old Masters, property of Her Majesty the Queen, stolen in broad daylight under the protection of special security advisor, Archibald Gibbs. The humiliation was absolute and the voice of his *alter ego* taunted him mercilessly: 'I have to hand it to you Gibbs. When you make a cock-up, it's spectacular. A wagonload of priceless art hijacked and two gendarmes blown to bits, right under your nose!'

He reached inside his pocket and pulled out the central

computer panel for the electronic tagging. The small flat handset was flashing N/A; the pictures were already out of range.

Feeling ridiculous stranded on the autoroute, Archie scanned the horizon; he saw a Renault 5 approaching in the slow lane. He blocked its path, shouting and waving his arms. The woman driver hesitated until she saw the two gendarmes in uniform also signalling to her frantically. Dutifully she pulled on to the hard shoulder.

'Get her out,' Archie shouted to the French police, who brusquely told the Frenchwoman that her car was being commandeered on matters of national importance. To the British soldiers he shouted, 'Stay with your vehicles,' and jumped into the back seat of the Renault, leaving the soldiers standing helplessly on the autoroute.

'We chase the stolen van?' the policeman behind the wheel asked nervously.

'Don't be so bloody stupid,' Archie said. 'Get to the nearest telephone for Christ's sake.'

They took the exit for St Omer and almost immediately after the *péage* found a public telephone box. Archie dialled Madeleine's private number, and prayed to God she would answer.

'*Commissaire Husson à l'appareil.*'

'Madeleine, this is Archie. There's been a hold-up.'

'*Qu'est-ce que tu racontes?*'

'We were held up by five masked gunmen who killed two gendarmes and hijacked the front wagon of the Royal Baggage Train, the one with all the paintings. Three vehicles, the Royal Baggage Train wagon, a blue Renault station-wagon and a black Peugeot left the motorway at a works exit two kilometres before exit 3, that's the turn-off for St Omer, eleven minutes ago. We need road-blocks on all main routes, helicopter patrols and an SOS to all local airfields.'

'I know my job, Archie,' Madeleine said testily. 'Tell your British soldiers to stay where they are. You go ahead to the St Omer Gendarmerie and give a statement to the officer in charge. I'll get an ambulance to the scene of the hijack right away. I'll be in St Omer within the hour.'

In the next-door telephone booth one of the *motards* was talking to his superior; now and then he held the receiver away from his ear as his chief roared insults down the telephone. Eventually the abuse ended and the young gendarme, mopping his forehead with a handkerchief, emerged from the booth.

'A police car is on its way,' he said. 'It will take us all to St Omer.'

'What about the wagon you were supposed to escort – ' Archie checked himself. There was no point exploding now; it would only be counter-productive. Gritting his teeth, he said, 'Get someone after it!'

'It's done, it's done,' the gendarme said apologetically. 'Our men from St Omer and Lille are in pursuit.'

Chapter 14

The normally sleepy town of St Omer was in turmoil with *motards* hurtling over the cobblestoned streets of the Place du Maréchal Foch; four Black Marias were parked in front of the majestic eighteenth-century town hall beneath a large *tricolore* flag which fluttered from the baroque façade. Overhead, a police helicopter patrolled the moody October sky, while barmen in white aprons stood at the doorways of their cafés cursing *les flics* who were frightening away customers.

The gendarmerie at St Omer had known little activity over the years, the occasional motorway accident, a drunken brawl on the 14th of July, an attempt by two Algerians to steal the candlesticks from the altar of the church. It had seen nothing like this. Archie arrived to find the local police station crawling with people, all in a state of high agitation. The telephone rang incessantly and officers gave urgent orders over their radio telephones.

Archie was taken to a room on the first floor which was hurriedly being transformed into an incident room. An Ordnance Survey map had been hastily pinned to the wall and engineers were busy installing a fax and three extra telephone lines. Archie was greeted sombrely by the head of the local gendarmerie, Captain Lefèvre, a short man with sharp features and a pencil-thin moustache. Lefèvre paced the room, thrusting his hands in and out of his pockets, telling Archie it was a black day for him and for France; two young colleagues were dead and the Queen of England had been robbed on French soil, in his district, under his authority. Eventually, Lefèvre calmed himself and after drinking two black coffees in quick succession he turned on the tape recorder and invited Monsieur Gibbs to give his account of the hijack.

Archie had just finished when a helicopter landed noisily in the car park below whipping up a whirlwind of dust. Moments later Madeleine walked into the incident room followed by two men; she introduced her assistant, Inspector Lamartine, and Commissaire Gérard d'Espous, head of the Brigade Criminelle, the French equivalent of Homicide. Tough bastards, Archie thought as he shook d'Espous's firm hand.

Madeleine flashed her eyes round the incident room and, using the jargon of her profession, said, 'The President of France has personally instructed me to use whatever measures I think necessary to apprehend the villains and recover the property of Her Majesty the Queen. Commissaire d'Espous has kindly agreed to assist me in my endeavours as we are dealing not only with a major art theft but also with the murder of two gendarmes.'

D'Espous was rugged and attractive and Archie sensed there was something between them; or was he being paranoid, imagining that every male colleague of Madeleine's was her lover?

Madeleine went on, 'We are all deeply shocked by what's happened and the President has instructed me to leave no stone unturned until the villains are caught and the paintings are recovered. The honour of France is at stake.'

Lefèvre nodded vigorously. Madeleine asked to listen to the recording of Archie's statement. It was as she expected, short and precise and delivered in near-perfect French.

'*Merci*, Monsieur Gibbs,' Madeleine said, switching off the tape recorder. Meanwhile, d'Espous had walked over to the wall map.

'We've traced the articulated truck that blocked the motorway. It was stolen. It belongs to a freight company based in Lille and the driver should have clocked into his depot this morning at eleven hundred hours. He never turned up. We've set up over fifty road-blocks on all main and secondary roads. We've got four helicopters patrolling a radius of three hundred kilometres and five regional police forces are on standby.'

'The pictures are probably in Belgium by now,' Archie murmured. 'The Union Corse doesn't hang about.'

D'Espous turned sharply. 'What makes you think the Union Corse is involved?'

'The weapons, especially the RPG7, it's a Union Corse favourite.'

'Russian weapons are two a penny since the end of the cold war,' d'Espous said tersely.

'The only thing we know about the nationality of the gunmen,' Madeleine intervened, 'is that according to Mr Gibbs and our own gendarmes the gang leader spoke French with a Parisian accent. If you don't mind, gentlemen, let's stick to facts. We're looking for a wagon from the Royal Baggage Train, a black Peugeot, a blue Renault station-wagon and four men armed with Heckler and Koch machine-guns, a RPG7 rocket launcher, six 9mm automatic pistols and six MAB sub-machine-guns belonging to our own gendarmes. In fifteen minutes I shall release details of the hijack to the press. It will go out on the lunchtime news, both radio and television. After that this place will be swarming with journalists. Mr Gibbs, I would ask you not to speak to them under any circumstances. One of my officers is dealing with that side of things.'

'Why should I want to talk to the press?' Archie said belligerently. 'I've got nothing to say. Nor have you. But I do know this wasn't your run-of-the-mill art robbery. Brutal and illogical. Why did they take only one of the wagons? Why not all three? The other two wagons are stuffed with silver, furniture, clocks, Renaissance bronzes, worth a fortune.'

'I agree, Monsieur Gibbs,' Madeleine said quietly. 'It is very strange. You have a theory?'

'My theory is we're not dealing with art thieves in general but art thieves in particular who carried out their operation with military precision and a very clear objective.'

Archie lit a cigarette and kept his eyes steadily on Madeleine as he blew a perfect smoke ring. He said, 'The gunmen knew the exact timetable of the Royal Baggage Train. How?'

'There was a leak,' Madeleine murmured.

'You're too damn right there was a leak.'

'But where?' Madeleine said slowly. 'Paris? London? We all had the copies of the movement order, the Pink as you call it.'

'Commissaire Husson, the hijack took place in France.'

He could feel Lamartine glowering at him from the corner. Madeleine drew herself up. 'As chief investigating officer I am keeping all my options open, Mr Gibbs, and as far as I am concerned everyone is suspect.'

Madeleine paused and levelled her dark eyes at Archie, who felt the anger rising in his throat. Cool it, boy, he told himself, she's only doing her job. She can't afford to trust you. For all she knows you're the mastermind behind this whole bloody caper. She's got to think the unthinkable; that's what she's trained to do.

'And now if you'll excuse me,' Madeleine went on, 'I have a press release to write. And no doubt you're anxious to contact your superiors in London. Captain Lefèvre, will you see Mr Gibbs has a telephone downstairs. And then perhaps he would join the others in the waiting-room.'

Archie tried and failed to reach Sir William Wardington by telephone; he was probably at a crisis meeting in St James's

Palace. In the end he left a brief message on Sir William's answering machine at his flat in the Albany. He called a friend at the Foreign Office and another in Special Branch. Then he joined a dejected Warrant Officer Phillipps and the rest of the escort, French and English, in the waiting-room.

Archie pumped Phillipps for information and found out that the other two wagons from the Royal Baggage Train with their shot-up tyres had been put on to low loaders and driven to a military garage on the edge of St Omer where a guard of twenty gendarmes with sub-machine-guns were on round-the-clock duty.

'Too bloody late,' Phillipps muttered.

With scrupulous courtesy Captain Lefèvre gave everyone coffee, took detailed accounts of the hijacking from each member of the escort, and explained that they would all be required to spend the night at a local hotel under police supervision.

'That's effing house arrest,' Warrant Officer Phillipps muttered to Archie. 'She can't do that.'

'She can,' Archie murmured. 'This is France and in France the police can do anything. Remember, in this country you're guilty until you're proved innocent. If you kick up a fuss we'll end up in the slammer.'

'The Queen's been robbed,' Phillipps reflected gloomily. 'And yours truly was Acting Baggage Master. I've got egg all over my bloody face.'

'I'm in the same boat,' Archie said. 'I was in charge of security so this isn't exactly my finest hour.'

'No,' Phillipps said, cheering up, 'I don't suppose it is.'

For once Madeleine thought she was wrong. By the end of the afternoon, despite news bulletins on radio and television no one had come forward; there were no clues, no witnesses; the road-blocks had produced nothing; the police at the airport and the docks had drawn a blank. The trail had gone cold.

Then, at 5.30 p.m. a Madame Gigot who owned the Bar de la Mairie at Nortquerque telephoned the gendarmerie at St Omer to say that three men had spent over an hour in her bar that morning. According to her husband they left in a blue Renault station-wagon.

'Why in God's name did she take so long to come forward?' Madeleine asked Lamartine, stubbing out her cigarette urgently.

'Monsieur Gigot doesn't like the police.'

'Who does?' d'Espous murmured.

'Get someone over there now,' Madeleine snapped, glancing out of the window at the crowd of television cameras and reporters on the pavement opposite.

The second breakthrough came at 5.50 p.m. when the head of station at the gendarmerie in Senlis rang to say the driver of the articulated lorry which had blocked the motorway had been discovered bound and gagged in a warehouse just outside the town. Apparently, early that morning, around 7 a.m., Henri Leblanc had stopped in a lay-by to use the lavatory and was getting back into his lorry when a tall Frenchman came up to him and asked for a light. That was the last he could remember. He was hit on the back of the head and when he came to he found himself bound and gagged. It was eight hours before a watchman found him.

Leblanc's statement was faxed through. Madeleine scribbled a note: did he see any other cars in the lay-by? The answer came back: yes, a black Peugeot.

'That's it,' she said to d'Espous urgently. 'There were two gunmen in the Peugeot. One coshed Leblanc, dumped him in a warehouse in Senlis, then tailed the Royal Baggage Train; the other gunman drove the lorry north arriving perfectly on schedule to blockade the motorway.'

At 7.20 came the bombshell. This time Lamartine didn't knock, instead he burst into the room, breathless. 'They've found the wagon! It's been dumped in an old farm building in the outskirts of St Martin au Lauret.'

'Get the forensic and fingerprint boys over there immediately,' Madeleine said, her dark eyes blazing. 'Things are moving, at last. Gérard, let's go.'

Downstairs she put her head inside the waiting room. 'Monsieur Gibbs, can you spare a moment?'

It was a brilliant October night and a crescent moon cast its platinum light on to the cobbled streets of St Omer. The main square was empty except for the sound of laughter in one of the bars and the disjointed song of a lonely drunk who sang as he lurched down the street. They drove the twenty-odd kilometres in silence, Archie in front, d'Espous and Madeleine behind. Lefèvre and Lamartine followed in a second car.

St Martin au Lauret was a picturesque old village of red-brick houses, a school, three bars and a church with a narrow grey spire. On the far side of the village was a derelict farm, a cluster of fine eighteenth-century buildings with a turreted dovecote and several barns with high slated roofs. The slates had been stolen, the roof beams were rotten and the window-panes smashed. The main farmyard was covered in weeds and rusty farm machinery: a plough, a harrow, a pre-war Massey Harris without its wheels.

They were greeted by the local gendarme, a tall, lanky Frenchman with pock-marked skin and brown, darting eyes, who informed them that the last owner of the farm, a Monsieur Gervais, had been killed in a car crash in 1986 and since then the place had been abandoned.

The fresh tyre marks in the mud had aroused the gendarme's suspicion and he followed the trail to the old granary where, beneath a gaping hole in the roof and surrounded by the sweet, rotting smell of wheat he found a very smart, highly polished dark-blue van which looked completely out of place in its derelict surroundings.

The forensic team had already arrived and set up spot-lights. A cat, its eyes gleaming in the dark, crouched still and hostile in a corner; through the hole in the roof Archie could see a million stars. The back doors of the Bedford van had been forced open and under the glare of a spotlight Archie counted twenty-three pictures crates, untouched, standing in their racks. Other crates – Archie counted twelve – had been hauled out of the van and forced open and the damp stone floor was littered with wooden splinters, bubble paper and hundreds of white nuggets of polystyrene packing filler. Archie spotted several electronic tags, all of them smashed. The barn must have been full of high-pitched, screaming alarms, heard by no one.

So that was it; twelve stolen pictures, each one priceless. Archie was digesting this horrible truth when he noticed a stack of paintings in gilded frames leaning against the damp wall.

'Use these polythene gloves,' one of the scientists said to Archie, 'we haven't checked them for fingerprints. And be careful. Only touch the edge of the frame.'

Madeleine crouched beside Archie as he slowly and carefully lifted up Van Dyck's triple portrait of Charles I. They scanned the varnished surface: it was undamaged, not so much as a scratch.

'One of the most valuable paintings in the world,' Archie said.

Madeleine turned to him. 'So why did they leave it behind?'

There were twelve oil paintings leaning against the damp wall. Archie ticked them off against the inventory. It was a roll-call of Old Masters: three Van Dycks, a Rubens self-portrait, a

Murillo, two Titians, a Van der Goes, a Van Eyck, a Perugino, a Rubens landscape and a Honthorst.

'Right, Madeleine,' d'Espous said, glancing at the smashed crates, 'what's the story?'

'The front wagon of the Royal Baggage Train contained thirty-five paintings in wooden crates, each one labelled. There are twenty-three crates in the back of the van, apparently untouched. Twelve crates have been taken out of the van and broken into, and there against the wall stand twelve paintings.'

'So what's missing?'

'Nothing.'

'That's absurd!' Lefèvre blurted out.

'Look here,' d'Espous said, the irritation beginning to show in his voice, 'there's only one possible explanation. These paintings are fakes.'

'Gérard,' Madeleine began, 'Monsieur Gibbs and I have made a preliminary identification but of course we cannot be sure, in this light, in these conditions. We must wait for the experts from the Royal Collection. However, our first impression is that these paintings are genuine.'

'If we're not dealing with fakes then it must be a clever case of substitution. Those crates inside the van, they're probably filled with straw.'

'Those crates haven't been touched,' Archie said emphatically. 'I tagged them electronically myself.'

He climbed inside the back of the wagon. 'I stapled a metal plate to the side of each crate, can you see? Then I punched individual codes into this central computer panel.' From his pocket Archie pulled out a small, flat handset. 'If any one of these twenty-three crates had been lifted out of the rack, an alarm would have gone off and the code would change automatically. But as you can see, everything is hunky-dory.'

Archie activated the central panel and checked crates at random; the codes were unaltered.

'Look, Madeleine,' d'Espous said, throwing up his hands in exasperation. 'The Royal Baggage Train was hijacked. Two men are dead. Are you telling me this was some sort of practical joke? These gunmen had an objective – theft.'

'I agree. But what did they take?'

It was dawn before the preliminary forensic examination was completed. Under Madeleine's supervision the Old Masters were wrapped in bubble paper and carefully stacked in the back of the van alongside the other unopened crates. The wagon was then driven on to a low loader, and under heavy guard – four police cars and a vanload of C.R.S. riot police – it was transported to the military depot at St Omer, where it was parked next to the other two wagons from the Royal Baggage Train.

'Well, gentlemen,' Madeleine said, pulling up the collar of her black suit. 'Tomorrow I shall need the services of a senior member of staff from the Royal Collection to complete a formal identification. Whom do you suggest, Monsieur Gibbs?'

'The Exhibitions Clerk, Flora Fenton. She put the catalogue together and knows the paintings backwards. You'll find her at the British Embassy, waiting to hang this lot.'

Madeleine turned to Lefèvre. 'I should like to see Miss Fenton here as soon as possible. And now, gentlemen, the best thing we can all do is get some sleep.'

As they drove back in the early morning light to St Omer a call came through on the police radio. Detective Inspector Burns had taken the night ferry and arrived by car from England and was waiting for Commissaire Husson and Mr Gibbs in the Hotel Étoile.

Burns was sitting in a faded velvet armchair in the lobby of the drab, provincial hotel.

'You're history, Gibbs,' he murmured. 'I'll make bloody sure your name is mud after this.'

'Good evening, Detective Inspector,' Madeleine cut in. 'This is a sad day for all of us but the situation is not very clear. If I may explain.'

She summarized the day's events in five minutes flat. She was tired and wanted to sleep.

'It doesn't make any bloody sense,' Burns said. 'Somebody's got it wrong.'

'Come and see for yourself tomorrow morning.'

'I will. Meanwhile, Commissaire Husson. Meanwhile, I'm sure you'll agree with me that this hijacking was well planned and well executed. It seems the gunmen knew every detail of the Royal timetable. How? That's what I want to know. The movement order was sent to your office, to Commissaire Rocard at the gendarmerie, to the Calais police and to the Paris police.'

'And to yourself, the British Embassy, and the Royal Household,' Madeleine added.

'Now wait a minute,' Burns objected. 'Are you suggesting that a member of the Royal Household —'

'I am suggesting nothing, Detective Inspector. I am simply exploring the ground. It seems to me unwise at this stage to assume the leak came from France, but you'll be delighted to know that Mr Gibbs is also of your opinion. At last you two have something in common. On this harmonious note I shall leave you. *Bonsoir, messieurs. À demain.*'

Alone in the gloomy foyer of the hotel, Burns turned to Archie. 'All right, Gibbs, what the fuck is going on?'

'Someone's playing games. But who and why, I haven't the foggiest.'

'It's all over the French Sunday papers,' Burns said, and thrust a copy of *Le Journal du Dimanche* into Archie's hand. His picture taken outside the gendarmerie at St Omer was on the front beneath a caption, 'Bungling British'. The article was a hatchet job on Archie.

'Sweet dreams,' Burns said.

Chapter 15

It was twelve o'clock on Sunday morning and while the good Catholics of St Omer were attending mass a small army of riot police with sub-machine-guns stood outside the military garage guarding the three wagons of the Royal Baggage Train.

Beneath its vaulted roof stood Archie, Burns, Lefèvre and d'Espous while Flora Fenton, who had arrived from Paris in a police car at 9.55 a.m., was hard at work in the corner of the hangar. She had set up a makeshift laboratory with two spot-lights beaming down on a trestle-table, where she laid one painting after another, inspecting them with an ultraviolet light. In all, she examined the entire contents of the front wagon, thirty-five Old Masters; the twenty-three pictures still inside the van had been uncrated to satisfy d'Espous.

'Well, Miss Fenton,' Madeleine said, 'what is your conclusion?'

'My conclusion is the same as yours, Commissaire Husson,' she said. 'Nothing has been stolen.'

'Strange, don't you think?'

'I don't know what to think,' Flora said evenly. 'All I know is that I'm enormously relieved. When I heard about the hijacking I went into shock. These paintings are an essential part of our British heritage – without them, as a nation, we would be culturally bereft.'

'I can see that art means a great deal to you,' Madeleine said, watching the girl closely.

'It's my life.' Flora blushed slightly and pushed back her hair.

'Commissaire Husson,' she went on, 'I do hope there will be no more delay. Our exhibition is supposed to open on Tuesday evening. The advertisements are all over Paris.'

'Don't worry, Miss Fenton,' Madeleine replied. 'The exhibition will open on time. The Royal Baggage Train will leave for Paris this afternoon under heavy police escort. I shall need to deprive you of those twelve paintings which were removed from their crates by the hi-jackers, but only for a short time. Inspector Lamartine will take them to the Louvre laboratories for further examination.'

'But those are some of the finest paintings,' Flora objected. 'The exhibition is nothing without them.'

'They will be returned to you within forty-eight hours, I promise.'

'And the Queen,' Flora said almost in a whisper, 'is she still coming to open the exhibition?'

'That's for the British to decide, not us. But we hope so.'

The girl levelled her green eyes at Madeleine. 'So everything will go ahead as if nothing has happened.'

'Not at all, Miss Fenton. The murder investigation will be pursued by Commissaire d'Espous and myself with the utmost vigour.'

'Of course,' Flora said solemnly.

'The inquest will be held on the day after the opening of your exhibition. You will all be required to give statements and answer questions from the Procureur de la République and myself. If for any reason you have to leave Paris, please let me know.'

The drive to Paris was majestic: a convoy of police cars, sirens wailing, motor-bikes, helicopters, even two dark-blue Panhard armoured cars armed with 30mm cannon. A bit late in the day, Archie thought, but they're like that, the French, great ones for theatre.

It was 11 p.m. by the time Archie got to the St James et Albany, one of those old-fashioned Paris hotels with arm-chairs in faded velvet, worn brocade curtains and a minuscule shuddering lift. Flora was avoiding him; why? At the British Embassy, where she supervised the unloading of the pictures, she spoke only to members of the Embassy staff. Now, in the hotel lobby, looking tired and tense, she nodded in Archie's direction, said a cursory good-night and went to her room. Archie watched her for a moment in the gloomy hall, then asked for his key.

In his sombre room with reproduction prints of old Paris and fading green silk bedcovers, Archie took a half-bottle of champagne from the mini-bar, filled a glass, lit a cigar and stood for a while on the balcony which overlooked the gardens of a convent, inhaling the sharp October air.

Madeleine stayed behind in St Omer. Later that afternoon she told the driver of her Safrane *banalisée* to head for the village of Nortquerque. It was a drab, soulless place, grey stucco houses lining the grey road; at the far end by a railway bridge stood a squat modern church with a thin black spire; there was one shop sporting *Alimentation* on its blue canopy, and a bar. Madeleine got out of her car in the main square, crossed the empty road and entered the Bar de la Mairie.

Two leather-jacketed teenagers were hunched over the Bar-barella slot-machine; a drunk man with a matted white beard stared into his absinthe glass.

'Monsieur Gigot?' Madeleine said to the man behind the bar. He was short with a bull neck and small, grey eyes. He looked suspiciously at Madeleine's identity card.

'We've had the police round once. I've said all I've got to say. I know my rights.'

'I was hoping to speak to your wife.'

'She's out shopping.'

At this moment a plump middle-aged woman marched into the bar carrying empty glasses. 'I need a hand with these, Jean Pierre,' she said. 'They weigh a ton —' On seeing Madeleine she broke off.

'She's police,' Monsieur Gigot said, nodding in her direction. 'I told her we've got nothing else to add.'

'Could you spare me a moment of your time, Madame Gigot? I just want to hear for myself what it was you heard and saw yesterday morning.'

Madame Gigot wiped her hands with a dish-towel and led Madeleine to the far end of the bar and pointed to a table by the window. 'That's where they sat. They came in about ten a.m., three men. The tall skinny one came over to the bar and ordered drinks. A round of Calvados and then beer.'

'The others, what did they look like?'

'Medium height. Broad-shouldered. I didn't pay much attention.'

'Did you hear anything they said?'

'They were playing cards. Some sort of patience. They didn't say anything. Except for the tall man who ordered the drinks.'

'And he was French?'

'As French as you and I, Madame.'

'And he spoke without any accent?'

'He spoke French, I am telling you, like a Frenchman. Come to think of it, I did hear something. One of the other two spilt his beer and swore, and it wasn't a word I knew. Sounded all guttural. Middle European perhaps.'

'How did they behave?'

'Nothing out of the ordinary. Now and then they looked out of the window at their car, a black Peugeot, according to my husband. He saw it when he crossed the street to buy his newspaper. The tall one kept looking at his watch. Eventually he went over to our public telephone box and made a call. One of the others, a big stocky chap, took a walk in the back garden. I was glad to get him out of the bar. He smoked like a chimney.'

Madeleine asked if she could see the back garden and was shown into a small, square patch, hemmed in by the backs of white bungalows. A potting shed stood in one corner, a dog basket in another and a neat bed of autumn crocuses. The grass was patchy, with long tufts sprouting on seeded brown earth. A glint of red caught Madeleine's eye. She took a plastic glove from her bag, put it on and picked up what looked like a cigarette butt which she then placed in a glassine evidence pouch.

'How often do you go into the back garden?' Madeleine asked.

'Very little. I put the dog out at night, that's about it. I'm afraid it's in a pretty bad state but I've told Jean Pierre I can't do everything. He's the gardener in the family.'

'Do you smoke, you or your husband?'

'Certainly not. Only an idiot smokes these days.'

'Thank you, Madame Gigot. You've been most helpful.'

It was 8 p.m. by the time she got back to Paris, to her office in the Ministry of the Interior. D'Espous was waiting. She produced the glassine evidence pouch and showed him the cigarette butt. 'One of the gunmen dropped this. I'll get it down to the lab for DNA spittle tests.'

D'Espous sniffed the derelict fag end without touching it. 'Afghan hash, probably top grade. Have you noticed these cigarettes have no filter, just a hollow cardboard holder? They're called *papierossi*, very handy for pot smokers and very popular among a nasty new breed of professional hit-men, Russian veterans of the Afghan war who can be bought for fifty thousand francs. Paris is crawling with these bastards. They shoot to kill.'

'Russian weapons, Russian hit-men, and a Russian cigarette butt. It doesn't get us very far, does it?'

D'Espous looked at Madeleine. 'Mr Gibbs has a charming smile.'

'Mr Gibbs? What's he got to do with it?' Madeleine said angrily, and pressed a bundle of papers into her briefcase. D'Espous came up behind her and placed both hands on her shoulders. Madeleine turned round. 'Gérard, I've told you many times that I treasure you as a colleague and a friend. But that is all. Please, we have important work to do.'

D'Espous watched as she picked up her briefcase and headed for the door. He pulled on his raincoat, threw a scarf round his neck and murmured, 'When a woman talks about friendship there is no hope, no hope at all!'

Chapter 16

The only thing Archie knew about the British Embassy in Paris was that it was built for Napoleon's sister, Pauline Borghese. It was a beautiful building with a yellow stone façade overlooking a large garden. The roof was ringed by an elegant balustrade. Behind the delicate columns and high chimneys Archie counted eight Royal Marine Embassy guards stalking the grey slate roofs like black cats, and on the neighbouring buildings he spotted a dozen CRS snipers; thirty marksmen would be on duty that night for the opening of the exhibition. With the Queen in Paris the French were taking no chances.

Archie had a rendezvous with Madeleine in the Embassy gardens at 10 a.m. For the last two days he had licked his wounds, wandered the *quais*, looked enviously at lovers kissing, and asked himself a thousand times what in God's name the whole bloody mess was about. Harry had telephoned to commiserate and faxed through cuttings from the British press, which had been kinder than the French, but either way Archie Gibbs came out bruised.

It was a garden of autumn colours; pink chrysanthemums filled the eighteenth-century Venetian urns, the beech trees had turned gold while the maple tree was a flaming red.

There was no escaping the noise, the furious hammering of a dozen or more workmen who were putting the finishing touches to the enormous white exhibition tent, in time for the opening that evening.

'You want to see me?'

Madeleine took Archie by surprise, coming up from behind and making no noise on the soft grass.

'I had nothing to do with the hijacking of the Royal Baggage Train.'

'Archie, I —'

'Nothing whatsoever, and if you don't believe me you're a fool. This isn't exactly a leg up for my career, for Christ's sake. I've got egg all over my face, have you thought of that?'

'Yes,' Madeleine said quietly, 'I have. Archie, this whole business is bad for you, bad for me and bad for France.'

'OK, but that's not what I'm trying to say. Will you get it into your head once and for all that I am not involved – any more than you are?'

Madeleine looked up and laughed. 'You're right, I'm a suspect too! For all I know, Lamartine is in touch with the Deuxième Bureau.'

'For Christ's sake, Madeleine,' Archie said, putting his hands on her shoulders, 'can't you see? This is something big and if we're going to get anywhere we've got to work together. The answer is somewhere inside those crates. That's where we're going to find the clue. Has the Louvre come up with anything?'

'Nothing.'

She had a mind to tell Archie the whole truth. The trail had gone cold on all fronts. D'Espous had issued an identikit of the head gunman based on descriptions given by Madame Gigot and the truck driver, but no witnesses had come forward. The checks at airports and seaports, the road-blocks, the helicopter searches had all produced nothing. The only clue so far was the Russian cigarette butt.

'You're telling me the Louvre has checked all twelve pictures?' Archie persisted.

Madeleine took a deep breath and straightened her back. 'The matter is under investigation. I cannot discuss it.'

'For God's sake, you're so bloody shortsighted! What if you're right and the leak came from England? Who's going to help you then? Burns? You think he'll deliver? And even if you're not right, and the leak didn't come from England, you're still going to need a Brit you can trust. But don't come to me because I've had it up to here.'

Archie walked with Madeleine across the lawn to the Embassy courtyard where Lamartine was waiting. He told Madeleine that Professor Barre at the Louvre laboratories wanted to see her urgently. 'We should leave at once, Madame le Commissaire,' Lamartine said. 'There have been some interesting developments.'

'Thank you, Pierre. I shall see you later at the office. Mr Gibbs will accompany me.'

Lamartine gave Archie a look charged with suspicion, and smiled. 'As you wish.'

A police car lurched out of the Embassy courtyard into the Rue du Faubourg Saint Honoré with Madeleine and Archie in the back seat.

'About bloody time,' Archie murmured.

They entered the Louvre through the glass pyramid, to find Professor Barre was waiting anxiously. He shook hands with his old friend Commissaire Husson and confessed that for one dismal moment he thought they were beaten, but at the eleventh hour, with the last picture, eureka!

The Professor led his visitors into his laboratory, a small room crammed with test-tubes and several microscopes. Here, on a table, lay the Honthorst.

'I started my examination of this painting yesterday afternoon in the presence of your colleague, Inspector Lamartine. I found dust patterns and compression marks in the wood and minute scratches on the inside of the frame which are only visible when magnified. Most important of all, I found traces of pigment and flakes of paint which are sixteenth century. As you know, Honthorst painted in the first half of the seventeenth century.'

'There was a second picture hidden behind the Honthorst,' Madeleine said, bringing her fist down on the table.

'Exactly.'

Madeleine asked to take the Honthorst with her; the Professor painstakingly wrapped the picture in bubble paper and carried it himself to the police car.

'Honthorst is very underrated,' the Professor said as he laid the picture in the boot. 'And this is a particularly fine example of his work. Not a picture worth dying for, mind you, unlike the second canvas which must be something quite extraordinary. Please let me know what happens.'

Madeleine thanked the Professor and took her place next to Archie in the back of the police car. She rested her head against the back seat, closed her eyes and spoke softly, almost to herself. 'In an investigation of this kind it's easy to lose sight of the wood for the trees. Let's start from the beginning. Whoever hijacked the Royal Baggage Train took a colossal risk. We're looking for someone with great ambition, a great ego and perhaps a contempt for the British Crown.'

'This wasn't political,' Archie said. 'I'm sure of it. The IRA would probably have taken everything and used the stolen art as blackmail. Whoever organized this robbery had only one objective in mind: the Honthorst, and behind it, something much more valuable. It's a classic case of stealing to order.'

'It's time to go on the offensive, start a fire, smoke out the guilty,' Madeleine said as the car sped down the Rue de Rivoli, its siren wailing. 'I need your help, Archie.'

'Of course you bloody do.'

*

The inside of the exhibition tent had been transformed into an exact replica of a Stuart manor house complete with oak panelling, Flemish tapestries, fireplaces and lattice windows.

'Flora, I congratulate you,' Sir William Wardington said, smiling affectionately at the Old Masters, meticulously hung and lit from above with the narrowest beams of light. The silver, the Renaissance bronzes, the parchment and the porcelain had been set out on highly polished oak tables. At the back of the house was an indoor garden with papier mâché Italian statues, a fountain cascading water surounded by shrubs and even trees: acacia, mimosa and holly.

'Superb,' Sir William said, inhaling the sweet air. 'And when I think of what those gunmen *could* have stolen, eight Van Dycks, the Michelangelo drawings, the Rubens, it doesn't bear thinking about. Instead, they kill two French policemen in cold blood and take nothing at all. It's rather baffling, don't you think?'

'I do, Sir William.'

'I daresay the police will come up with something before long. It'll turn out to be the devilish work of some anti-royalist crackpot. Meanwhile, the whole thing leaves a very unpleasant taste in the mouth. Stafford took to his bed for twenty-four hours when he heard the news. Even now he looks pea-green. Have you seen the poor fellow?'

'He looked round the exhibition this morning, criticized almost everything, and said he'd be back for the opening.'

'Typical! Well, my dear, you've nothing to worry about. He's accepted the visiting fellowship at Yale, which means he's off at Christmas.'

Sir William picked up a stray exhibition catalogue. 'You've seen your name? In bold, that's what I said to the printers.'

They walked back to the oak-panelled dining room; facing the massive stone fireplace was a magnificent Flemish tapestry of a deer hunt. In front of it stood an empty easel.

"Where *is* the Honthorst? If that picture isn't here in the next half-hour I shall call the delectable Commissaire Husson myself; she promised to get it here before lunch.'

'She always keeps her word, does Commissaire Husson,' Archie said, walking into the room carrying the Honthorst. He took off the bubble paper, placed the picture carefully on the easel and stepped back.

'*Voilà*, the rakish Duke of Buckingham. By the way, there's been an interesting little discovery.'

Archie spelt out the details of Professor's Barre's laboratory findings. Sir William was astounded and asked a great many questions about the second, hidden painting which Archie couldn't answer. Flora shook her head and said very little.

'We all need time to grasp the implications of this news,' Sir William concluded. 'I would ask you, Archie, and you, Flora, to exercise absolute discretion. Tell no one.'

The grandfather clock struck a solemn cascade of notes.

'Oh dear, it's a quarter to one. The Ambassador's giving a lunch for the Queen and I simply can't be late. He's invited the French Prime Minister and half the Cabinet.'

At that moment the silhouette of a tall, elegant man appeared at the entrance of the tent. In a deep, melodic voice he said, 'William, I've been sent to fetch you.'

Archie noticed that Flora drew in a sharp breath.

'Dicky,' Sir William said, shaking his hand warmly, 'may I introduce our security consultant, Archie Gibbs. Archie, this is Lord Sulgrave.'

A cold smile crossed Dicky's face as he stared Archie straight in the eye. 'We've met before. Dear me, you have been having a difficult time.'

'All's well that ends well,' Sir William said brusquely, and was about to introduce Flora when Dicky leant forward and kissed her lightly on the cheek.

'We're old friends. Come on, William. You can't keep the Queen waiting.'

'Indeed I can't. Archie, I forgot to tell you the chief security officer at the Embassy is most anxious to see you.'

Flora pleaded with her eyes for Dicky to stay but he smiled at her vacantly and left the exhibition tent.

In her office at the Ministry of the Interior, Madeleine sat behind her Louis XVI desk, facing Lamartine. The ormolu clock behind her struck one. By now, Madeleine thought, Archie would have broken the news about a second, hidden canvas. The news would travel like wildfire through the Royal Household and the Embassy and before evening the press would have the story; and, with luck, someone would be feeling very uncomfortable.

'You know what I think,' Pierre Lamartine said eagerly. 'This is smuggling at the highest level. A painting of great value which had been refused an export licence was placed behind the Honthorst in order to get it out of the country.'

'Rather an elaborate plan, don't you think?' Madeleine said. 'Why not put the picture in the boot of a car? It's so easy these days.'

'Because this has a political motive. The aim is to embarrass the British Monarchy. The IRA is behind this.'

'Before we get on to the IRA let me understand what you're saying. Someone with access to the Royal Collection placed a second canvas behind the Honthorst and arranged to have the Royal Baggage Train hijacked by gunmen. Is that right?'

'I don't know if it's right but it's possible,' Lamartine said, a shade arrogantly, Madeleine thought; he was getting too big for his boots. 'The British packers, Ellis and Sons, are prime suspects. Those sorts of places are easy for criminals to infiltrate.

On the other hand, the brain behind this operation could be someone in the inner sanctum of the Royal Household. But if this is a British conspiracy then we'll never get to the bottom of it. Look at Blunt. He was disgraced as a spy but even to this day no one knows what damage he inflicted. The British always protect their own.'

'And we don't?' Madeleine said, smiling.

Lamartine shrugged and went on, 'More likely it's someone on the fringes of the Royal Household and I would say there's an obvious suspect.'

'And who is that?'

'Mr Gibbs. He was brought in as an outsider and he knew every detail of the operation.'

'But what's his motive? This whole affair is a black mark for him. He may not recover.'

'That's what he wants us all to believe. It's the perfect cover. And of course he's operating from a position of strength, enjoying your confidence.'

Madeleine shot Lamartine a warning look. One more word and she would pull him off the case and hand him an official reprimand. Lamartine felt her fury and retreated to his desk behind a pile of papers.

'Pierre, you're a cynic,' she said, recovering her composure.

'I'm a professional.'

She could have said the words herself. How many times had she told Lamartine to keep an open mind, suspect everyone until one by one you are able to eliminate them from the enquiry? Had she eliminated Archie too quickly? She rummaged in her bag for a cigarette.

Flora stared miserably at the entrance to the exhibition tent. If only Dicky had stayed behind to talk, just for a moment;

couldn't he see she was terribly worried? She couldn't sleep; almost every morning she woke around 4 a.m., her mind bursting with questions about the hijack; why and how had it happened?

She walked through the oak-panelled dining room and library of the mock-Stuart house, noticing nothing, to the indoor garden with its Italian fountain, and here she scooped handfuls of cool water and splashed her face. Her head was throbbing. Suddenly she looked up and Dicky was standing in front of her.

'Lunch is delayed,' he said. 'The French Prime Minister is stuck in a traffic jam on the *périphérique*. You look troubled, my sweet. What is it?'

'Do you know what's happened?' Flora whispered.

'According to the papers not very much.'

'The Titian's been stolen.'

Dicky plunged both hands into his pockets and stared thoughtfully at his feet. 'That explains everything. Now, Flora, think carefully before you answer. Who else did you tell apart from me?'

'No one.'

'Think really carefully. Not a friend, not your father?'

'My father. Why would I tell him?'

'He's in considerable financial difficulties.'

'Dicky, what are you saying? My father's not a criminal. I told no one. Only you.'

'Are you suggesting – '

'You're the only person I told.'

A pained expression crossed Dicky's face. 'I'm sorry, Flora, but I'm not prepared to go on with this conversation.'

He strode angrily towards the exit but Flora ran after him. 'Dicky, don't go, please. I'm just trying to make sense of it all.'

Dicky heaved a long-suffering sigh and turned to face Flora. 'If the only person you told was me, then it's obvious what's happened. Someone else found the Titian.'

'What do you mean?'

You're not the only person with access to the Royal Collection. Someone else found the hidden canvas, put two and two together and got there first. It's very bad luck.'

'Bad luck! Two men were killed.'

'Yes. It's a dreadful business.'

'I don't know what to do, Dicky. The inquest opens tomorrow. I'm going to be cross-examined by the police. They're going to ask the most detailed questions.'

'Don't answer them, Flora,' Dicky said quietly. 'That's my advice to you.'

'You don't understand. They've found traces of sixteenth-century pigment. They know there was a second canvas hidden behind the Honthorst.'

'So what? You don't know anything about a second canvas. You found the Honthorst, you cleaned the Honthorst. You noticed nothing unusual. Just keep your nerve, Flora, and everything will be fine.'

'Lunchtime!' a voice shouted.

'I'm sorry but I've got to go. *Lèse-majesté*.'

Chapter 17

At 6.30 p.m. sharp, Sir William Wardington led the Queen, the President of France and the rest of the Royal party into the exhibition tent. Everyone was in evening dress including Madeleine, Archie and Detective Inspector Burns who looked on as the French President thanked the Queen profusely for bringing such exquisite treasures to Paris. The Queen, in turn, congratulated Sir William Wardington and Stafford Hardinge on a magnificent exhibition. It would not have been possible, Sir William insisted, without the dedication of the Exhibitions Clerk; he summoned Flora Fenton to be formally introduced.

Flora curtsied low and unsteadily. Archie watched her closely; the girl was a bag of nerves but she looked ravishing in a russet silk dress with her mass of auburn hair coiled in a chignon.

The guests arrived at 7.15 p.m. Almost immediately Archie was summoned outside to deal with a friend of his, an obstreperous Englishman in the Embassy courtyard. Beneath the glare of television spotlights beaming down from the Rue du Faubourg Saint Honoré they found Harry Wardington shouting at a French policeman.

'My name is Harry Wardington and my father, Sir William Wardington, organized this entire exhibition. Here is my invitation. Miss Setsu has one too, but she's lost it!'

Minako Setsu stood by his side, obviously embarrassed. The moment Harry saw Archie a huge smile crossed his face.

'Thank God you're here. Will you please tell these jokers

123

that Minako's name is on the list. I had the blasted invitation in my hand this morning. God knows what I've done with it.'

Archie got hold of the Social Secretary and within five minutes the problem was solved. Archie led Harry and Minako into the exhibition tent where he introduced them to Madeleine.

'You are without question the prettiest policewoman I have ever met,' Harry announced with a broad grin.

'Put a sock in it,' Archie groaned, but Madeleine was smiling and obviously amused. She had a quick word with the police on duty and Harry and Minako were allowed through the cordon of police and security.

'You wanted to know who bought the Renoir,' Archie said to Madeleine as they walked across the Embassy courtyard. 'He's a Japanese called Seiji Hakomoto, and that girl is his assistant.'

'Seiji Hakomoto,' Madeleine murmured. 'Never heard of him.'

'No one has.'

Inside the exhibition tent a small crowd stood in front of the Honthorst. Sipping her drink, Madeleine edged forward to hear the random comments. A Frenchman was speaking with author- ity; this, he said, was the painting which had been hijacked and was it not astonishing, out of all the treasures belonging to Her Majesty the Queen, that this picture alone had been stolen and then mysteriously returned? Clearly it was the work of an anti- royalist crackpot. Or perhaps a sexual pervert, because you know of course the Duke of Buckingham was homosexual and worse, oh yes, much worse.

Archie was admiring the massive silver tureen with Harry and Minako when a shrill burst of laughter cut into their conversation. Archie turned round to face a blonde American with a deep cleavage talking to Dicky Sulgrave.

'Your friend Sulgrave seems to be enjoying himself,' Archie murmured, taking Harry on one side. 'What's he really like?'

'I like Dicky but he's a dark horse. He never talks shop. No one know who his clients are or what he's got in the way of pictures. In the seventies and early eighties he made a lot of money but he's a name at Lloyds and people say he's taken a hell of a beating. His wife is loaded but they row all the time. Oh, and they say he's having an affair with your colleague, Flora Fenton.'

'Do they?' Archie said, raising an eyebrow.

'That hijack was bloody bad luck. I don't suppose it's helped your security business. If there's anything I can do – '

'Give me a good lunch while you're in Paris.'

'You're on.'

Flora was standing beneath a row of copper pots in the mock-Stuart kitchen, looking out of a lattice window at Dicky. He was still with the American woman, laughing. She was probably an old girlfriend, Dicky had so many. Never mind, Flora told herself; later that evening she would be alone with him holding hands across a table at the Tour d'Argent. She lifted another glass of champagne from a passing tray; the dry, sharp taste made her feel better. Suddenly Dicky turned and looked in her direction; Flora smiled and raised her hand, but Dicky turned away.

She felt a wave of panic flood through her whole being. Dicky was avoiding her; why? She watched in dismay as he moved from one beautiful Frenchwoman to another and took another glass of champagne. Dicky had no business ignoring her like this; she must speak to him. She made her way through the crowd to the oak-panelled dining room where he was standing by the Rubens self-portrait.

'I must talk to you.'

'Really, Flora,' Dicky said, smiling apologetically at the American woman, who moved discreetly away. 'This is very tiresome.'

Flora was breathing heavily, twisting her fingers. 'I'm going to tell them everything. I owe it to Sir William.'

Dicky gripped her by the arm and led her to the back of the tent, stopping by the papier mâché statue of Venus; he stared at her angrily. 'Are you out of your mind? Do you want to see your career go down the drain? You know nothing, do you understand? You did your job, compiled a catalogue, organized an exhibition and you have no idea how or why the Royal Baggage Train was held up. That's what you tell the French police.'

'And what will you tell them?'

Dicky let go of Flora's arm. 'Why on earth should the French police want to talk to me?'

'Because you knew about the Titian.'

'But they don't know that, Flora.'

'But I know it, and it bothers me, Dicky, it bothers me terribly. Don't get angry, please, but did you tell anyone else about the Titian? Someone got hold of confidential information and it wasn't through me.'

'Flora, you disappoint me,' Dicky said, shaking his head.

'All the same,' Flora said, focusing once more on her hands, telling herself to keep calm and in control, 'when Commissaire Husson finds out we're lovers she'll want to talk to you.'

'And when she finds out that we are no longer lovers?'

Flora's jaw dropped.

Dicky's voice was cold and steady. 'I wanted to break this to you gently, but sometimes one has to be cruel to be kind. You're a beautiful young woman and you must find a boyfriend your own age, and do all the conventional things, get married, have children. I'm too old and too tired for a young family. I won't deny I've thought about us, together, but it wouldn't work. Don't cry. Please don't cry.'

Dicky offered a beautifully ironed silk handkerchief which Flora took and wiped her eyes.

'And our dinner tonight?'

'Did I say we'd have dinner? How dreadful! I'm afraid I have to dine with my hostess, Lotti von Arnim. I'd love to ask you, but she's an old friend of Cordelia's.'

Archie had been watching Flora and Dicky from the Venetian fountain. What was all that about? he wondered as he walked over to Flora, who was standing by herself, looking desolate.

'Are you all right?'

Tears were glistening in her eyes but on seeing Archie she laughed and said, 'As right as rain.'

Archie put his arm round her shoulder. 'Look, why don't we go to the inquest together? We can have breakfast first in the café opposite. Let's meet tomorrow in the lobby at nine. OK?'

'OK. And thanks, Archie.'

Harry wasn't in a mood to look at pictures, all the same he went through the motions of showing Minako the exhibition, but he wasn't concentrating; his mind was on the Japanese girl, her scent, her hesitant smile, her exquisite green silk dress which showed off her small and perfect figure. Later that evening he took her to a small restaurant behind the Pantheon and after that home, to the flat he'd been lent by a photographer friend, a penthouse on the Ile St Louis overlooking the Seine and the floodlit spire of the Sainte Chapelle.

That night Harry didn't have to seduce Minako, she seduced him with Japanese precision; her love-making was delicate and tender. She undressed Harry slowly, kissing every part of him;

127

she then undressed herself and rubbed her body against his back and began to massage his neck, and then his arms, and then his thighs until the desire in him became unbearable. He felt almost too big for her, she was so small and frail; she moved with him in perfect harmony, as if nothing could separate them, moaning softly, while her long red nails dug into his back. Later she trembled in his arms and whispered 'Harrysan', and he felt infinitely protective.

'What do you want out of life, Minako?' he said as he cupped her small soft breast.

'So many impossible things,' she whispered. 'I have a son of nine – Yuji. His father was American. We didn't marry. In Japan I am dishonoured. It is my dream to live in France with my son, somewhere deep in the countryside like the Massif Central. Do you know it? I have seen pictures; it is wild and beautiful and there are no skyscrapers and no cars and very few people. I would have a house with green shutters. Would you come and see me, Harrysan?'

But Harry didn't answer. Instead he said, 'Is Hakomoto cruel to you?'

Suddenly the dark eyes were frightened.

'No,' she whispered. 'Not any more.'

Abruptly her mood changed. The fragile, pliant Minako hardened into a porcelain doll. In a matter-of-fact voice she asked Harry if he would be so kind and take her back to her hotel as Mr Hakomoto had a habit of telephoning at all hours of the night. She sat stiff-backed and frozen in the corner of the taxi. Harry broke the silence. 'How did Mr Hakomoto make his money?'

'Construction.'

'What sort of construction? Hotels, houses, hospitals?'

'I know very little about his business affairs. He has many secrets.'

128

Harry kissed her long and tenderly but there was no response. She hurried out of the taxi into the Plaza Athénée.

She took the lift to the third floor, opened the door to her hotel bedroom, and started.

'Where have you been?' Hakomoto said, sitting in the armchair holding a glass of brandy in his hand.

'Harry Wardington took me to the opening of an exhibition at the British Embassy. The Queen was there . . .'

'Was she?' Hakomoto said sarcastically, and he let his empty brandy glass slip from his hand and roll gently on the floor. Minako bent down to pick it up and felt Hakomoto's hand grip her hair.

'You like him, don't you, Mr Wardington? Have you slept with him?' And he pulled on her head, harder, and she cried out in pain. Hakomoto released his grip and closed his eyes; he was half drunk. 'Westerners!' he drawled. 'The scum of the earth, and my little Minako lusts after them. She hasn't learnt anything after all these years.'

He opened his eyes wide and gripped her chin, pressing his fingers into her white skin. 'You owe everything to me. Don't forget that. Now get me a girl.'

The doorman at the hotel knew where to find the girls but at this time of night he was doubtful. 'It's late, Madame.'

'Please, please try. It's terribly important and he'll pay five thousand francs an hour.'

'Five thousand francs,' he murmured.

'And five thousand for you, of course.'

The doorman nodded gravely. 'I'm sure I can help,' he said.

Minako waited for what seemed an eternity; in fact it was twenty minutes. The doorman produced a tall baby-faced blonde chewing gum and dressed in expensive clothes. Officially the hotel did not allow 'visitors' in the rooms after eleven; in practice the night concierge turned a blind eye to well-dressed call-girls. Minako and the prostitute took the lift to the third floor.

Minako knocked on the door of Hakomoto's suite. A voice barked, 'Come in,' and they entered to find Hakomoto wearing his most expensive silk Sulka dressing-gown. The champagne was on ice. Minako bowed and left.

It was just before midnight and slowly Archie climbed the hotel steps. He was tired. He had closed the exhibition shortly after 10 p.m., crossing swords with Burns, who made it clear he was not welcome at the British Embassy. It was Royal Protection Group territory and Gibbs was *persona non grata*. For over two hours Archie had walked along the *quais*, watching the cargo boats slip silently through the grey waters of the Seine, now and then sounding their mournful horns.

In the hotel corridor he passed Flora's room and noticed the light was still on. As he got to his bedroom the telephone was ringing. It was Harry, downstairs in the lobby with a taxi waiting and a table booked in a Provençal supper club, Le Mistral in Saint-Germain. The night, Harry said, was young.

Flora had been sitting for over an hour at the desk in her hotel bedroom writing to Dicky. Her eyes were red from crying and several crumpled sheets of paper lay on the floor. She twisted the metal top off a miniature bottle of poire and took a large gulp. Earlier she had taken two sleeping pills but they seemed to have no effect. She wasn't tired at all. Two half bottles of champagne from the mini-bar and a miniature brandy stood empty on top of the fridge. She went to the bathroom and took two more sleeping pills and if they didn't work she would take another two. She lay on her bed and waited for the blissful oblivion of sleep. The telephone rang; Flora answered it.

In his official statement the night porter said that he put a telephone call through to the English girl's room at 12.50 a.m. and at 1.05 a.m. she left the hotel.

Chapter 18

It was one of those glorious October days in Paris; bright sunlight flooded the boulevards and the brittle brown leaves on the chestnut trees glinted gold, but Archie was not impressed. His head throbbed violently as he sat in the hotel lobby waiting for the Anadin Extra to take effect. God knows what they had put into the sangria last night, but his hangover was 9 on the Richter scale.

By 9.15 a.m. there was no sign of Flora so Archie rang her room; she didn't answer. He walked across the road to a brasserie where he ordered croissant and *café au lait*. Flicking through the pages of the *Herald Tribune* and sipping the frothing coffee, he kept his eye trained on the entrance to the hotel.

Burns came through the swing doors and walked briskly in the direction of the Rue des Saussaies. Archie ordered another coffee and waited. By 9.45 a.m. he decided Flora wasn't coming; he paid his bill and left.

The inquest was held at the Ministry of the Interior, on the floor above Madeleine's office. The room was bleak, with plain wooden furniture and posters of the châteaux of France on the walls. Madeleine, in her most official black suit, sat next to the examining magistrate, the Procureur de la République, a small, pedantic man who sat hunched over his papers and wrote in a tiny, spidery hand. At 10 a.m. precisely the Procureur de la République asked to see Miss Fenton, to be told by Inspector Lamartine that she had not yet arrived.

132

'In the absence of Miss Fenton,' the Procureur announced, 'I shall begin my enquiry with Detective Inspector Burns.'

The interview with Burns lasted ten minutes. Lamartine took notes while a junior officer operated the tape recorder. Madeleine then questioned the Baggage Master and the three other soldiers. Then it was Archie's turn. By the time he had finished his account of the hijacking it was 11.40 a.m.

The magistrate turned to Lamartine and said, 'Has Miss Fenton arrived yet?'

'No, Monsieur le Procureur, she has not. I rang her hotel five minutes ago. She isn't in her room and there's no message.'

'I told her ten a.m.,' Madeleine said. 'Mr Gibbs, you didn't see her in the hotel this morning, by any chance?'

'We were supposed to meet at nine a.m. for breakfast but she didn't show up.'

'Pierre, check with the police that there has been no accident involving an English girl. There is nothing to do but wait.'

At 12.30 p.m. the news came through that a body of a young woman had been found near the Pont St Louis. Madeleine, Lamartine, Burns and Archie hurried down to the morgue near the Gare St Lazare. Outside, the world was sunlit and cheerful; inside, the morgue was cold; water trickled along the sluices round the dissecting slabs. An attendant pulled back the refrigerated drawer and lifted the sheet which covered Flora's naked body.

Archie stared at Flora's alabaster face, bloated from drowning, at the swollen eyelids shut for ever; he touched the cold cheek. He was asked to make a formal identification and the attendant wrote the name Flora Fenton on a label and tied it to Flora's big toe on her right foot.

'Any witnesses?' Madeleine asked the pathologist.

'No one has come forward.'

'Any indications as to how or when she died?'

'Death was between one a.m. and three a.m. this morning. The complete autopsy is not yet ready but preliminary examinations show no violence to her body, indeed no injury at all. The lungs are filled with water, which points to drowning. The blood shows a high alcohol content and also traces of sleeping pills, not many, two, perhaps four, not enough to kill the girl but enough to make her too drowsy to swim if she fell into the Seine.'

'Thank you, Monsieur.'

In the hall outside, Madeleine turned to Archie and said, 'Mr Gibbs. Where were you last night?'

The question was fired without warning. Madeleine, grim and impassive, kept her eye fixed on Archie; Lamartine smiled. Archie could have killed the bastard but he kept his cool.

'After the exhibition closed I walked along the *quais*. I got back to the hotel at 12.15 a.m. The night porter gave me my key. I just got to my room when he – the night porter – rang me to say Harry Wardington was downstairs in a taxi waiting. We went off to a Provençal night club called the Mistral near the Boulevard St Michel. We both got plastered and were the last to leave around four a.m. Harry danced on one of the tables. There's no way the waiters won't remember us.'

Madeleine turned briskly to Lamartine. 'Cancel all other appointments for today,' she said. 'Call the Quai d'Orsay to inform the British Ambassador, Detective Inspector Burns and Sir William Wardington, but ask them to keep the information to themselves at least for today. Inform Commissaire d'Espous of the girl's death and ask him to meet me in my office in an hour. Tell the forensic boys to get over to the girl's hotel, and call the hotel manager and tell him not to touch the room. Tell him to get hold of the night porter for questioning. Mr Gibbs and I will go straight to the girl's room. Mr Gibbs knew the girl well. He can assist me in my enquiries.'

What am I doing justifying myself to my assistant? Madeleine asked herself as she got into the police car. Am I so riddled with guilt?

Between gritted teeth Archie said, 'What are you playing at, breaking my balls in front of that slimy toad Lamartine?'

'I'm not breaking anybody's balls but the question had to be asked, and when your story is corroborated I can eliminate you from my enquiries.'

'Cut the crap, Madeleine. It's me you're talking to.'

'Archie, you must understand I have a duty to France to act impartially. Justice must be seen to be done, especially in front of Lamartine. He doesn't like you.'

'The feeling's mutual. And you're too suspicious for your own good.'

'I have to be,' Madeleine said, and tapped the woman driver of the police car on the shoulder. 'Marie, I'm in a hurry.'

The police car jerked forward and darted through the Paris traffic, siren wailing and blue roof-light flashing. Eight minutes later Madeleine and Archie stood in the musty, old-fashioned bedroom where Flora had spent the last hours of her life. The empty half-bottles of champagne and the brandy and poire miniatures stood on top of the fridge. A catalogue of the exhibition lay by the bed next to two photographs, one of an older man, who resembled Flora and was laughing; the other was Flora in Venice, lying back in a gondola on the Grand Canal, resting her head on the shoulder of a man. Archie looked closely; it was a face he knew.

'Look at this,' Madeleine said, carefully unravelling a crumpled sheet of paper which she had picked up from the floor. She read the letter aloud: 'My darling, Don't cut me out of your life. Please, I beg you, don't say our relationship must end. I love you and I know you love me. My heart is breaking. I can't imagine my life without you, my darling Dicky.'

The writing stopped suddenly and there were tear-stains on the paper.

Madeleine said, 'Who's her lover, do you know?'

'This man,' Archie said, picking up the Venice photograph. 'The Earl of Sulgrave. He's in Paris for the exhibition and I saw them together last night. They had some sort of row. Flora was in tears. Pull him in, Madeleine, but whatever you do don't tell him Flora's dead.'

Madeleine was about to ring Lamartine when he arrived at the hotel with a small army of forensic scientists. Madeleine told him to pick up the Earl of Sulgrave – the Embassy would know where he was staying.

'It's not an order, it's an invitation,' she stressed. 'Don't say why. Suggest that it's all part of the inquest into the hijacking. Play it down and above all be discreet.'

In the hotel lobby Madeleine questioned the night porter who had put a call through to Miss Fenton's room at about 12.50 a.m. Shortly after 1 a.m. he had seen her hurry out of the hotel. As for Mr Gibbs, he had come in just before midnight and collected his key but he hadn't been in his room for more than a couple of minutes when a friend of his, an Englishman, had arrived at the front desk and telephoned Mr Gibbs in his room. The friend was a real gentleman and they had talked about horse-racing. The two Englishmen had left in a taxi at 12.10 a.m.

Lamartine handed Madeleine a statement from the manager of Le Mistral who confirmed that Archie and Harry arrived at the club at 12.25 a.m. and stayed there until 4 a.m.

'Archie,' Madeleine murmured as they walked the short distance to her office in the Rue des Saussaies, 'I can now eliminate you from my enquiries.'

Chapter 19

'It could have been suicide,' Madeleine said to Archie, back in her office; she was sitting on the edge of her desk smoking while Archie paced the room.

'How?'

'What do you mean "how"? There's a letter saying she can't live without the man.'

'*Façon de parler*, Madeleine. The modern woman doesn't die from a broken heart and Flora was too ambitious and too successful to kill herself for a lover.'

'If she didn't jump then she was pushed, and she would have put up a fight. But there's no sign of a struggle.'

'Not necessarily. She'd taken sleeping pills and her reactions were slow. A strong man could have tossed her in, hand over her mouth to stop her screaming. And anyway, the Pont St Louis was deserted.'

'Not quite. Lamartine took a call this morning from a barman on the left bank who was walking home last night at 1.50 a.m. and who saw a man and a woman arguing on the Pont St Louis. He didn't get a good look at their faces but he overheard the odd word and he swears they were speaking English.' Madeleine took a long, deep drag of her Gitane and went on, 'All right, she was pushed. By whom? Someone she knew. There was a telephone call at twelve fifty a.m. and she left the hotel at five past one. Did she go to meet her lover, or a friend perhaps, or a colleague? That's a scenario we haven't discussed, the Fenton/Hardinge axis. They both find the hidden

137

canvas, arrange the hijack together, they argue in Paris and he kills her. How does that sound?'

'Unlikely. They were daggers drawn. Professional jealousy, mutual dislike, you name it.'

'All the same, I think I'll call him in for questioning.' She talked to Lamartine over the intercom, at the same time grinding her cigarette butt into the ashtray.

'What did Professor Barre say?' she said wearily. 'The hidden canvas must be something extraordinary, a picture worth dying for. It's a picture worth killing for, that much we do know. As for the rest, perhaps the Earl of Sulgrave can shed some light on this delicate matter.'

'It wouldn't hurt you to have some background detail on the Earl before you grill him. Can I use your telephone?'

Without waiting for an answer Archie sat down at Madeleine's desk. Commissaire Gérard d'Espous was surprised to find the Englishman chatting on the telephone with his feet on Commissaire Husson's desk when he arrived five minutes later. Madeleine briefed d'Espous and they agreed that Madeleine alone should question the Earl. Eventually, Archie handed her a sheet of paper with various facts and figures and took up his listening post in the next-door office, behind a desk, earphones clamped to his head.

A composed, urbane Earl of Sulgrave followed Pierre Lamartine into Madeleine's office.

'Lord Sulgrave, I am grateful to you for coming at such short notice,' Madeleine began. 'May I introduce a colleague – Commissaire d'Espous. As you know, we are carrying out an inquest into the hijacking of the Royal Baggage Train and I must ask you about your relationship with the Exhibitions Clerk, Flora Fenton.'

'I'm sure you already know, or I wouldn't be here, that we were having an affair. Nothing very serious on my part;

in fact I'd already told her in London that it was over. But she didn't believe me. She imagined that she was in love with me.' He shrugged his shoulders and smiled. 'You know how it is.'

It was the observation of an attractive man who is used to success with women, Madeleine thought to herself. She kept her eyes trained on Dicky's face. 'You were seen talking to her yesterday evening at the opening. Can you tell me about this conversation?'

'By all means. She wanted me to take her out to dinner. But I couldn't. I'm staying with the Baroness von Arnim, who had organized a dinner party. I simply couldn't let my hostess down.'

'And you couldn't invite Flora?'

'No, I couldn't. Lotti went to school with my wife. They're old friends.'

'Is your wife in Paris?'

'No.'

'Why not?'

'My wife gets a little too fond of her drink, especially at parties. I encouraged her to stay at home.'

'Please go on.'

'I told Flora I couldn't have dinner with her but she wouldn't take no for an answer. She kept following me about. Well, it simply wasn't on. So I told her.'

'You told her what?'

'I told her she must leave me alone.'

'Is that all you said?'

'No . . . no.' Dicky Sulgrave paused. 'I tried to make her understand that our affair was over. I put it as kindly as I could. I said I was too old for her and she should find a younger man. It wasn't the ideal time or place, I admit. She was very shaken by the robbery, and I don't blame her. I mean, you don't really

139

expect the Royal Baggage Train to be hijacked in broad daylight on the French motorway, right under the nose of the French police and an ex-army security specialist, now do you?'

Lord Sulgrave was on form, Archie thought.

'Did she say anything about the robbery?'

'Not yesterday, but I talked to her last Sunday evening after she'd spent the day in St Omer identifying the pictures. She was appalled and of course hugely relieved that nothing was taken.'

'She said that, did she?'

'Said what?'

'That nothing was taken.'

'Well, it wasn't, was it?'

'Lord Sulgrave, if you could answer the question. What exactly did Miss Fenton say to you?'

'She said that everyone in the Royal Household was enormously relieved that nothing was taken. At the same time they were mystified. What was the point of it all, two men shot dead and nothing taken, unless it was an act of bravado by criminals who wanted to make fools of you all?'

Madeleine kept staring at Dicky Sulgrave until he looked away, staring vaguely out of the window.

'Has Miss Fenton ever talked to you about any discovery she had made in the Royal Collection?'

'Yes, as a matter of fact, she has. She found this lovely painting of the Duke of Buckingham by Honthorst. At least that was *her* attribution. Stafford Hardinge disagreed, but Flora stuck to her guns. She sat up late one evening in the picture store and gave the picture a surface clean, and hey presto she found the signature.'

'She cleaned the Honthorst herself, alone, in the picture store? No one was with her?'

'Why should anyone be with her? She's a qualified restorer.'

'Lord Sulgrave, behind the Honthorst it seems there was a second hidden canvas. In the Louvre laboratories we have found traces of sixteenth-century pigment which don't match the seventeenth-century pigment of the Honthorst.'

'I had no idea,' Dicky said coldly.

'Miss Fenton was informed of this at lunchtime yesterday by Mr Gibbs. Did she say nothing to you?'

'Nothing at all.'

'Lord Sulgrave, this morning the body of Flora Fenton was recovered from the Seine.'

Dicky stared at Madeleine uncomprehendingly, in a state of shock, his eyes wide and staring. Eventually he whispered, 'How perfectly frightful.'

'Lord Sulgrave,' Madeleine said quietly, keeping her eye trained on Dicky. 'Do you think Flora killed herself?'

'I don't know what to think. Things were getting out of hand and that's why I tried to break it off. Of course I didn't realize she was ready to take the ultimate step. If I had known, I'd have – ' He stopped speaking and stared into his hands.

'You'd have what?'

'I don't know. What can one do in these cases? Sometimes one has to be cruel to be kind.'

'Not that cruel, surely?' Madeleine said as she handed Sulgrave Flora's half-finished letter. He read it slowly and buried his face in his hands, unable to finish the sentence. Dicky looked up, his eyes wet with tears. 'I feel responsible, of course I do! I should have waited until the exhibition was over, until she was back in London. I shall never forgive myself, it was terribly thoughtless of me.'

Dicky pulled out a handkerchief and wiped his eyes. Archie, the earphones clamped to his head, heard a muffled sob and began to wonder; the Earl was so plausible, so convincing.

In a businesslike tone Madeleine continued: 'Lord Sulgrave, when was the very last time you spoke to Flora?'

'At the opening of the exhibition. It must have been around eight o'clock.'

'According to the night porter someone telephoned Miss Fenton at twelve fifty a.m. Was it you?'

'No, Commissaire Husson, it was not me. I am not in the habit of ringing people that late.'

'She left the hotel at one ten a.m. Where were you at that time?'

'With Baroness von Arnim.'

'Where exactly? I am sorry to press you but you understand the gravity of the situation.'

'If you must know we were in bed together.'

'Is she prepared to confirm this statement?'

'Why don't you ask her? She's waiting for me downstairs, in her car, a black Mercedes convertible.'

'Pierre, ask the Baroness if she would join us at this enquiry. Lord Sulgrave, what else can you tell me about Flora Fenton?'

'She was beautiful and bright and kind—' He broke off and held his head in his hands. He composed himself and went on, 'She was remarkable for her intelligence. She came from a very simple family. Her father was a truck driver. I never met him but Flora told me quite a lot about him. He made some money in the eighties and started his own trucking business but the recession knocked him sideways and he declared bankruptcy. He seemed to go off the rails, talked about doing anything to make money. One day he said he was going to rob a bank. It was a joke, of course, but Flora didn't like all this wild talk and in a way she felt threatened. A bankrupt father wouldn't go down well in the Royal Household.'

'How close was she to her father?'

'Very close.'

'In your view is it possible Flora found the second hidden canvas and arranged the hijacking of the Royal Baggage Train?'

'I find that very hard to believe. Flora always struck me as so honest, but I suppose anything is possible when people are under financial pressure. Her father could have got at her. I simply don't know.'

'But you're under financial pressure yourself, Lord Sulgrave.'

Dicky flinched and dug a nail into the palm of his hand. Madeleine went on, 'As a member of both Gooda Walker, Feltrim and Outhwaite syndicates at Lloyds your losses so far exceed two million pounds.'

'Nice one,' Archie thought, listening to every word next door. The Earl's voice was calm, almost casual.

'Lloyds has been a disaster and a great many people are ruined. Fortunately, I am not one of them. My wife is a very wealthy woman. And I deeply resent the implication of what you are saying, Commissaire Husson.'

There was a light knock at the door and Baroness von Arnim was led into the room. She was big-boned, with a broad, generous mouth and large breasts. She spoke perfect French with a soft German accent.

'Baroness von Arnim, thank you for joining us. Can I ask if the Earl of Sulgrave was staying in your house last night?'

The Baroness glanced affectionately at Dicky and said, 'He was.'

'I am sorry to ask such a personal question but was he in a separate room from yours?'

'No. We spent the night together in my bed.'

'In the early hours could he have left your bed for any length of time, an hour or so, without your knowing?'

'Not really. You see,' and again she glanced coyly at Dicky, 'we made love until four o'clock. I know it was four o'clock

143

because I said to Dicky, look at the time, it's so terribly late and we'll be so tired in the morning.'

'Thank you,' Madeleine said, 'I shall not need to detain either of you any further.'

Dicky Sulgrave followed the Baroness out of the door, down the stairs to her car.

'You were wonderful, Lotti darling, I don't know how to thank you.'

The Baroness trailed a long red nail down the lapel of his suit. 'We should have got married all those years ago when we were young and in love. I always told you Cordelia would never make you happy.'

Stafford Hardinge watched the touching scene, contemplated saying hello to Dicky Sulgrave, decided against it and marched into the Ministry of the Interior. It was, he told Madeleine, a most inconvenient moment to be called away from his duties, but he understood it was urgent.

'Miss Fenton's body has been found in the Seine,' Madeleine said abruptly. Hardinge's eyes widened and he craned his neck like a bird.

'I always thought the girl was unstable.'

'It may not have been suicide. Tell me, Mr Hardinge, did she have any enemies?'

'She and I were not the best of friends. We were, how shall I put it, opponents on the academic field of battle. We clashed repeatedly but I don't make a habit of killing those I disagree with.'

'We all have secrets, Mr Hardinge. Perhaps Miss Fenton had found you out?'

'I'm not blackmail material, Commissaire Husson. I came out of the closet a long time ago.'

'All the same, I must ask you to give an account of your movements last night.'

'I spent the evening at the Tarzan. It's a gay bar. There was a floor show which ended at two thirty a.m. I stayed on till the place closed at three thirty a.m. Plenty of people saw me. After that – do you really want to know?'

Madeleine had no further questions and Hardinge left the room. Next door, Archie took off his earphones and went into Madeleine's office.

'Pierre will check out Hardinge's statement,' she said. 'He's a nasty piece of work but I suspect he's telling the truth. The man to watch is Sulgrave. What did you think?'

'He's lying.'

'But he lies very well. I was almost convinced, except for one thing. He said too much. There was no need to go into all that detail about Flora's father. The man was being too clever.'

'Do we have Mr Gibbs to thank for those revealing figures about the Earl's difficulties at Lloyds?' d'Espous asked, glancing at Archie with an ironic smile.

'We do,' Madeleine said drily. 'Lord Sulgrave didn't like his financial problems being so openly discussed. But in the long run we're none the wiser. If he killed Flora Fenton he's not admitting it and he has an alibi. And if he didn't kill her there are two possibilities, either she killed herself or someone else killed her. There are no fingerprints on her personal effects except her own, we've checked and double-checked them and Detective Inspector Burns spent an hour going through her belongings and found nothing of any interest.'

'I'd like to see them,' Archie said.

'I don't really think—' d'Espous began.

'Why not?' Madeleine interrupted. 'We've got nothing to lose.'

Ten minutes later Flora's suitcase and briefcase were brought into Madeleine's office from the police safe in the basement of the building. Archie pulled out the russet silk dress she had worn the night before, her shoes, her evening bag. He emptied the contents of her briefcase on to the table and glanced at Flora's catalogue of the exhibition and her pocket diary.

'Detective Inspector Burns has made a xerox copy of the girl's diary,' d'Espous said wearily. 'With the greatest respect, Mr Gibbs, I'd be surprised if anything has escaped us.'

'Could I make copies of some of these documents? I'd like to study them in my own time.'

Madeleine and d'Espous exchanged glances.

'By all means,' Madeleine said, and instructed Lamartine to help Archie, which he did grudgingly while she paced the floor of her office, smoking.

'So let's go through it once again,' Madeleine said eventually. 'What have we got? The hijacking of the Royal Baggage Train, the death of two French gendarmes, the theft of an unknown sixteenth-century painting, and now the death of the Exhibitions Clerk in the Royal Household. And where are we in our investigations? Nowhere! We have no idea who is behind this, what exactly they have stolen nor why. Have we any hard evidence? Nothing whatsoever except sightings of men who may or may not have been the gunmen, and one cigarette butt filled with hashish. Someone is dancing rings around us laughing his head off.'

Angrily she stubbed her cigarette into the ashtray and went on. 'We release nothing to the press until the Queen is on her way back to London. She's had enough scandal for one Royal visit. The Queen's Own Flight takes off at eleven a.m. After that, Pierre, you can go public.'

Archie broke the news of Flora's death to Sir William in the gardens of the British Embassy that afternoon. He was devastated.

'That girl had the makings of a great art historian. How could she throw it all away?'

'I don't think she did, Sir William. I think she was murdered.'

'What on earth for?'

'To shut her up. She knew about the hidden painting and told someone who planned the hijacking with or without Flora's knowledge. Either way she was sitting on dynamite information.'

'Archie, you must get to the bottom of this, for Flora's sake,' Sir William said. After a long, troubled silence he went on, 'I can't help feeling sorry for Dicky Sulgrave. You say they were having an affair? He must be shattered.'

'I don't know if he's shattered or not but he spent last night in the arms of Baroness Lotti von Arnim. Flora wasn't his only girlfriend.'

'Really?' Sir William was shocked. 'I've always wondered about Dicky. I knew his father, the old Earl, Bertie. They didn't get on, you know.'

Archie went back to his hotel room and studied the xerox copies of Flora's papers. At 9.15 p.m. he called Madeleine on her portable telephone and asked to see her at once. They met in a small bar on the Avenue Velasquez in front of the Cernuschi Museum and Archie showed Madeleine the xerox of Flora's exhibition catalogue. On almost every page she had scribbled notes in pencil. Next to the illustration of Titian's drawing of Mary Queen of Scots she had written, 'Hair, burnished gold, hands, lily white, ring, gold, dress, black velvet.'

'I don't understand, Archie. What's odd about this? These are the jottings of an art historian.'

'Flora's talking colour when the drawing is black and white with just a touch of red chalk.'

'But the drawing was a sketch for an oil painting and Flora must have been familiar with that picture.'

'You're too right. But read the footnote. The Titian portrait of Mary Queen of Scots, one of the great masterpieces of the sixteenth century, went missing after the execution of Charles I. It hasn't been seen since. But Flora knew exactly what it looked like. How? She found the Titian and it cost her her life.'

Madeleine stared at Archie. 'A picture worth dying for,' she murmured.

They shared a taxi to Madeleine's flat in the 17*ième arrondissement*. She got out and hesitated; Archie paid the driver and followed her into the quiet, dark building; it was 1 a.m. He pressed the button for the lift.

'Not in Paris,' she murmured as he took her face in his hands and kissed her eyelids, her lips, her forehead.

'Close your eyes and imagine we're in London,' he said, and his mouth closed over hers as the lift shuddered to the sixth floor.

Chapter 20

Why must our inner cities be so bleak, Archie thought; wastelands of crumbling tower blocks and rubbish tips. Flora Fenton came from the slums of Birmingham. She got out. It can't have been easy. Nothing's easy round here.

Archie watched as Flora's coffin was lowered into the earth in St Michael and All Saints graveyard, a massive red-brick Victorian church which once stood in acres of green; now it was surrounded by a council estate and the vicar had to shout above the roar of traffic. The immortal words, 'From dust to dust, ashes to ashes,' were drowned by the roar of a jet coming into land at Birmingham airport.

There weren't many people, just a few girls Flora's age and a woman who resembled Flora, except she was older and unattractive. She blew her nose loudly into a handkerchief. A broad-shouldered man, with untidy hair, a cheap grey suit and Flora's green eyes, was crying openly. Archie walked over to him.

'John Fenton?'

The man looked up.

'Archie Gibbs. I worked with Flora.'

'She told me about you,' he said, shaking Archie's hand.

'We were colleagues and became friends. I admired her very much.'

'They've sent a wreath,' John Fenton said, nodding towards the flowers by the headstone. Archie read the card; it was from William Wardington.

John Fenton shook his head and muttered, 'They've all been

here, Special Branch and the Royal Protection Group, asking me questions, taking my flat apart, looking in all my papers. They wouldn't tell me why. One of those detectives, a pompous git called Burns, told me it was probably suicide. Not bloody likely. A couple of weeks ago I got a letter from Flora saying she was taking me to Rome this summer. I've never been to Rome.' He paused for a moment, the tears welling in his eyes. After a long, deep breath he went on, 'Flora wouldn't kill herself. She had too much to live for. What was he getting at, the Burns fellow?'

'She did what a lot of girls her age do, she fell in love with a married man and when he broke it off she was very unhappy. Listen, we could talk about this over a drink, or do you want to be with your family?'

'The wife,' he said, nodding towards the woman who looked like Flora and who was leaning on the arm of a man in a cashmere coat, 'she doesn't want to know me now I'm bankrupt. That's her new husband over there, a company lawyer. He's raking it in with all these closures. The girl next to him is my wife's daughter by her first marriage, Flora's half-sister. She and Flora didn't get on. No, Flora was my family. I'll have that drink, thanks.'

Across the car park the Coach and Horses smelt of tobacco and lager; they sat in a far corner and sipped neat whisky.

'He didn't come then, the boyfriend?'

'No.'

'A coward and a bastard.'

'Yes. He's both those things.'

'You haven't told me the half of it, have you?'

'No. And I can't, not for the time being. But when I find out what happened, I'll come and tell you everything, I promise.'

Wearily John Fenton drained his glass and got to his feet. Archie handed him a business card and explained that he would have to go back to Paris in a few days' time to pack up the exhibition but if John Fenton needed him for anything, he could reach him through his London office.

Archie caught the 2.10 to St Pancras and went straight to his office in Vigo Street, where he found a message that stopped him dead in his tracks. It was the last person he expected to hear from, the Countess of Sulgrave, asking him to ring immediately. He did.

'Mr Gibbs, how very kind of you to return my call.'

Archie reckoned she'd been drinking; the voice was thick.

'Could I trouble you to come and see me as soon as possible? I'm afraid I can't tell you what it's about over the telephone.'

'I can be with you in fifteen minutes.'

'Perfect,' she said, and hung up.

He got to Rutland Gate just after 5.30 p.m. Cordelia Sulgrave opened the door herself with a drink in her hand and a labrador rubbing itself against her legs, tail wagging.

'Thank you for coming,' she said. 'Nelson, behave! Do come in.'

Archie stepped into the hall and before he could shut the door the dog pushed past and pressed his nose against the door and closed it.

'Who taught him that?' Archie said.

'Nelson is a guide dog for the blind. He belonged to my father, who died last year and now he lives with me in the country. But Dicky hates him and I can only bring him to London when Dicky's away. Nelson is the cleverest dog I've ever met. I'm always teaching you new tricks, aren't I?' And she crouched down beside the dog and stroked him affectionately.

The drawing room was as Archie remembered it, elegant and cold.

'That picture,' she said, turning round to face the portrait of her mother. 'You remember *that*?'

151

'I do.'

'My husband took it off the wall to be photographed. You were here when he brought it back. He said it was the same painting, and you believed him. Well, it's a fake.'

'How do you know?'

'I know because I have eyes in my head. That painting is not by Augustus John and that woman is not my mother. She's an impostor and with your help I can prove it. Have a drink, Mr Gibbs, help yourself.'

Archie poured himself a malt whisky and sat in a deep armchair. Nelson shuffled over and settled his chin on Archie's knee.

'He likes you.' Cordelia Sulgrave drained her glass and in a new, almost sober voice she said, 'Will you help me? I'll pay you whatever you want. But you're not to tell the police. I don't want them involved.'

'What do you want me to do?'

'Take the picture away and show it to an expert.'

'So you're not sure, after all.'

'I'm quite sure but who's going to believe me, Cordelia Sulgrave, that old soak? They'd laugh in my face. I need the opinion of an expert. Dicky's away today and tomorrow. You've got two days. Come back tomorrow evening and tell me that I'm right.'

'And if you're right,' Archie said, slowly stroking the dog's soft fur, 'what are you going to do?'

'I don't know. Maybe something rather unpleasant. You see, I'm old-fashioned. I believe in an eye for an eye. Oh, by the way, that girl who died in Paris, she was Dicky's mistress.'

'I know.'

'She wasn't the only one.'

'I know that too.'

'Goodness me, you are well informed.'

She smiled and raised her glass to Archie while Nelson nuzzled up to her legs.

An evening class on Michelangelo was the last thing Archie felt like after a long day, but on a Thursday it was the one place he knew he could find Hewitt. He made it to the Cundy Street Adult Education Centre shortly after 6.30 p.m. and settled into the empty chair next to the Chief Inspector, who was taking notes, now and then glancing up at a shaky image of the Vatican *Pietà* on the projector screen while the teacher eulogized about the world's greatest sculpture. Archie sat back and closed his eyes.

After the lecture they walked down Queen Anne Street to the Green Man for a pint. A juke-box was playing sixties music and the air smelt of stale beer.

'I need your help, Paul,' Archie said. 'Who knows about fakes?'

'Depends which period.'

'Twentieth century.'

'Abstract?'

'Figurative.'

'Artist?'

'Can't tell you.'

The Chief Inspector leaned forward over his beer. 'And why not?'

'The client wants to keep this under wraps.'

Paul Hewitt leant his head against the wooden panelling behind him, and stared at the man at the next-door table who was blowing neat smoke rings into the stale air.

'Geoffrey Hunter. Lives in Maida Vale. Went down for two years on a forgery charge, in this case Modigliani but he's forged almost everything in his time. Now he's doing very nicely thank you in his own business.'

'Which is?'

'Reproduction of twentieth-century masters. It's all above board. By law the paintings have to be a smaller size than the originals with Geoffrey's name stamped on the back. He's bought himself a flat in Torremolinos with his profits. That's the official story.'

'And the unofficial story?'

'He's still forging. Probably from the flat in Spain. But the Spanish police, well, you know how it is. The Costa del Sol is full of British villains. If he's in London you'll find him in flat A, twenty-three Sutherland Avenue.'

'Thanks.'

For five hundred pounds plus expenses the Countess of Sulgrave had bought one day of Archie's time. He'd kept the Augustus John in his safe overnight and the next morning he drove to 23 Sutherland Avenue and rang the bell opposite the name-plate: 20th-Century Masters.

'Who is it?' a voice barked through the intercom.

'I've got a picture. I want you to look at it.'

'Who are you?'

'Archie Gibbs. Security consultant.'

It was one of those videophone entry devices and the eye of the small camera was on Archie's face as he waited while Hunter decided whether or not to let him in.

'Come in.'

The small flat was flooded with light from windows which opened on to a communal garden with flowerbeds of autumn crocuses and Michaelmas daisies. A dog bounded across the neatly mown lawn, darting in and out of rose bushes. There was dandruff on Hunter's collar, his skin had an oily sheen and his eyes were faintly bloodshot.

'So, who sent you here?'

'Word of mouth.'

'Whose mouth?'

Archie didn't answer. He lifted the parcel on to the table, tore off the brown paper and held up the Augustus John of Cordelia Sulgrave's mother.

'What do you think?' he said in his most offhand manner.

'What do I think about what?'

'Is it genuine, or a fake?' Archie was staring intently at Hunter.

'My opinion isn't cheap.'

'How much?'

'Three hundred and fifty.'

Archie pulled out three hundred and fifty pounds in fifty-pound notes and handed them over.

'It's an oven job,' Hunter said.

'What's that?'

'You coat the canvas with a binding agent, usually gesso. Print on to it. Bake it in the oven. If you get it right you can fool most of the people for most of the time.'

'But you can spot the difference?'

'Now and then.'

'Have a good look at this picture. Are you sure?'

'As sure as eggs is eggs. I knocked it up myself.'

Archie caught his breath. Hunter was grinning, showing two gold teeth.

'How did you do it?' Archie said. 'From a photograph?'

'A negative. It's dead easy. Now don't get me wrong, there was no intention to deceive. I never tried to pass it off as the real thing. Can't get me on that one. Just did a friend a favour, that's all.'

'The Earl of Sulgrave.'

'The Earl of who?'

The bloodshot eyes were expressionless. Hunter began to count the money.

'Thanks anyway,' Archie said, picking up the picture. Clever bastard, he thought as he walked down the street with the picture under his arm. Earned himself three hundred and fifty quid in less than five minutes.

At 6 p.m. the next evening Archie rang the doorbell at 4 Rutland Gate. Nelson was waiting by the door, wagging his tail. Cordelia poured them both stiff whiskies and listened to what Archie had to say. When he'd finished she blew a long puff of smoke into the air.

'An oven job,' she murmured. 'What does Shakespeare say? "Conscience does make cowards of us all!" Well, not Dicky. He's as brave as a lion. He doesn't stop at anything. Here's your money, Mr Gibbs, and the three hundred and fifty pounds you paid the forger.'

Cordelia handed Archie a brown envelope.

'Thank you for all your trouble. I'm enormously grateful.'

'What for?' said a deep, irritated voice. Dicky Sulgrave was standing in the doorway in a dark suit, wearing a Garrick Club tie. Nelson growled.

'I've told you a thousand times, Cordelia, I won't have that dog in this flat!'

'Be quiet, Nelson,' Cordelia said kindly; reluctantly the dog lay down on the floor beside her.

Dicky gave Archie a long, hard look and said, 'Shouldn't you be in Paris looking after the Royal Collection?'

'I came over for Flora Fenton's funeral.'

Dicky glanced at Archie with cool indifference, went over to the drinks tray and poured himself a large whisky. 'That doesn't explain why you're in my flat.'

'You're wife asked me to get the Augustus John looked at by an expert in twentieth-century figurative art.'

'She did what?'

'She thought it was a fake and asked me to consult an expert, so I did. He pronounced it a forgery, what is known in the trade as an "oven job".'

'Who is this man?'

'I can't tell you his name.'

'Then I'm not interested in his opinion. An expert who doesn't dare reveal his name is hardly a man to take seriously.'

'On the contrary, Lord Sulgrave. He has to remain anonymous because he was the forger.'

Archie kept his eyes trained on Dicky as he took a large gulp of whisky.

'I suggest you hand him over to the police.'

'He'd deny everything. But he knows what he's talking about. Take the painting to any of the top galleries and they'll say the same.'

'In that case you're the bearer of very bad news, Mr Gibbs,' Dicky Sulgrave said, sinking into an armchair, distress written all over his face. 'I'll get my people on to it at once. But if it *is* a forgery then it's quite obvious what happened.'

'Tell us, Dicky,' Cordelia said sarcastically.

'I don't exactly know how you make an "oven job" but I imagine it's a photographic process, is that right, Mr Gibbs?'

'That's right.'

'About a month ago the picture was photographed. Obviously someone stole the negative, made the forgery, did a quick substitution and walked off with the original. Quite clearly this was an inside job. I'm going to call the police.'

Archie got up and shook hands; he could feel the Earl's sweating palm.

'I'll see myself out,' Archie said. As he was closing the front door he heard Cordelia's guttural voice.

'You'll pay for this, Dicky, I swear to God!'

157

Chapter 21

The next day Archie was on duty at the British Embassy; by the evening he was out of a job. He should have seen it coming but he didn't. Instead he caught the first flight to Paris and went like a lamb to the slaughter.

It took a team of specialist art packers less than five hours to dismantle the exhibition, pack up the art treasures and crate them up ready for the journey home. Stafford Hardinge barked orders as the silver tureens were laid in beds of polystyrene chips and Old Masters were lifted off the imitation oak panelling and laid in bubble paper ready to be crated up. Meanwhile, an army of workmen dismantled the mock-Jacobean manor house and uprooted the indoor garden, carrying off the papier mâché statues under their arms and switching off the fountains.

Archie got the sack at tea-time. As sackings go it was done in a very gentlemanly way by Sir William Wardington while ambling across the Embassy lawn.

'I'm afraid there's been a Palace revolution,' Sir William announced. 'Detective Inspector Burns has been working overtime bending the Chief Commissioner's ear, with the most unfortunate results. The Queen's Private Secretary is now persuaded you're more of a liability than an asset. I've argued as forcefully as I could that it's in our interest to retain your services but the tide's against you, dear boy. I must terminate your contract as of now. We'll pay you to the end of the month, of course. I'm very sorry about this, Archie, a most unfortunate conclusion to this troubled affair. What will you do? Go back to London?'

'Maybe, maybe not. I don't like leaving business unfinished. Sir William, it's been a pleasure working for you.'

'I wish you the very best of luck,' Sir William said, and shook Archie's hand warmly.

In the Embassy courtyard Madeleine and Lamartine were watching as the crates were loaded into the gleaming blue vans of the Royal Baggage Train. Madeleine hurried over. 'The more I think about it,' she said, her dark eyes glowing, 'the more I'm sure we've got to tap Sulgrave's telephone. I'll have a go at Burns but Sir William is the key. Talk to him. He'll listen to you.'

'Not any more, he won't. I've just got the sack. That bastard Burns has been working overtime behind my back. Sorry I can't help, Madeleine, but I'm out of a job.'

'No you're not,' Madeleine said with a dazzling smile. 'You can work for me.'

Archie left the Embassy and made his way back to his hotel, where he found Harry Wardington waiting in the lobby. The moment he saw Archie, Harry jumped to his feet.

'The old man's off his head, giving you the sack. I told him, "What could Archie do against sub-machine-guns? Bare his chest and wait for the bullets?" According to Pa they were after a canvas hidden behind the Honthorst. Any idea what it was?'

'Maybe.'

'A lot of *Sturm und Drang* for one picture, if you ask me, not to mention those two gendarmes who were blown away. Very nasty. Anyway, I went down on bended knee for you, Archie, but Pa told me they were twisting his arm and a head had to roll. Yours. God, I was furious.'

'Lay off your old man. I like him. Anyway, I've got myself a new job, so relax.'

They had dinner at a local bistro and washed down sirloin

steak with two large carafes of red wine which brought out the maudlin in Harry.

'Do you ever think, what the fuck am I doing? I mean, look around. Men our age have settled down, Archie. They've got wives and children and all that family baggage; birthdays and anniversaries and school holidays. Do you ever feel your life is one gaping hole?'

'No,' Archie lied. He wasn't in a sentimental mood.

'Well, I do. I've been playing the field for years and the girls are a sort of blur. Not long ago I was in bed with Lorna and in my sleep I called her Kate. She wasn't pleased. I tell you, Archie, it's time we settled down.'

'Have you got someone in mind?'

'Not really. I'm having a most unsuitable affair, as my father would say, with Seiji Hakomoto's concubine. Lovely body, lovely face, but a devious mind. Nothing's clear-cut with Minako. Hakomoto's asked her to find a top picture restorer who's prepared to spend a month in Tokyo. The fee's outrageous. A thousand dollars a day.'

'It must be one hell of a picture. What is it?'

'I don't know, nor does Minako. Hakomoto is being very hush-hush. All she knows is that it's sixteenth century and in lousy condition. Jesus, this wine is filthy. I'm going to have the most God-awful hangover tomorrow morning.'

He didn't look good at 8 a.m. when Archie and Madeleine marched Harry out of his flat in the Rue Bonaparte for a breakfast of *café au lait* and croissant.

'What's the blinding hurry?' he said, blinking unhappily at the bright morning sunlight. In the Café Bonaparte, Archie produced a variety of hangover remedies but Harry settled for Alka Seltzer and drank three espressos in succession, burped loudly and told Madeleine she should be a film star not a policewoman.

'Mr Wardington—'

'Harry, please.'

'I need your help. I'm interested in your friend Miss Setsu and in her employer Seiji Hakomoto. I'd like to ask you a few questions, off the record of course.'

'Look, I'm a simple soul, especially when I'm hung over. What's this all about?'

Madeleine took just under five minutes and one cigarette to spell out the salient facts, by which time Harry was wide awake.

'The idea's incredible. The Earl of Sulgrave, gentleman thief, supplies stolen art to the Japanese construction king, Seiji Hakomoto. You're off your rocker, both of you.'

'Minako's looking for a sixteenth-century-picture restorer and it's all very hush-hush,' Archie murmured.

'We can't prove anything,' Madeleine said firmly. 'All we have is a mountain of circumstantial evidence, coincidence after coincidence which points to a joint operation between Sulgrave and Hakomoto. But as for hard evidence, we haven't got any. We don't even know if Sulgrave and Hakomoto know each other.'

'They do.'

Madeleine and Archie looked up sharply at Harry.

'How do you know?' Madeleine asked, her voice urgent.

'Because I was in the lobby of the Plaza Athénée the morning after the opening, ringing Minako's room – we had a date to have breakfast and I was standing in this telephone booth, ringing and ringing her room – there was no answer – when someone comes into the next-door booth and begins to dial. The voice says, "Seijisan, this is Dicky, I'll meet you at the usual place." I got a quick look. It was Dicky Sulgrave.'

'"Seijisan", that's very chummy,' Archie murmured.

Madeleine didn't react, she was draining her espresso and thinking. 'Has Minako ever mentioned Dicky?' she asked.

'Never. And when they met after the Shackleton auction

they both behaved as if they'd never met, which is possible. After all, she's new to the job. On the other hand, it could have been a little show for my benefit.'

'You don't trust her?'

'I'd like to but . . . listen, she's pretty and clever and I saw myself supplying her boss with an endless stream of pictures so I've been extra specially nice to her, foot-slogging round Paris looking for Mr Oliver Dashwood.'

'Who's he?'

'A top picture restorer and expert on sixteenth-century painting. He used to work at the National Gallery but left under a cloud of suspicion. For some reason Minako thinks he's the man for the job in Tokyo.'

'Have you found him?'

'No. But we're going to have another crack this afternoon. God knows why but he keeps changing flats.'

'I need twenty-four hours,' Madeleine said. 'Can you post-pone your meeting with Minako until tomorrow afternoon?'

'Probably,' Harry said. 'Look. I'll do anything I can to help. This blasted hijacking is a sorry end to my Dad's glorious career and there's nothing I'd like more than to surprise him with the long-lost Titian of Mary Queen of Scots.' He drank his fourth espresso in one gulp. 'I don't want to teach my grandmother to suck eggs, and by the way you don't look anything like my grandmother, but it's quite obvious what you should do next. Get inside the Hakomoto camp.'

Madeleine sat back in her chair and smiled.

'That's exactly what we're going to do.'

Chapter 22

'Harrysan, this is the number.'

Minako and Harry were standing beneath a large black umbrella surveying the unpromising exterior of 381 Boulevard Raspail, a concrete block from the 1950s. They took the lift to the fourth floor, rang the bell, and the door was answered by a man with a shock of brown hair and a bushy brown beard; he wore an old, stained smock smeared with paint.

'Mr Dashwood?' Harry said.

'Who are you? What do you want?'

'My friend here wants to talk to you.'

'I have a job for you,' Minako intervened meekly. 'A restoring job.'

The man hesitated, then he said gruffly, 'You'd better come in then.'

It was a typical Parisian studio, one large room with a skylight. The gentle thud of rain tapped on the glass roof. A painting stood on an easel; canvases large and small leant against the wall and everywhere there were bottles and rags, palette knives and paints, and the air smelt of chemicals.

'I work for Seiji Hakomoto, he is a Japanese industrialist and he has just acquired a new picture. It is sixteenth century and the condition is poor. He wishes you to come to Tokyo and clean it. Please name your price.'

'What is this? Some sort of joke?'

'I am not joking, Mr Dashwood.'

'You walk in here off the street, ask me to go to Tokyo and

tell me I can name my price. If that's not a joke I don't know what is!'

'Mr Dashwood, I am not joking.'

'Why me? Out of all the restorers in this goddam world, why me? No one wants to know me these days.'

'Mr Hakomoto understands that sixteenth-century pigment is very delicate. You are an expert. And very famous.'

'Very infamous, isn't that what you mean? Sacked from the National Gallery. A drawing went missing, and they said I stole it. Well, I didn't, but professionally I was finished. That was two years ago.' His voice trailed off.

Minako went on softly, 'Mr Hakomoto estimates that the work will take at least a month. He is happy to offer a thousand dollars a day, and of course all your expenses will be paid. He hopes very much you will accept.'

'Who's the painting by?'

'We don't know. Mr Hakomoto was hoping that you would be able to find out.'

'Landscape or portrait?'

'Portrait.'

'Man or woman?'

'Woman.'

'You said the painting is in poor condition. How poor?'

'It is black except for a small portion which has been cleaned.'

'By some amateur, no doubt. Do we know the artist or the identity of the woman?'

'No.'

'All right, I accept. I want the money sent to my account in the Channel Islands. I want a letter confirming these arrangements and an advance of three thousand dollars. But I have to tell you now, I can't leave for four weeks. I've got a lot of work to finish for the galleries before Christmas.'

'That is not a problem,' Minako said. 'There is no great

hurry. I am leaving for Japan on Monday. Until then I am at the Plaza Athénée. Here is my card. I shall send you a letter confirming our arrangements.'

'I don't answer the telephone when I'm working but you can leave a message.'

'Goodbye, Mr Dashwood,' Minako said, holding out her slim, soft hand.

'Goodbye,' the man said.

Minako and Harry hurried down the four flights of stairs, anxious to get out of the stale, unhealthy air of the building. Outside, in the dreary October rain, Minako was elated. 'Harry-san, our long search is over. Mr Hakomoto will be very pleased. It is a shame Mr Dashwood cannot start sooner, but never mind. It is worth waiting to get the best, I think, don't you?'

She was late for a lecture at the Louvre and hailed a taxi. Harry waved until she was out of sight then hurried back into the buildings, took the lift back up to the fourth floor and marched into the flat where the bearded man and Madeleine were laughing.

'Archie, you deserve an Oscar.'

The real Oliver Dashwood didn't have a chance. Madeleine came down on him so hard he collapsed and agreed to everything. She mobilized half the Paris police force and found him within a matter of hours. Detectives were sent in to dig up the dirt and by nightfall she had all the ammunition she needed. She called on Dashwood at 8 a.m. the next morning, flashing her police card in his anxious face as he stood in his jogging clothes ready to go out for his morning run.

'Tax evasion is a criminal offence, Mr Dashwood,' Madeleine said, picking her way between the newspapers, tubes of paint and bottles of white spirit which littered the studio floor.

Meanwhile Lamartine stood by the grubby window staring out over the Boulevard Raspail. 'You've been taking cash payments for your restoration work. And more cash from your bookstall on the *quai*. You're in trouble, Mr Dashwood. A prosecution would mean a heavy fine, and, as a British subject, expulsion from France.'

'I couldn't pay the fine. I don't have any money.'

'Then you could go to prison.'

Madeleine watched the gaunt, bearded face twitch at the news he might go to jail.

'Why are you picking on me like this? There must be plenty of other people who cheat on a bigger scale than I do. You know as well as I do, in France everyone cheats.'

'That is not true, Monsieur.'

'Isn't it?' Dashwood said wearily. 'Times are hard, you know that. Work is very scarce. It's no use asking me for a fine. I can't pay it. But that's not why you're here, is it?'

'No. I need your co-operation, Mr Dashwood. People tell me you were the best restorer in England—'

'I'm still the best restorer in England, but these days I only get the dregs, the sort of rubbish people find in their attics, moth-eaten portraits of ancestors by second-rate followers of Kneller or hack stuff from third-rate galleries.'

'I can offer you a first-class painting to restore, Mr Dashwood. The army academy in Saint Cyr has a fine collection of Meissonier battle scenes which badly need restoring. Will you take it on?'

'Of course I'll take it on but what's the catch?'

'The catch is, for the next four weeks I want you to teach a friend of mine how to restore paintings. Teach him everything you know. Make him practise eight hours a day. Turn him into a professional. Can you do it? We will pay you generously.'

'In four weeks? I can make him pass for a professional, sure, but not for long. Without experience or training he's bound to slip up, especially if he can't draw or paint.'

'He's a gifted amateur, as they say.'

'That helps, but he'll be caught out sooner or later.'

'Yes, of course, but I'm interested in the first impression. Can you make it convincing?'

'Maybe.'

'I want him to move in here and live with you.'

'That's out of the question. I will not have my privacy invaded.'

'In prison there is no privacy at all. Think about it, Mr Dashwood.'

For a moment, Dashwood looked bewildered, then he capitulated: 'All right. I agree.'

'Excellent. Now. I have a favour to ask. I need to borrow your studio for a few hours this afternoon. Don't worry, we won't touch anything. By five p.m. we'll be gone.'

'All right.' The voice was dull, flat. 'This friend of yours, my flatmate, what's his name?'

'Andrew Guthrie.'

'Andrew Guthrie! Why did you pick such a terrible name?'

'It's a good name,' Madeleine said as they walked beneath the massive iron labyrinth of the Eiffel Tower. 'And it means you don't have to change your initials. Anyway, it's only for three weeks. After that your name is Oliver Dashwood. I've taken a long and careful look at the real Oliver Dashwood; he's the same build as you and he keeps himself fit jogging. The good thing is Hakomoto has never met him.'

'Hakomoto may not have met Dashwood but he's met me at the Clermont with Harry.'

'Did you talk to him at any length?'

'No. We exchanged a few words then he challenged Harry to a game of backgammon. Minako was there. And don't forget that you and I met Minako at the opening of the exhibition.'

'All right, you've met them, but only briefly and the human memory is easily deceived. We have the most highly skilled make-up artists, as they like to be called. Several of them trained with the Comédie-Française and I can assure you, give them half a day and they can turn you into anything, a hunchback, a great-grandfather, even a woman! Now, I've made some notes.'

Madeleine pulled out a small black book from her pocket. 'Dashwood wears his hair long, he has a beard, it's brown and bushy. His eyes are a dark brown. Yours are a light hazel so you'll have to wear coloured contact lenses. The other details are easy: his hands are dirty, especially his fingernails. When he sits he slouches, and he drags his feet when he walks and he's always frowning. He's a man in a permanent crisis, at odds with the world. You'll notice these things for yourself, and of course pick up many other details when you live with him.'

'Live with him?'

'Yes, you're moving in tomorrow.'

'I'd rather live with you.'

Chapter 23

Needles pricked his eyes; his spine felt calcified. For three hours Archie had been sitting in front of an eighteenth-century copy of Titian's *Diana and Actaeon* on loan from the Louvre. Oliver Dashwood, on the other hand, was feeling fine. He paced his studio floor, a glass of wine in his hand, giving instructions.

'Gently, gently. You roll the cotton wool, you don't scrub. This isn't a shirt collar, Andrew. It's a poor copy, I grant you, but worthy none the less of your finest effort, not your contempt. His finest paintings, in my view, are portraits. There was no one better. Ah, but Rembrandt touches the soul, I hear you say. Yes, indeed, and old age has never been the same. But his range was narrow, Dutch burghers, hundreds of them, all dressed the same. Titian had a glorious sense of theatre and he loved kings and queens and all that pageantry. Who didn't he paint? The Emperor Charles V, Pope Paul III, Margaret Queen of Spain and the most beautiful monarch in Europe, Mary Queen of Scots. Alas, the picture is lost, hacked to pieces by Puritan fanatics, at least that is my interpretation.'

At last Oliver Dashwood drew breath.

'That was a *tour de force*,' Archie said.

'I graduated in Fine Arts at Cambridge and I used to lecture at the Courtauld. I'm an art historian as well as a picture restorer. I had a brilliant career. I was going right to the top until . . .' His voice trailed off. He banged his fist hard on the wooden table. 'I wouldn't mind so much if I'd stolen the bloody thing, but I didn't! I was innocent. But no one believed me. The drawing was found in my briefcase, an exquisite sketch by Raphael of the Virgin and Child. Someone put it there, someone who wanted to destroy me. Well, they did. End of story. But enough of me and my woes, back to work! Now, leave the tree and start on the shield in the right-hand corner.'

Archie's hands smelt of white spirit. Even at night it wouldn't wash off. All day he seemed to be mixing chemicals, dipping cotton wool in ammonia, coaxing off layers of varnish.

After the first week they moved into the Louvre laboratories, where Professor Barre gave him a crash course in the mixing of pigments and in distinguishing the countless different shades of green and blue and red.

Dashwood was wary of too much theory and he threw Archie in at the deep end, sitting him in front of a damaged canvas and telling him to get on with it. Gingerly Archie dipped his fine sable brush into the small patch of dark paint he had mixed on the corner of his palette; hesitantly he touched the canvas.

'For God's sake, Andrew, don't be so tentative!' Dashwood urged. 'The picture won't eat you. Be firm but exact. One stroke at a time. You are breathing life back into the canvas, repairing the ravages of time, stopping the rot, holding fast to the artist's dream.'

Dashwood and Archie spent whole mornings examining paintings with an ultraviolet lamp, followed by long afternoons studying the same pictures under infrared light. In the third week, Archie tackled his first relining.

'Your job is to get this new linen canvas on the back of this old flax,' Oliver Dashwood explained. 'You use one of three things: animal glue, wax resin or the latest invention, Beva 371. Watch carefully, and I'll show you and then you have a go.'

They went to all the museums: the Picasso Museum, the

d'Orsay, the Marmottan, the Louvre again and again; the Guimet with its extraordinary collection of Indian and Khmer sculpture; the Rodin Museum, the Orangerie, the Jeu de Paume and Beaubourg. In museums Oliver Dashwood was transformed; when he stood in front of great art he radiated happiness and waved his hands about as if he were conducting an orchestra.

Archie filled two notebooks with details about the way Dashwood dressed, held his newspaper, smoked his cheap, thin cigars; how and when he laughed (very seldom). He wrote down his most frequent words (excruciating, cerebral, derivative) and analysed the structure of his sentences. They were short. To the point. And without warmth. There was a coldness in his speech and in his character. He enthused only about art, never about people.

In the evenings they would wander down the Boulevard Raspail to Montparnasse and sit in the Coupole, a vast art-nouveau brasserie which could seat over five hundred people.

'You should write a book,' Archie said to Dashwood one evening at the Coupole, sipping white wine which was cold and good.

'I started a book on the Venetian painters, Titian, Giorgione, Bellini and Carpaccio. I even employed a researcher, my star pupil at the Courtauld. I used to invite him home for supper, introduced him to my wife. Little did I know! One day I came home early and found them at it, in my bed, heaving away, grunting and groaning with a passion and pleasure I'd never experienced. Neither with my wife nor with anyone else. I've never really enjoyed sex, and my first thought was one of envy. I wanted to feel like that, until I realized that she was my wife and he was my student, and then I hit the roof.'

Archie was about to say something and then changed his mind, picked up his glass and drank.

Dashwood looked at him and said, 'I know what you're thinking. No, I'm not gay.'

They ate a cheap supper of beef and mashed potato and wandered back around midnight.

'I wasn't always like this, a crusty old bore. I was quite a lad in my youth. The girls fancied me, especially on the ski-slopes. I was a downhill racer. Skied for Cambridge.'

'Really,' Archie said. 'That's very interesting.'

'I found everything amusing,' Dashwood went on, warming to his sentimental theme. 'I was full of goodwill. My cup overflowed. I had a loving wife and two children, a career in teaching and restoring of art. I loved my subject and I had the brains to make a name for myself as an academic. But I didn't have the luck, and now my life's a washout!'

'The job in Saint Cyr is serious. Those Meissoniers are good pictures. It could lead to something.'

'I doubt it.'

The operation was codenamed Fleur-de-lis. It was Archie's idea to invoke the emblem of the kings and queens of France; after all, when Titian painted Mary she was the French Queen. Madeleine did her own meticulous background research and found out that Interpol had nothing on Hakomoto. Her counterpart in Japan said Hakomoto had some pretty unsavoury friends but he wasn't part of Yakutza, the official Japanese mafia, although rumour had it that in the last year he had been bribing politicians to get himself large construction deals. He kept his art collection entirely to himself, refusing to show or lend a single painting to any museum.

This information and much else was discussed at planning meetings held over lunch in a private room at the Coupole. 'Laws of title – by that I mean ownership – are extremely complicated in Japan,' Madeleine explained one day, as Harry and Archie finished a hearty meal of twelve oysters and fillet steak. 'Our biggest problem will not be finding the picture but getting it back.'

'But the Titian was stolen from the Royal Baggage Train!' Harry objected. 'It belongs to the Queen. Don't tell me if Archie finds it hanging on Hakomoto's bedroom wall he can't get it back legally?'

'I'm telling you Archie's got a problem,' Madeleine said. 'First he has to prove the Titian was part of the Royal Collection. How? It doesn't appear in any of the catalogues for the last four hundred years. Officially this picture belongs to no one because officially it doesn't exist.'

'Then Hakomoto's laughing,' Harry said gloomily.

'Even if we could prove the Titian was stolen,' Madeleine went on, 'that still doesn't mean we could get it back. All Hakomoto has to say is that at the time of purchase he had no idea the picture was stolen, he was an innocent buyer, and under Japanese law he'd be allowed to keep it.'

'The law's an ass,' Harry said.

'The law's an ass world-wide, not in Great Britain or the United States, mind you, where Anglo-Saxon law is on the side of the original owner, but in France, Germany, Italy, Switzerland, title passes to the most recent buyer. Now, we in France try to be fair. If your picture is stolen and you discover it hanging on someone else's wall, you have the right to buy it back.'

'Buy back your own picture?' Harry blurted out. 'What's fair about that?'

'At least you get it back. In Germany if your picture is sold at public auction, that's it, you've lost it for ever. The new owner is under no obligation whatsoever to sell it back to you.'

'It seems like an *Alice in Wonderland* nightmare,' Harry said.

'It is,' Madeleine said with feeling. 'And try being a police-woman in the middle of this legal chaos. Take the statute of limitations. A simple idea. After X number of years – each country sets its own standard – an art object legally belongs to its current owner. Well, it won't surprise you to know that the banks in Geneva, Zurich and Bern are stuffed with stolen art, just sitting there waiting for the Swiss statute of limitations to expire.'

'I wouldn't be in your shoes for anything,' Harry said, pouring Madeleine another glass of wine.

Archie, who knew all the legal ramifications of stolen art backwards, had only been half listening while nursing a large bowl-shaped glass of Armagnac and inhaling the powerful smell. 'If Hakomoto's got the picture,' he said thoughtfully, 'there's only one thing to do. Steal it back.'

It was early November and the Paris boulevards were carpeted in a thick bed of leaves, some damp, some brittle, whipped up now and then by sharp gusts of wind into spiralling tornadoes.

Whenever possible on a Friday night, Archie met Madeleine at the Place d'Iéna and they drove out of Paris to a cottage near Chartres which belonged to her brother, a diplomat stationed in Prague. They pretended everything was all right, but it wasn't. The light-heartedness had gone. They were both on edge, counting the days until Operation Fleur-de-lis began.

'I'm afraid for you,' Madeleine said one evening. 'Our plan is very dangerous, especially for you.'

'So is Northern Ireland. So is crossing the street. Why the doubts all of a sudden? Where's the Iron Lady?'

'I'm getting too fond of you, Archie.'

'Good,' he said, leaning forward and kissing her neck. 'That's what I like to hear.'

One evening when they sat huddled by a log fire sipping red wine, Archie looked into Madeleine's anxious eyes and said, 'Stop worrying.'

'You're a British civilian. I've got no right to ask you to do this.'

'Look, Madeleine, my reputation is shot to pieces. This is a chance to make amends. Don't you see, I've got nothing to lose. It's a waste of time talking about the pros and cons when we could be in bed.'

Archie telephoned Paul Hewitt every week, but the news on Sulgrave was always the same: the man was being good as gold; he hadn't put a foot wrong. Once, he took a pretty girl from the Sotheby's English watercolour department to lunch at Claridge's but that was all. He didn't appear to have a mistress and went home to bed every night. His drawing-room light stayed on late, and now and then you could hear shouting, but as far as Hewitt could tell the wife wasn't being knocked about.

At the end of November, Archie went back to England and met Hewitt in the Green Man.

'You've been in Paris for nearly two months. Doing what, or need I ask?' Hewitt said, grinning.

'They've sent me back to school,' Archie said, and he briefed Hewitt on Operation Fleur-de-lis. It was, he explained, a two-man, one-woman show. Archie was going into the lion's den as Dashwood; Harry was himself in Tokyo for the International Art Fair; and Madeleine, in Tokyo ostensibly for the same reason, was directing the operation unofficially and without the knowledge of the French Ambassador but with the help of the Deuxième Bureau and the French Head of Station.

'Jesus,' Hewitt muttered. 'Be careful. It's all very well having Madeleine Husson in Tokyo, but how much back-up can she give you? The Japanese don't muck around. Remember the war.'

'I've been undercover before.'

'Listen, mate, this plan of yours is illegal, dangerous and daft but I suppose you've got nothing to lose. You're pretty much at rock bottom.'

'That's nicely put, Paul.'

Hewitt agreed to keep up the surveillance on Sulgrave and to report anything interesting to Madeleine via the British Embassy in Tokyo.

Archie had never travelled first class before. In the army whenever he was on close-protection duty guarding VIPs, he travelled with the RAF in VC10s, seats facing the rear. Now he took off his shoes, put on the slippers provided and sat back in his seat waiting for take-off, remembering his long night of love-making with Madeleine; already he ached for her.

There was a last-minute passenger who stumbled on to the aeroplane breathless and dishevelled and took his seat at the back near the lavatory. There were no slippers for economy passengers and he sat squashed between two large businessmen. Not my scene at all, thought Harry Wardington.

The aeroplane took off. Archie leant back in his seat and thought of Oliver Dashwood. He could see him now on the pavement of Boulevard Raspail.

'I only hope I can remember the half of what you've taught me,' Archie had said as he took the indifferent hand.

'Don't worry. You'll forget it all in a month. I don't believe in crash courses. Goodbye, Andrew.'

Dashwood's face was solemn as he spoke. Was he ever human, Archie wondered. Would his face break into a smile, just for once? It didn't. Dashwood climbed into the Citroën waiting to take him to Saint Cyr; in the back seat Lamartine was reading *Le Monde*.

'*Bonne chance!*' Archie called out, but Oliver Dashwood looked straight ahead.

Over the loudspeaker the pilot announced they had reached a cruising altitude of thirty-seven thousand feet. Archie took a glass of Bollinger from the white-gloved hand of the cocktail steward and opened his book, *The Cleaning of Paintings* by Helmut Ruhemann.

Chapter 24

'I hope you will be comfortable,' twittered the doll-like Japanese receptionist as she showed Archie into his hotel bedroom.

'Comfortable,' Archie said, throwing himself on the sumptuous double bed, 'is the word.' This was the Seiyo Ginza hotel, where a standard room cost five hundred dollars a night. But there was nothing standard about his room. It was palatial. Archie kicked off his shoes and his feet sank into inches of Wilton carpet. Waiting for him on the imitation Louis XIV desk was letter paper embossed with his name, and the fridge was full of champagne. As for the bathroom, he'd never seen anything like it: gold fixtures, two telephones and television fixed to the wall. He soaked in stephanotis bubbles from Paris, sipped a glass of Bollinger and watched a Japanese game show.

At 6.45 p.m. he wandered into the executive lounge on the first floor. It was decorated in the Japanese idea of an English country house with deep armchairs, imitation Chippendale mirrors and sporting prints. 'Land of Hope and Glory' was playing discreetly in the background. A waiter came over to Archie, bowed and took his order for a neat whisky; thank God he and Oliver Dashwood liked the same drink.

Archie had dressed the Dashwood part to perfection: his clothes were old and shabby, his beard had been dyed a shade darker than its natural chestnut, his long hair, also dyed, curled over his collar, and half-moon spectacles added to his eccentricity. He was a shocking contrast to the overblown opulence of his surroundings, and the other guests stared at him with disapproval but Archie feigned indifference. He was Oliver Dashwood and Oliver Dashwood didn't care; he was an embittered, neurotic man, dissatisfied with himself and with the world. Archie lit up a cheap, thin cigar and waited.

At exactly 7 p.m. Minako arrived accompanied by the hotel manager, who bowed low and said it was a great honour to receive a guest of Mr Hakomoto.

'Thank you,' Archie said without warmth, holding out a coarse hand with paint under the fingernails. He turned to Minako. 'I am hoping to start work as soon as possible. Is the painting here in Tokyo?'

'I am not at liberty to say, Mr Dashwood. My orders are to collect you tomorrow morning at nine a.m. if that is convenient.'

'I shall be ready.'

'You must be tired after your long flight. I shall leave you to your rest.'

Minako and the hotel manager bowed and left Archie to his drink. On their way out of the hotel lounge, Minako murmured, 'You will follow Mr Hakomoto's instructions?'

'Of course.'

Minako bowed; she didn't understand why but Hakomoto-san wanted Dashwood's telephone tapped and any contact with another person reported.

At 6 a.m. the next morning Archie set off for an early morning jog. It was bitterly cold and he wore layers of sweaters, a track suit and a Sony Walkman clamped to his head. The headset had been carefully modified by the Deuxième Bureau and acted as a voice-activated short-wave radio transmitter/receiver when switched to zero. At a traffic light Archie checked the dial: it stood at zero.

It was still dark and the December sky was starless. Already the traffic was building up and one by one the garish neon lights in the Ginza district were going out as the all-night strip clubs

179

closed and the coffee shops opened, ready to give commuters their first shot of caffeine.

He jogged through Marunouchi, the business centre of Tokyo, past clusters of skyscrapers, across the huge highways that slice through the city to the public gardens of the Imperial Palace, where the mist was lifting, giving way to the clear, sharp light of winter. The park glistened with an early morning frost and under this shimmering sheen of white Archie could see that everything was scrupulously neat: the lake meticulously edged with weeping willows; the rocks strategically placed in the burbling streams; the clipped lawns and freshly painted park benches and pristine litter bins.

As he skirted the lake, wishing to God he had played more tennis in London, he was joined by other joggers, many of them foreigners, heading up the hill. Someone called out in English then in French and Archie realized that the path through the Imperial Gardens was the international jogging circuit. At the top of the hill, overlooking the Imperial Palace with its moat, he sat down on a bench and tightened the laces of his left shoe. A jogger wrapped in a thick scarf sat down beside him; suddenly Madeleine's voice was in his ear.

'Don't look up. I'll meet you here every morning. If you think you're being followed have a jersey round your neck over your track suit. If you need help, tie up your left shoe-lace when you see me and I will spring you immediately. If the restoration work turns out to be too difficult and if you need to get out, order olive-oil-based Burnt Sienna from the art supplier.'

By the time he looked up Madeleine was jogging downhill towards the lake, which was coated in a thin layer of ice.

Seiji Hakomoto's office was on the fifth floor of the Hakomoto Trust Building with a magnificent view of downtown Tokyo, a mighty jumble of crazed buildings, impressive skyscrapers and six-lane highways. The room was spartan, with a desk, two chairs and on the wall one hanging scroll. Next to Hakomoto stood a stocky Japanese with protruding temples and a stupid cruel face; he wore the traditional black kimono.

'You're a man who likes to take exercise,' Hakomoto said, shaking hands. 'So does Akira here. May I introduce my personal bodyguard.'

Akira bowed, his face impassive, eyes fixed to the floor.

'Am I being spied on?' Archie said testily, glancing at Minako, who blushed and stared at her hands. 'Picture restoration is extremely tiring on the optic nerve. The body, like the mind, must be fit.'

'That is my philosophy also, Mr Dashwood. Every morning at five a.m. Akira and I do an hour of kendo, an old Japanese martial art. Perhaps you would like to join us one morning?'

'I'm too old to learn a new sport.'

Hakomoto smiled and inclined his head at the man's lack of grace. He had been warned that Dashwood was impossible. Brilliant but impossible.

'You are anxious to start work. But first I thought you might like to see one or two of my paintings.'

'Yes, of course,' Archie said in his blandest voice.

Hakomoto led Archie into a large room with two dark-red velvet ottomans in the middle of a shining parquet floor; on the walls, hung so close the frames were almost touching, were forty-odd paintings.

'As you can see I have focused on the Post-Impressionists. They haven't suffered from overexposure and they still contain mystery. And mystery is very important to me.'

The word is well chosen, Archie reflected, looking at Cézanne's portrait of his tight-lipped wife; a breakfast scene by Vuillard in brown and brooding colours was next to an understated yet sensuous Modigliani nude; mystery was every-where.

'Magnificent!' Archie burst out, with the unnatural vehem-ence of a neurotic.

'Thank you, Mr Dashwood. I'm glad it meets with your approval. This is a very personal collection, and a very private one. I do not lend my pictures, ever.'

'The public doesn't appreciate art,' Archie said with feeling. 'They troop around galleries but what do they see? Nothing! It takes a trained eye to know what one is looking at, to under-stand, and above all to love.'

'Our views on art are very similar,' Hakomoto said, looking at Archie with interest.

'There he is!' The voice was unmistakably English and unmistakably Harry. 'You know what they told me downstairs? They said Mr Hakomoto was abroad. That's laying it on a bit thick, isn't it?'

'I am well protected, Mr Wardington,' Hakomoto said, shaking hands, while Akira looked on uneasily.

'I knew you were here. There's a vast black Mercedes outside which has to belong to you.'

'It does,' Hakomoto conceded. 'May I introduce Oliver Dashwood. This is Harry Wardington. Perhaps you know each other?'

'I don't think so,' Harry said, shaking hands indifferently. 'This is all very wonderful,' he went on, glancing round the room. 'Let me see. Madame Cézanne, Sotheby's 1988, seventeen million pounds if I remember right. The Matisse, that fetched a record twenty-two million dollars from Christie's New York in May 1987. Van Dongen, Vuillard, three Picassos, two Braques, and there's my old friend the Renoir. Eleven million, two hundred and fifty thousand pounds thanks to some brilliant bidding on my part! Now let's add it all up. I would say on a fairly conservative estimate you've laid out a hundred and fifty million pounds for this lot. Which is going to make the picture I've come to sell you ridiculously cheap.'

'You have something to show me? Perhaps you would like to come into my office. I'm sure Mr Dashwood will forgive us for a few moments. Miss Setsu will look after you.'

'The lovely Miss Setsu!' Harry cried, throwing out his hands extravagantly. 'I'm counting on her to show me the sights.'

Minako blushed and bowed.

'Mr Wardington, if you would care to come this way,' Hakomoto said firmly, and led Harry into his office.

'I don't know the first thing about Japanese art,' Harry said, standing in front of the black and white monochrome painting of a duck paddling in a lotus pond, 'but this is exquisite.'

'Sotatsu. Eighteenth century. Ink and wash. Look closely and you will see infinite variation of tone, achieved by one fluid sweep of the brush. In Japanese monochrome painting the artist cannot make a mistake. If he does the picture is ruined. This is very much my philosophy. No mistakes. I have been following your father's misfortunes in the newspapers. There was loss of face, I'm afraid.'

'My dad's a tough old bird,' Harry insisted.

'You wish to show me a painting?'

'I've brought a photograph to whet your appetite. The picture's with me in Tokyo. I can bring it round any time you like. If you don't buy it someone at the International Art Fair will. People tell me there's an awful lot of cash sloshing around Japan in spite of the recession.'

Hakomoto stared at the photograph: the girl was blonde, naked, lying on a rock, her head thrown back; the breasts were ripe, the lips slightly parted.

'Yes,' Hakomoto said slowly. 'I would like to see the picture. Why don't you come to my house the day after tomorrow at three p.m.? I shall send a car for you. Where are you staying?'

'With a cousin of mine who's Commercial Attaché at the British Embassy,' Harry said, scribbling his number on a piece of paper. 'Thanks for letting me drop by. I must be off now.' And he left.

Alone in his office, Hakomoto didn't know whether to laugh or be angry. The cheek of it, he thought, barging into the Hakomoto Trust Building and more or less demanding an interview *and* getting it. How arrogant they were, the English, and how he hated them for bringing shame on him and his family!

Archie was pacing the parquet floor of the gallery, frowning and glancing impatiently at his watch.

'Mr Dashwood, I am sorry to have kept you waiting,' Hakomoto said. 'Shall we go?'

In the back seat of a brand new Mercedes, Archie sat next to Hakomoto as they drove to Haneda, the internal airport. Akira and Minako followed in a second Mercedes. It was obvious to Archie that Minako didn't like the bodyguard and she did her best to avoid him, whereas Akira stared at her with a mixture of lust and admiration.

In choking traffic they drove through the Tokyo suburbs, a chaotic jigsaw of wooden flats, flickering television screens and washing strung across cramped backyards; but never a tree, a park, a flower. Nature had been suffocated beneath layers of concrete.

At Haneda they boarded the Hakomoto corporate jet. 'We're going to Hokkaido,' Minako whispered to Archie. 'I wasn't permitted to tell you before. We return this evening.'

It was a relief to soar above a thick bank of cloud which obliterated greater Tokyo with its oppressive concentration of eleven million people. Archie slept. As the aeroplane came into land, he had a good look at the savage coastline; thick forest, smouldering volcanoes and towering mountains plunging into a cold sea.

A black Nissan was waiting for them at the airport. They drove for miles through rich brown arable land dotted with shiny new aluminium storage tanks; and on the horizon loomed magnificent snow-capped mountains.

'I grew up in Hokkaido,' Hakomoto said. 'Have you heard of the Ainu? No? An aboriginal tribe, perhaps the oldest inhabitants of Japan. There are fifteen thousand of them living in the north of the island. No one knows where they came from. If we had time I would take you there.'

'Really,' Archie said in a cultivated monotone.

'People don't interest you, Mr Dashwood?'

'The human race doesn't interest me *per se*, but genius, above all artistic genius, that's another matter. I can spend hours looking at a great painting. It is a spiritual experience. I enter the world of the gods and shut out what people call reality. Look around, what do you see? A world that is mediocre and unjust; terribly unjust!'

Dashwood was exactly what Hakomoto had expected, a man poisoned by failure. He was disgraced, his career had been ruined, all of which made him the perfect man for the job. He would take his money and say nothing. He had no reputation to save.

Fifteen kilometres before Sapporo the black Nissan lurched into the mountains and climbed steadily for the next half-hour. There had been heavy snowfalls in the first days of December and the upper slopes gleamed white. A good year for skiing, Archie thought. The car drew up alongside a high brick wall spiked with broken glass and stopped in front of reinforced steel gates. A guard appeared with a Rottweiler straining at the end of a chain. The dog lurched forward, dragging the guard for a foot or so until his owner pulled him up with a violent jerk, shouting angrily. The guard stared into the car and then spoke to the driver.

'I am sorry but we must get out,' Hakomoto said. Archie was impressed: this was the correct procedure in case Hakomoto had been kidnapped and was sitting in the back seat with a gun pressed to his ribs. They all got out of the Nissan and the guard bowed low to Hakomoto, inspected the car and held the door open as they climbed back in.

The Nissan slid up the drive. It was early afternoon and the lawn was covered in a smooth blanket of snow which glinted in the brilliant winter sun. In front of the villa they were met with a curious sight. Four men in long black padded tunics, their heads covered by thick protective masks, were practising kendo, one of the oldest of the Japanese martial arts. They lurched forward and back, slashing, thrusting and parrying with the five-foot iron-bound bamboo staves. Archie knew that one blow from this weapon would paralyse a man for life.

'My security staff,' Hakomoto said. 'I encourage them to keep fit.'

Two villas stood side by side, one larger than the other. Fifty yards behind was a bungalow complex, for the staff, Hakomoto explained. The smaller villa was the guest house and the main villa was his own residence.

They followed Hakomoto into the main chalet. In the hall Archie noticed several crates marked Banque Weber. They stepped into the lift and Archie registered the markings on push-buttons: −1, −2, −3; Akira punched in a computer code and the lift hissed downwards, till it stopped three floors underground.

'I also have a swimming-pool, a gymnasium and a cinema,' Hakomoto said, stepping out of the lift. 'You are welcome to use any of them.'

He led the way down a corridor to a small, windowless room brightly lit by strip lights. The room was empty except for a stool, a low table and a canvas standing on an easel, completely black except for two small circles where the surface had been cleaned.

'Over to you, Mr Dashwood,' Hakomoto said.

'Who's been tampering with the picture?'

'I acquired it in its present state.'

'I shall start work at once,' Archie said, opening his leather bag and taking out his equipment: a magnifying glass, a second magnifying glass known as a high-definition loupe, an ultraviolet light which he plugged into a wall socket, various bottles, swabs and brushes. He adjusted the canvas on the easel, put on surgeon's gloves, and on his head a magnifying glass attached to a headband, like a miner's lamp, and set to work.

'We shall leave you to your labours,' Hakomoto said. He barked an order at Akira, who took up his position outside the room. Archie rolled the swab carefully across the canvas, and as he worked inch by inch he could hear Oliver Dashwood's firm instruction: 'Slowly, carefully, nothing in a hurry. When in doubt stop.'

The hours passed. At 6 p.m. that evening Hakomoto reappeared.

'What are your first impressions, Mr Dashwood?'

'I have established two things – the painting is sixteenth century and of excellent quality. The stretcher is screwed oak, typical of the period and the canvas is made from the most expensive flax, which indicates this picture is of some import-ance. My immediate task is to remove several layers of varnish and dirt. It's possible there will be chemical complications but I hope not. The paint itself seems to be in extraordinarily good condition; there is no fading of primary colours, as one would expect if a picture had been exposed to normal light. But this picture has not seen the light for several hundred years I would say.'

'How would you like to proceed, Mr Dashwood?'

'First I want to examine the samples of paint I have taken from the canvas – this means studying them under a microscope and then making a chemical and spectrographic analysis. I shall then begin to remove the varnish and dirt. For this I'll need other materials which I'm told I can buy in Tokyo. Sixteenth-century paintings need special solvents. It's so easy to damage pictures from this period by careless cleaning. In those days pigment was not generally synthetic as it is today, but organic, and must be treated with the greatest of care. I will not be hurried.'

'No one is pressuring you, Mr Dashwood.'

'I've done all I can do for today,' Archie said, putting his equipment back in the leather bag. 'She's a noblewoman. On her hand is a signet ring with the initial "F". The dress is velvet and silk and she seems to have the most extraordinary-coloured hair. It's not red, and it's not blonde but somewhere in between.'

Archie took off his gloves and the headband and closed his restorer's bag. He glanced round the enclosed, claustrophobic room. 'It would be better if I had natural light.'

'I'm afraid that is not possible,' Hakomoto said. 'But if you would like to come upstairs I can give you a drink. We leave for the airport in twenty minutes.'

As he followed Hakomoto to the lift, Archie noticed a steel door at the far end of the corridor which had been shut when he first arrived but which now stood ajar. Archie thought he glimpsed a wall packed with paintings but before he could get a better look Hakomoto ordered Akira to shut the door.

'You keep part of your collection here in Hokkaido?' Archie said casually.

'Yes, I do. Paintings particularly close to my heart.'

'I should like to see them.'

'Another time perhaps,' Hakomoto said brusquely.

Akira led the way into the lift and once again punched in the code, 8917, Archie noted. They hissed upwards and stopped on the ground floor and followed Hakomoto into the spacious sitting room furnished with heavy antique Japanese furniture. Minako joined them, moving soundlessly across the wooden floor, her head bowed, avoiding Akira's lustful stare.

Archie admired the spectacular view of the mountains and the ski-slopes from the panoramic window in the sitting room. Directly opposite was a downhill slalom course marked out with poles and flags. Far below in the valley Archie could see the flickering lights of small villages. The garden wall surrounding the villa was floodlit and soft banks of snow glistened in broad shafts of light. Archie counted two sentry boxes but as far as he could see the sitting room was not protected by infrared detectors.

In front of the window, on a maroon lacquer display rack, Archie noticed a magnificent samurai sword. The two-handed grip was covered in green sharkskin. The guard was intricately carved and embossed with gold, while the gently curved scabbard was decorated with designs of dragons and warriors applied in gold relief.

'This sword was one of a pair,' Hakomoto explained. 'The other is now in the Northumberland home of the late Field Marshal Sir Francis Festing.'

Hakomoto waited for Dashwood to ask why and how, but the Englishman said nothing.

'It belonged to one of my ancestors who served under Iemitsu, the third *Shōgun* of the Tokugawa period. It was forged in the seventeenth century by one of the great sword masters. It is a superb piece of work, perfectly balanced and perfectly sharp. It has killed many men, and passed the ultimate test.'

'Which is?'

'This very sword, this very blade cut a criminal from skull to hip with one single blow. That is Japanese craftsmanship for you! In this case I have some of the finest samurai daggers. No European could match such work. Not the sword-smiths of Toledo, or Milan, or Solingen or even your precious Sheffield.'

'Weapons don't really interest me,' Archie said indifferently.

'A drink, Mr Dashwood?' Hakomoto said, showing Archie into the library lined with oak bookcases; above the large desk hung the Augustus John portrait of Cordelia Sulgrave's mother. 'Whisky and soda?'

'No soda,' Archie said, staring at the painting. 'I don't usually like Augustus John but this is very fine. And it's dedicated to the sitter, that's unusual. "To Margaret". Who was she, do you know?'

'No,' Hakomoto said firmly, and handed Archie his drink. 'Shall we get down to business? While you are working for me you'll stay in my guest house, which is linked to the main house by an underground tunnel. Minako is also staying there with her son.'

Minako shuffled forward in tiny hesitant steps. 'Hakomoto-san has been most kind and arranged for Yuji to go to school for a term here in Sapporo so that I am not separated from my son while I am here with you. I have no words to express my gratitude.'

'Minako will remain with you throughout your stay in Japan,' Hakomoto said. 'She will see that you have everything you need. As you requested, your salary is being sent directly to your account in the Channel Islands. I do not expect you to work all the time. You must relax and have free time, and with that in mind I have provided Minako with a car so she can take you out for a drive now and then, and you might like to go skiing. I understand you were captain of the Cambridge ski team, and set a British record for the giant slalom.'

'It's been beaten many times since,' Archie said gruffly.

'Still, a competitive spirit. I like that, Mr Dashwood. I'm afraid the runs here in Hokkaido are very crowded at the moment; the Japanese Olympic trials begin here on the fifteenth of December and end on the twenty-fifth. We don't celebrate Christmas here in Japan.'

'I don't celebrate Christmas either,' Archie said sourly.

'Good, then you can enjoy the wonderful view of the men's downhill slope from my sitting room. From time to time I shall drop in on you. I hope you will not be bored.'

'I won't be bored. I have my work and that is everything to me. And you are paying me well, Mr Hakomoto.'

'I must ask you to talk to no one about your work for me, and when you return to France you will never refer to this assignment. I am a very private man, Mr Dashwood.'

'And I don't need a lesson in discretion,' Archie snapped.

It was time to leave for the airport. As they stepped into the cold night air, two more security guards stood to attention at the front entrance to the villa. They climbed into the chauffeur-driven Nissan and headed towards the perimeter fence. A brilliant moon had burnt a hole in the night sky and the stars were as sharp as diamonds. The car stopped in front of the steel gates and they waited while the guard stepped forward and shone a torch into Archie's face. The Rottweiler growled, saliva dribbling from its mouth. The guard bowed to Hakomoto, stepped back and the gates slid open.

It was 10 a.m. by the time Minako got back to her small flat in Minato-ku. Her son, Yuji, was in his pyjamas doing his home-work, and her young cousin who lodged with her in return for babysitting was working at her desk. Work, work, work, that's all we do in this country, Minako thought, and for what? From her bedroom window she could see the Tokyo tower, pavements choking with people, streets jammed with cars, a million moving beams of light, lights and people, people and cars, cars and noise, endless noise. Even the air was torn to shreds by the shriek of aeroplanes. She closed her eyes and thought of the rolling hills of France, and fields covered with poppies and sunflowers. There was a knock at her door. Suddenly she was frightened; the idea flashed through her mind it might be Akira. How she hated his leering stare! Minako put the chain across her door and opened it an inch; it was her neighbour, a tetchy old woman in her sixties bent double with arthritis. In her hand was a large bunch of red roses.

'A man brought these round earlier,' the woman said, handing over the flowers. She stared at Minako with the utmost disapproval, then added contemptuously, 'An Englishman.'

Chapter 25

It was 6.30 a.m. and pitch-dark. Only the faintest glow of peach on the eastern horizon gave a promise of daylight. Archie sat down on the same bench in the Imperial Gardens, his Walkman clamped to his ears, the dial set at zero, and waited. At 6.35 a.m. Madeleine's voice crackled down the airwaves. 'Good morning, Mr Dashwood. How was Hokkaido?'

'The Titian's there, and the Augustus John. God knows what else he's got in the villa. There are three underground floors.'

'Where exactly is the villa?'

'Sankakuyama. Sixteen kilometres from central Sapporo, to the west, on the road to Hokkaido village ski resort. Just before the village there's a supermarket where you turn left up a mountain track, keep on for two kilometres till you come to the steel gates, electronically controlled. You can't miss them, it's a dead end.'

'And the security?'

At that moment a Japanese in a dark-blue track suit slumped on to the bench next to Archie; he was panting heavily. Archie got to his feet and resumed his jogging.

'Se-cu-ri-ty,' Archie sang, 'is bloody tight. What else do you want to know?'

'Details, Archie. Details.'

'You sound like my commanding officer in the Green Jackets.'

Archie sat on the icy stone seat of a summer-house.

'Six security guards, maybe seven. Infrared alarm system which also at a guess works on vibrations. Flood lighting round

193

the house. A very nasty Rottweiler at the entrance. A lift that works on a computer coding system.'

'Have you started work on the picture?'

'I've taken a pigment sample and started on a surface clean. Nothing much, yet.'

'So what's your timetable?'

'A few days in Tokyo to get sorted out. I take the pigment fragments to the lab for analysis, order my materials, then we move to Hokkaido.'

A young woman was staring at Archie inquisitively, wondering why he was talking to himself; Archie got to his feet and began to jog, rocking his head from side to side and singing, 'I can't get no . . . satisfaction.'

Madeleine cut in, 'Sulgrave left for Tokyo yesterday. We've had a message from Hewitt.'

'I can't get no . . . girlie action. Thanks for the tip. And I try . . . and I try. . .'

Madeleine watched Archie jog downhill towards the lake. She sucked in a deep breath of cold air and headed in the opposite direction, to the main road jammed with rush-hour traffic where a black Renault with French diplomatic plates was waiting. Serge Noailles, officially Political Attaché at the French Embassy, unofficially Head of Station, opened the door for her.

'So far so good,' Madeleine said.

That morning she decided to be seen at the International Art Fair just in case people wondered what she was doing in Tokyo. She changed out of her jogging clothes into a Dior suit and took an Embassy car to the huge glass exhibition hall in Ueno Park. She wandered from booth to booth inspecting Renaissance drawings and pre-Colombian sculpture and asking herself how much of it was stolen. She was admiring a Boucher drawing in the Colnaghi stand when a man came up behind her.

'Commissaire Husson, I hope you're not following me.'

'Why should I follow you, Lord Sulgrave?' Madeleine said, turning round. 'Have you got a guilty conscience?'

'Not at all,' Dicky said, smiling broadly and offering his hand. 'What brings you to Tokyo?'

'The same as you.'

'I tell you she's on to me, I can feel it.'

'Dickysan, please calm down,' Hakomoto said.

'She's on to me and perhaps she's on to you. Have you thought of that?'

'But who am I, Dickysan? An innocent collector. I buy paintings in good faith and if they turn out to be stolen, I throw up my hands in horror and cry, "I didn't know. I am the unsuspecting victim." She can't touch me, Dickysan, and she can't touch you. The law is on our side!'

'Don't push your luck, Seijisan. Take my advice. Get Dashwood to Hokkaido as soon as possible and get this picture restored. Then you can pay me my money, and we can all go home.'

'I will pay you as soon as I'm certain the painting is what you say it is, Mary Queen of Scots by Titian.'

'The picture is right. Dashwood will tell you.'

'We shall see.'

'He will, and when he does, what do we do then? He knows our little secret. And when he gets back to Paris what if he decides to go and tell our friend Commissaire Husson?'

'He's not going back to Paris.'

'Oh?'

'How tragic that a man of his extraordinary talent should die so young. But accidents do happen.'

'Indeed they do,' Dicky said, and a slow smile crossed his face.

The conversation was taking place in Hakomoto's house in the heart of Tokyo, one of the few to survive the fire-bombing of the Second World War. In the sitting room, separated from the rest of the house by a sliding screen, there was no furniture except for a low wooden table; on it stood a vase with an orchid. Hakomoto and Dicky faced each other, sitting Japanese style, cross-legged on the tatami mat. Hakomoto was wearing a dark-blue kimono.

'Did I tell you,' Hakomoto went on, 'your friend Mr Wardington is in Tokyo. He wants to sell me a picture. I've asked him here for tea.'

'That's a bloody stupid thing to do!' Dicky burst out. 'His father is Director of the Royal Collection. Harry's bound to know about a hidden painting behind the Honthorst. What if he talks to Dashwood?'

'Dashwood will be dead; and it's possible the same sad fate will strike Mr Wardington. He's beginning to annoy me. Now, about the girls.'

'Don't worry, I'll find you girls.'

It was the same every year, an invasion of leggy blonde secretaries who come to Tokyo for the International Art Fair. There was always a handful who wanted money, badly, and could be bought if the price was right.

'And now if you'll excuse me,' Hakomoto said, 'I must begin my hour of meditation. We shall see each other tonight.'

Hakomoto's eyes glazed over as he contemplated the Zen garden he had designed himself, focusing his mind on three rounded boulders, one large, one medium size and one small, set in a sea of carefully raked pea gravel.

Dicky got to his feet, slid out of the room in his stockinged feet, put on his shoes and climbed into the back of one of Hakomoto's chauffeur-driven cars.

The Earl of Sulgrave didn't think of himself as a criminal; he was a man driven by necessity. He was a victim of an incompetent father who had dissipated his inheritance; of Lloyds, that British institution which had suddenly gone belly up in a cataclysm of fraud, negligence and stupidity; of his wife, who at twenty-five had been sweet and compliant and promised him the earth and by thirty-five was transformed into an aggressive alcoholic. He was a victim of high taxation, bad government and bad luck, and when Hakomoto gave him the chance to make serious money he took it.

The proposition had been delicately put one June day in Geneva. On the bridge across the lake, Dicky was standing next to Hakomoto watching the brightly coloured spinnakers dance on the choppy water.

'Provenance is everything to me. Perhaps you think I'm stupid?'

'Eccentric. Not stupid.'

'How can I explain? If a work of art has changed hands often, been subjected to the vulgarity of the saleroom or sold by dealers, it is tainted, its beauty is tarnished. But if a painting has remained with the same owner for decades, even centuries, and if it has been cherished by generations of discerning collectors, then it is even more beautiful and more precious than ever and there is nothing I would not pay for such art.'

'The market's flat at the moment, Hakomotosan. Good pictures just aren't coming up.'

'But don't you see,' Hakomoto said, laying a thin hand on Dicky's arm, 'we need to find a new source of supply. Your friends, for example. The owners of great art. Pure art which has not been bought or sold. Art which I would love to own.'

'I don't think my friends would want to sell.'

'Then we must make other arrangements.'

It was all surprisingly easy. Dicky Sulgrave knew a bent art dealer in Portobello Road who knew a gang in the Brighton

Lanes ready to 'do' anyone's house, anytime. Dicky got his team together although he and they never met. The Portobello dealer who knew Dicky as 'George Simpson' acted as a middle man and Dicky was very, very careful.

Of course the Royal Baggage Train was a different matter. He was out of his depth and so he had left the details to Seiji Hakomoto, who had planned the operation, recruiting Russian veterans from the Afghan war, trigger-happy thugs who killed for fun and in Dicky's view made a mess of the whole operation. But at least they had got the Titian; it had been flown out to Switzerland from Arras airport on one of Hakomoto's corporate jets registered in Panama, deposited with the Banque Weber, and a few days later air-freighted to Tokyo on Hakomoto's private jet.

Flora was another matter. He had always thought of her as reliable and strong and it had come as a shock to discover she might crack at any moment. He had been so careful to keep her out of it, and what had she done? Lost her nerve and threatened him! He was furious with her; how could she let him down at a time like this? And when she had stood on the bridge that night in Paris, drunk and crying, he had felt revolted. The rest was easy.

Chapter 26

Seiji Hakomoto knelt before the small Shinto shrine in the corner of his sitting room and bowed three times to the photograph covered by a plain black silk cloth embroidered with a yellow chrysanthemum. Slowly he lifted the cloth and met the stern gaze of his father, Shunzei Hakomoto, an officer in the Imperial Guard during the Second World War, and once again he repeated the oath he had taken so many times over the past two decades: Britain had hurt his father, he would hurt Britain.

After the war, in 1947, Shunzei Hakomoto had been charged with the murder of several hundred Australian prisoners of war at the fall of Singapore in 1942. (Who can talk of murder in war? War *is* murder, any Japanese knows that. The end is justified by the means; there is no middle path.) Shunzei Hakomoto was tried for war crimes at the express orders of Admiral Lord Mountbatten, the Allied Commander-in-Chief in South-East Asia, and found guilty. He asked to be allowed to commit ritual suicide but the British refused his request. His four-hundred-year-old samurai sword was taken from him by the late Field Marshal Sir Francis Festing to whom he had surrendered, and in December 1947 he was hanged as a common criminal by a Sikh executioner in Changi jail. An Imperial guardsman and a samurai hanged; the shame was complete! The family was disgraced and Seiji's mother fled to a remote provincial town in the northern island of Hokkaido where they had changed their name and lived in obscure poverty.

At the age of twelve, in a mountain shrine in remotest

Hokkaido, white prayer flags fluttering in the cold wind, Seiji swore he would be revenged.

At eighteen he was sent to England by a rich uncle to the London School of Economics, where he perfected his English and took a First. He returned to Tokyo, assumed his father's name, clawed his way back into Japanese society and climbed the ladder of success. He cultivated amorality; he had been shamed, he would shame others; he had been wronged, he would wrong others; but first he must establish his power base. He paid his protection money, built a construction empire, mastered the art of insider trading, insurance fraud and the manipulation of currency markets. Several senior politicians were on his payroll making sure his affairs were not inspected too closely by the Fraud Squad which came sniffing at his doors. The law is for little people, he would scoff. I do what I want and I prosper. I pull strings and people dance!

The Nissan dropped Harry outside the front gate of Hakomoto's house. His black folder with the Van Zoorn was carefully inspected by the security guards before he took off his shoes at the entrance and was ushered into the sitting room by a silent servant.

'Welcome to my house, Mr Wardington.'

Hakomoto bowed low. Harry Wardington was his equal, the son of an English baronet, while he was the son of a Japanese baron, a samurai. As for the Earl of Sulgrave, he was a traitor to his class and to his country. But Wardington was pure. Pure enough to hate.

'We can look at the painting later. Sit down. Do you like my Zen garden? If you look at it for long enough, the troubles of this world evaporate.'

Hakomoto clapped his hands and barked an order. Akira emerged from the shadows carrying several boxes wrapped in material which he carefully laid on the floor. Reverently Hakomoto untied the ribbons on the silk damask and lifted the carved wooden lids.

'I come from a long line of samurai. For centuries we have been custodians of the honour of Japan, of its traditions and its arts. Take this spoon – ' and he held up a bamboo spoon not more than nine inches in length, exquisitely shaped, 'it was used by Sen-no-Rikyu, the great sixteenth-century tea master. So great was his integrity and his art that today this spoon is worth one hundred and fifty thousand dollars.'

'Good God.'

'This was his cup,' Hakomoto said as he held in his hands an earthenware bowl, unevenly shaped, with a rough, grainy texture. 'Made by a craftsman from Korea. Korean potters were the best. They came to Japan and taught us. We have always learnt from others, Mr Wardington. That is the secret of our survival.'

Hakomoto caressed the bowl in both hands.

'Later I shall perform the tea ceremony with my tea master. It's an act of faith, you understand. The individual must surrender his will to the ritual. Ritual, tradition, these things are very dear to me, Mr Wardington, and to many Japanese of the old school. But you British, you have abandoned your traditions, you have lost your national will and your discipline and as a result you will not survive. You have diluted your Aryan blood with blacks. Our country is still racially pure. That is its strength. I do not think your monarchy will last. Everything will be swept away in a chaos of adultery and riot!'

'I don't think so.'

'It is true you won the war and we lost. But now? Look at Britain, look at Japan. Who is the victor now?'

'With all due respect, Mr Hakomoto, you have power, but

what else? You make products the world wants to buy, but you don't write books it wants to read, or music it wants to play. We don't envy you. Your people are slaves to the work ethic.'

'It's the price of power,' Hakomoto said angrily. 'Do you see that photograph at the shrine over there? That was my father. You British hanged him.'

'My uncle died in a Japanese prisoner-of-war camp. He was beaten and starved to death like thousands of other British soldiers. To the eternal shame of Japan not one article of the Geneva convention was observed.'

'You talk to me like this and you still think I will buy your painting?'

'Yes, I think you probably will.'

Suddenly Hakomoto burst out laughing. 'Your nerve is remarkable, Mr Wardington. One of the few British qualities I admire. I do not like the British.'

'So I gather.'

Akira reappeared with two bowls of Japanese green tea. Harry winced as he tasted the bitter green glutinous substance. Hakomoto watched Harry's hands as they held the bowl; they were steady. The Englishman is not afraid, he thought. He should be but he is not.

'Come,' Hakomoto said, getting to his feet and pulling back the sliding windows which led directly on to raked gravel. 'Let me show you my garden. It's the finest in Tokyo. You will need your coat. It is cold.'

Harry's hot white breath spurted into the cold winter air as he followed Hakomoto round the edge of the Zen garden to the spacious lawns beyond covered with a sugar coating of light snow. They walked through the most intensely cultivated garden Harry had ever seen, a labyrinth of rock gardens, miniature evergreen trees and an endless variety of plants and shrubs, each one meticulously labelled. A thin film of ice covered the streams of water which filtered slowly and silently through this oasis; the only distinct sound was the rhythmic high-pitched ping of a single drop of water as it dripped steadily from a bamboo pipe carefully poised above a pond.

'This house and garden belonged to my father,' Hakomoto explained. 'After his execution it was confiscated. I always swore I would buy it back and I did, eight years ago. You see that wooden house over there? It is an open air Noh stage. Let me show it to you, Mr Wardington. Shall we put on our own little play, if you're not too cold, that is? We have the costumes, and the masks. We even have the swords.'

The floorboards of the stage had been polished to a high finish. At the back stood several large wooden chests. Hakomoto lifted a lid and pulled out two yellow silk robes; they were full-length, padded and elaborately embroidered with clouds and dragons in brilliant blues, greens and reds.

'Put this on. You needn't do up the fastenings, they take hours. Here's a mask for you.'

Hakomoto helped Harry into one of the robes and passed him a white mask for his face. Through the eye slits Harry could see Hakomoto putting on his own embroidered robe. He put on a similar white mask, then opened another chest and took out two swords, both in their sheaths.

'The sword is heavy.'

Harry held the double-handed sword with both hands.

'You have seen a Noh play?' Hakomoto asked.

'Never.'

'There is no real fighting, only the symbolic gestures of battle. Movements are slow and rhythmic and there is chanting.'

Hakomoto began to howl in a monotonous flat pitch. The noise wafted out into the garden. He pulled the sword from its sheath and raised it slowly above his head and advanced towards Harry, who faced him, his legs apart, his hands on the hilt of his own sheathed sword. Hakomoto's naked blade came crashing down, slicing the air less than a foot away, pinning the end of Harry's robe to the floor.

There was a frightened cry, like a mina bird. Both men turned to see Minako standing on the edge of the stage. Hakomoto shouted at her, spitting out his angry words. She bowed her head and answered meekly in Japanese.

'It seems that I must leave you, Mr Wardington. The tea master is here. Leave the painting with me. I'll give you an answer tomorrow. My car will take you wherever you wish to go.'

Still wearing his mask, Hakomoto put a hand on to Minako's shoulder. His grip was tight.

'My little Minako, she likes Westerners. She had a child by one, you know. The boy is racially impure. We don't like hybrids in this country, Mr Wardington. We are very old-fashioned. Minako is disgraced, banished from her father's house. But I have taken pity on her and her half-caste bastard. You see, I too have been humiliated and I know what it's like.'

'I am most grateful to Hakomotosan—' Minako began.

'Yes, yes,' he interrupted. 'Look after Mr Wardington. And he can report back to his father, Sir William, that we are civilized after all!'

Hakomoto took off his mask and robe and hurried across the lawn, his sandals crunching on the light snow, to greet his tea master, an elderly Japanese with white hair and a white beard wearing a simple grey kimono. They bowed low to each other several times before hurrying into the bamboo tea house which stood under an acacia. Minako led Harry back into the sitting room and warmed him with a cup of Earl Grey tea. From behind the sliding windows they had a perfect view of the tea ceremony: Hakomoto and his tea master sat on their heels, straight-backed, the palms of their hands on each thigh and the tea ceremony instruments laid out in perfect order on the tatami mat. The tea master bent over to pick up the bowl, each movement of his hand perfectly controlled, the result of years of practice. A blackbird settled on the skeleton branches of a birch tree and watched.

Suddenly a boy burst into the room carrying a hamster in the palm of his hand, and for the first time Harry saw an expression of sheer delight on Minako's face as her son crouched down beside her stroking his pet. He was a beautiful Eurasian boy with almond-shaped eyes and a delicate nose, and Minako spoke to him softly in Japanese. The child bowed to Harry, pressing the hamster to his chest, kissed his mother and ran off laughing.

'He's a lovely boy,' Harry said.

'I was seventeen when I had Yuji. His father, an American banker, wanted us to get married, but he was killed in a car crash. That was nine years ago and still my father has not forgiven me. I am banished from the family home. Now and then I meet my mother in secret; I miss her so much. It has been hard for me, Harrysan. I had no money, no job. Until I met Mr Hakomoto.'

'Are you happy?'

'I do not expect to be happy.'

From next door came the angry sound of Akira's voice; he was shouting at the child, who ran into the sitting room crying, clutching the hamster in both hands. Minako jumped to her feet, her eyes blazing, and in a torrent of furious Japanese she defended her son. Akira looked at Minako sullenly and walked away, leaving Yuji sobbing. Minako sat with him and stroked his head.

'Akira told Yuji he would kill his hamster,' she said to Archie. 'What a horrible thing to say.'

'Have dinner with me.'

'Harrysan, Mr Hakomoto does not —'

'He told you to look after me, I heard him. So why don't you cook me dinner in your flat? I'll be there at nine p.m.'

'Mr Dashwood, you don't like raw baby squid?' Hakomoto said, glancing at Archie's plate.

'No. I don't.'

'It is a delicacy in Japan.'

'Well, I can't help that, can I?'

Hakomoto smiled; the man never ceased to amuse him with his absolute lack of charm. They were sitting cross-legged on the floor at a round table. Sulgrave was getting cramp, shifting from side to side. Dashwood sat quite still. That was because he ran, he was fit, Hakomoto decided. Poor Dicky, unable to endure even the slightest discomfort. How he despised him! And how he needed him. The Earl of Sulgrave was one in a million, well connected, well informed and without the whisper of a conscience.

In that respect we are alike, Hakomoto reflected. What distinguishes us is our ambition. Look at a man's ambition and you look at his soul. Dicky's ambition is limited, whereas mine is infinite!

Akira shuffled towards them in his white-stockinged feet, holding the Ming porcelain plate with peeled prawns. He wore a loose-fitting black kimino and Archie noticed his enormous biceps.

'I understand you spent the day in the laboratory,' Hakomoto said.

Archie took from his pocket a small red notebook and opened it. The raw baby squid was untouched.

'I took two pigment samples, yellow and blue. I set the pigment in resin, ground it down, examined it under the microscope and I found that in the case of the blue it was smalt, or ground blue glass. There was no trace whatsoever of Prussian blue.'

Archie shut his notebook with an air of finality and waited for a reaction but there was none. 'It's highly significant,' he explained. 'Prussian blue was invented in 1706 and was universal thereafter. One is therefore able to deduce that your painting is earlier than 1706. It is almost certainly sixteenth century. Everything points to it, even the yellow which is lead tin, a pigment base used extensively in the sixteenth century. Later it became yellow ochre.'

'What's your next step?' Sulgrave asked eagerly.

'Well, now that I can date this painting, albeit approximately, I am in a position to choose my materials for cleaning and for restoring. My next step is to go shopping.'

'You shall, Mr Dashwood,' Hakomoto said. 'Minako will take you first thing tomorrow morning. I have revised our timetable. There really is no point wasting any more time in Tokyo. If you have no objection you will be leaving for Hokkaido tomorrow afternoon.'

'That suits me. I'm very anxious to get on with the job. Can I ask a question? Who does this painting belong to? You or you?' And he turned his head first to Hakomoto and then to Dicky Sulgrave.

'Does it matter?' Dicky said.

'I'm curious, that's all.'

'The painting is mine, on approval,' Hakomoto said, and clapped his hands. 'Akira will see you out. Oh, by the way, Mr Dashwood, I have decided to lend you my faithful Akira for the rest of your stay in Japan. He will go jogging with you tomorrow.'

'I prefer to jog alone,' Archie said.

'It's for your own safety, Mr Dashwood. You jog in the early morning when it is still dark and this makes me anxious, but with Akira by your side I shall rest easy.'

Archie thanked Hakomoto for dinner and followed Akira out of the room.

Hakomoto turned to Sulgrave. 'Are you satisfied?'

'No. But it's a step in the right direction.'

'Dicky, Dicky, you must learn to relax.'

'When you've paid me my ten million dollars I shall, Hakomotosan, I shall!'

Dicky knew exactly what he would do with the money: buy back Redgorton Castle, the ancestral home which had been sold to Arabs and converted into a hotel. All he had been able to keep was a 'bothy' wing, a couple of rooms by the kitchen. It was the ultimate humiliation.

He had grown up at Redgorton, a massive red-brick castle on a hill overlooking the river Tay where he used to fish as a boy. He got his first gun at eight and he remembered the cold sharp mornings when he stood in his father's butt, waiting for the grouse, watching the mist rising off the moors and feeling the heather hard against his shins.

He would buy back Redgorton Castle, pay his Lloyds debts and divorce Cordelia. The Titian solved all his problems!

'Let's drink to Mary Queen of Scots,' Dicky said, raising his glass of warm sake.

'To the purest painting of them all,' Hakomoto said, touching glasses.

'You cannot stay, Harrysan. My son gets up early.'

'Your skin smells of flowers.'

'You must go. He will wake any moment.'

Above the bed was a large poster of the French countryside, showing a field of sunflowers. Harry got dressed, kissed Minako and slipped out of the flat down the stairs. The old woman next door pulled back her curtain and watched him cross the street. It was 6 a.m.

At 6.10 a.m. Archie jogged towards the Imperial Palace, Akira at his side. The bodyguard was fit; he took the hill in his stride, his white breath steaming in the cold December air. Archie had put his cassette to zero and clamped his earphones to his head. He'd thrown a polo-neck sweater round his neck, over his tracksuit.

Madeleine's voice crackled over the airwaves: 'You're being followed?'

'Tea for two, and two for tea,' Archie sang.

'Roger, out,' Madeleine said.

Chapter 27

'Hakomotosan, you're hurting me,' Minako cried as Hakomoto pulled her by the hair, forcing her down on her knees. Hakomoto was shaking with anger; he hit Minako hard across the face, twice, with the back of his hand. His large signet ring caught the edge of her mouth and a drop of deep-red blood trickled down her white skin. He waited for her to cry but she knelt in silence, her face a livid red from the blow.

'Whore! You opened your legs for the Englishman, didn't you? He spent last night in your flat and it wasn't the first time, was it? All those days in Paris, you fucked him then, didn't you? Japanese men aren't good enough for you, are they? Well, we'll see about that.'

Hakomoto was standing in his sitting room overlooking his Zen garden, towering over the trembling woman. He'd sent for Minako early that morning, the moment the old woman rang. He was going to teach her a lesson, a lesson for life.

Later that day, Minako, her son, Yuji, Akira and Archie took the evening flight to Hokkaido. Minako's lip was bruised and swollen.

'What happened?' Archie said.

'I fell.'

It was a deadly routine: eight hours a day in front of the easel until Archie's back was sore and his eyes ached. To make matters worse, Akira shadowed him all the time; he sat on a stool in the corridor while Archie worked on the Titian, sat with him in the evenings when he played cards with Minako and her son or read a book; followed him at lunchtime when he strolled in the gardens of the villa, his boots sinking into the deep snow. The only time Archie was free of Akira's haunting presence was for an hour each morning when he and the other security guards practised their kendo in the snow, dressed in black padded robes and protective masks and wielding with ferocious force the lethal iron-bound bamboo staves. It was surreal: large black shapes dancing against the pure white of snow. Surreal and sinister.

One morning there was an accident. Archie was watching the deadly ritual when one of the security guards lost his footing in the snow, and Akira's stave came down on his arm, breaking it in one strike. The guard yelled in agony, clutching his arm which hung limp by his side. Archie watched the crippled man stagger into the guard house and made a mental note: don't tangle with an iron-bound stave, especially when it's wielded by Akira.

During these kendo sessions, Archie walked with Minako in the snow-covered garden; it was their only time alone together. Archie looked at the purple bruise on the corner of her mouth.

'It was Hakomoto, wasn't it?'

'Mr Dashwood, this is a private matter.'

'If I can help . . .'

'Thank you,' she whispered.

A strange man, Minako thought to herself. Distant and cold and yet underneath so kind. Her eyes filled with tears.

'Isn't she ravishing?' the Earl of Sulgrave said to Seiji Hakomoto as they stood in front of Archie's easel in the airless studio. The two men had flown into Hokkaido for the day.

The central part of the painting had been cleaned, to reveal a young woman of exceptional beauty; her hair was an extraordinary reddish-gold. Her dress was magnificent, black velvet, hooked and slashed, and studded with pearls, and more pearls were coiled around her long elegant neck. But it was her almond-shaped amber eyes that were mesmeric. Hakomoto moved a step to the left and a step to the right and discovered that whichever way he moved the bewitching eyes followed.

'Do you have any idea who she is, Mr Dashwood?'

'A lady of the highest rank, that's obvious. Spanish possibly, or French. A princess, perhaps.'

'A queen?' the Earl suggested.

'Possibly. I have a feeling there will be clues in the background. This looks to me like the outline of a banner but I can't see anything until I take off the varnish which is unbelievably stubborn. There's not one layer but three, with dirt in between, like a sandwich. Propanol alcohol is useless so I've changed to diacetone alcohol and at long last I'm getting somewhere.'

'What about her signet ring?' Dicky said eagerly. 'It's an "F". "F" for Francis, perhaps?'

'Or Fides, or Felicitas. There's no point jumping to conclusions at this stage,' Archie said testily. 'What I can tell you is that the paint is in remarkably good condition. I suggest we strengthen the fingernails on the left hand and the pearls round her neck and fill in the hair-line cracks above her head. That should do it.'

'Take your time, Mr Dashwood,' Hakomoto said. 'You're making excellent progress. Please, join us for a drink when you've finished your morning's work.'

Archie didn't answer, instead he leant forward, his nose almost touching the canvas, and rolled the cotton-wool swab carefully over the surface.

'When I'm finished,' he said dismissively.

That evening Hakomoto and Sulgrave flew back to Tokyo and Archie resumed his punishing routine. As Sunday approached, Minako suggested to Oliver Dashwood he might like to take the day off and go skiing. He accepted readily, complaining that he was suffering from a permanent headache from the solvents and toxic chemicals in his airless underground studio. On Sunday, thick white cloud hung low in the valley and it was snowing but they decided to ski all the same.

'Tell Akira he doesn't have to come,' Archie said to Minako. She translated the message; the bodyguard answered angrily.

'What does he say?' Archie asked.

'He says, where you go he goes.'

'How touching. Can he ski?'

'He was born in Sapporo.'

It was a white-out. Visibility was nil and there was almost no queue in front of the chair lift. Akira stayed close to Archie, making it clear that he intended to ride with him on the chair lift. Suddenly there was a shout and out of the dense mist two skiers appeared, one of them out of control. The stranger ploughed into Akira, toppling him. In the fall Akira's bindings came undone and by the time he had sorted himself out Archie was on the three-seated chair lift between Harry and Madeleine. It was, he admitted, neatly done.

'How are you?' Madeleine said, her dark eyes smiling through the yellow goggles.

'I've got backache, eye ache, headache and heartache. What else do you want to know?'

'Everything.'

'There's an underground room full of pictures. I've got to get inside. See what he's got. Decide what to take.'

'You take the Titian, Archie,' Madeleine said firmly, 'no more and no less, if possible this Friday when the Emperor's nephew, Prince Hito, opens the Olympic trials.'

'You remember Hitosan,' Harry interrupted, turning to Archie, 'he was at Oxford with us. Had a passion for doughnuts.' Archie had often seen the eccentric Prince who spurned Western clothes for a traditional black kimono, flying down the High Street, books in one hand, a bun in the other.

Madeleine went on, 'On Friday just at six p.m. there's a black-out in the whole valley for an hour for the torchlight procession and a massive firework display. That's just the cover we need.'

'Hakomoto and Sulgrave are due back this afternoon. What if they decide to stay on next week?'

'Leave them to me,' Harry said.

'And the girl?' Madeleine said.

'She's frightened of Hakomoto. Sometimes I think she hates him. Her son means everything to her. Every day she drives him to the high school near the Imperial Hotel, and picks him up.'

'She's told Harry she dreams of living in France. Do you think there's a deal to be struck?' Madeleine asked.

'Yes,' Archie said thoughtfully, 'I do. But you must talk to her, woman to woman.'

'If we're wrong —' Madeleine murmured.

'It's a calculated risk,' Archie cut in. 'We need her.'

By the time they got to the top of the chair lift the cloud was breaking. Harry took off his goggles to wipe them. As he was doing this Akira caught up with them, furious at being left behind. The Japanese saw Harry's face for the first time, scowled and followed Archie down the mountain. As soon as he got back to the villa Akira told his boss that Harry Wardington was in Hokkaido.

'You got him here, didn't you?' Hakomoto roared at Minako, who stood in front of him, her head bowed. 'And I suppose you've planned secret meetings while I'm away? Well, I'm not going away. I'm staying right here to organize your engagement party. You're getting married, my dear. Akira, come here.'

The bodyguard shuffled forward on his white-stockinged feet, his long black kimono rustling.

'How old are you?'

'Twenty-six.'

'A good age to be married. You like Minako, don't you? Yes, I can see from the way you look at her. Well, I give her to you, as your wife. Be sure you have several pure Japanese children. And don't worry about the little half-caste. You can send him away to boarding school!'

Akira bowed low to Hakomoto and murmured, 'To have an arranged marriage at your hand, Hakomotosan, it is an honour I never dreamt of.'

Minako was staring at Hakomoto, horrified. 'I am not worthy—' she began.

'You will do exactly as I say,' Hakomoto said. 'Akira, tell your parents the good news; we shall celebrate the engagement as soon as possible. Beg them, for my sake, to overlook Minako's past stupidity.'

Akira was smiling broadly, staring at Minako, taking in the perfect figure beneath her tight black dress.

'Don't get any ideas!' Hakomoto said sharply. 'You don't lay a finger on her until she's your wife, do you understand? Now get out of here, both of you.'

Akira was given the evening off and he went to celebrate with the other security guards in their quarters. Archie found Minako sobbing in the small sitting room where she sat with her son in the evenings; the child was comforting her, whispering, 'Don't cry, Mama, please don't cry.'

Archie brought her a glass of water, and eventually she calmed herself and said, 'Mr Dashwood, if I did not have Yuji then it would be an easy decision. I would kill myself. But I cannot leave my child alone. And yet, I have nowhere to go, no visa to live in a foreign country. In Japan I am banished from my family home and I can't get a job because . . . Oh, Mr Dashwood, what can I do?'

'Something will turn up,' Archie said cautiously.

The next day Minako collected her son from school at the usual time of 4 p.m. She was late and she parked her Nissan in the school car park forgetting to lock the car and hurried off to fetch the child. As they walked towards the car Yuji was chattering about a prize he'd won at mathematics when he stopped mid-sentence and stared at the European woman who was sitting in the passenger seat of their car. Madeleine turned round. Minako recognized the French policewoman from their meeting in the British Embassy, on the opening night of the exhibition.

'It's all right, Yuji,' Minako said, 'this is a friend of mine.'

Chapter 28

'Does Mr Dashwood always work so late?' Hakomoto asked Minako, sipping his neat whisky. It was 7 p.m. on Tuesday. Dicky Sulgrave was reading yesterday's *Times* by the crackling fire, now and then glancing through the panoramic window at the floodlit *piste*. It was a brilliant starry night and very cold; the barometer read minus thirty. Akira stood in attendance by the bar, wearing, as usual, his traditional Japanese kimono.

'Sometimes. He works very hard.'

'He does not like our food, I understand.'

'I make him omelettes,' Minako said, 'and he seems happy.'

'You are good at making a man happy, Minako. You will make a good wife to Akira here.'

The bodyguard smiled but Minako hung her head. Her only hope was to escape with Mr Dashwood, who was not Mr Dashwood at all but Mr Gibbs, Harrysan's good friend. It was all so dangerous and so difficult! She had managed to talk to him only once, when Akira was practising his kendo. 'Commissaire Husson has told me everything,' she had said. 'I am with you to the end.'

'Akira,' Hakomoto barked. 'Ask Mr Dashwood if he would like to join us for a drink.' The bodyguard hurried out of the room. Hakomoto turned his gaze on Minako, his eye lingering lasciviously on the small swell of her breasts. Minako, uneasy at his sensual scrutiny, whispered an excuse and hurried into the library, but Hakomoto got up and followed, shutting the sliding doors behind him.

Minako was leaning over his desk.

'Running away?' Hakomoto said, turning her round. 'Let me look at you. Pretty!' He trailed his manicured nail down the side of her face and neck to her breast. 'Please wear your kimono tonight, the blue one. There's nothing like a kimono to arouse a man's desire. So much material, so many folds, a man's hand slips so secretly inside. Is Minako's breast still so white? So soft? It's a long time since you gave me your softness.'

He pulled her to him, holding the back of her neck in a vice-like grip, and pressed his lips on hers. She could feel him hardening against her. Suddenly he pushed her away.

'Minako has changed,' he said angrily. 'She is contaminated by the embraces of her English lover. She has forgotten that Japanese women are obedient. But she will remember.'

Once again he pulled her to him and kissed her, this time forcing his tongue into her mouth. He took Minako's hand and pulled it down to the front of his trousers where she could feel the hard swell.

'Perhaps it's my fault,' he said, breathing heavily. 'I've neglected you. Tonight I shall make amends. Don't forget. Wear the blue kimono.'

They returned to the sitting room in silence. Moments later Akira came back into the room, bowed and announced: 'Mr Dashwood cannot come.'

'Cannot come!' Hakomoto said angrily.

'He wants all of you to come downstairs. He has found something very interesting.'

They found Archie leaning against the wall, his arms crossed, staring at the painting on the easel.

'The mystery is solved,' he said. 'See the scarlet and gold banner in the background? It's the *oriflamme* of St Denis, the banner of the kings of France. See the signet ring with the letter "F"? Lord Sulgrave was right, it's "F" for Francis II and this is his Queen. They called her Marie Stuart but later she moved to Scotland where she became —'

'Mary Queen of Scots!' Dicky Sulgrave burst out triumphantly.

'We know that Titian painted her but the painting went missing in the Civil War. It's a fascinating picture, a magnificnt copy.'

'A *copy*,' Hakomoto whispered incredulously. 'A copy of *what*?'

'Of the Titian commissioned by Francis II and once owned by Charles I. It's in the 1635 inventory.'

'What on earth makes you say this is a copy?' Dicky Sulgrave asked belligerently. 'In my view it's the original!'

'I really don't think so. Look at the brushwork, it's too tentative, too mannered, don't you find?'

'No, I don't,' Dicky objected. 'The brushwork is magnificent.'

'Is it? Look at the hands, and the hair and those pearls coiled round her neck; too neat, too precise. And the mouth is weak. Oh, I don't know. These things are largely instinct. It's a long time since I've looked at work of this quality. Send it to London, to the National Gallery. Or to the Louvre. They'll tell you.'

'Mr Dashwood,' Hakomoto said, ignoring Archie's last remark, 'I am interested in your opinion. Minako, take Lord Sulgrave back to the sitting room, will you. Akira, wait down here.'

Hakomoto walked along the corridor towards the forbidden door, stopping in front of the panel of numbers where he punched in a code. 1940. His date of birth, Archie guessed. The steel door clicked open and Hakomoto led the way into a dark-red room covered with paintings, their frames almost touching. Concealed lights beamed precisely on to each canvas.

Akira was shadowing them as Hakomoto walked briskly on towards a second room. Archie lingered in front of an Oudry still life stolen from the Marquess of Cholmondeley in 1993; next to it he took in the Rembrandt self-portrait stolen from the Isabella Gardner Museum in 1990; a Gauguin of a Tahitian woman stolen in transit at London airport in 1989. And there were a dozen or so Impressionists, including a Sisley of Paris, a Degas of a woman ironing shirts and a Pissarro of cliffs by the sea, which Archie recognized as being stolen from French museums – he remembered the photographs Madeleine had brought to the Art Loss Register that day in London.

'If you would care to follow me, Mr Dashwood,' Hakomoto said impatiently. The second room was smaller and the paintings were hung sparingly, and there was a sofa, a low table and a vase of silk flowers. Archie glanced at the ceiling and saw infra-red lights in the corners. There was an internal alarm system inside the stronghold itself.

Archie found himself looking at portraits of women; blonde women. Paul Hewitt would have been electrified.

'What do you think of my ladies, Mr Dashwood? Give me your professional view, if you will.'

It was a test and Archie knew it and his mind raced back over the hours he had spent with Oliver Dashwood in the Louvre and the Musée d'Orsay.

'It's a pageant of blonde beauties throughout the ages,' Archie began.

'Pageant,' Hakomoto murmured thoughtfully. 'I like that word.'

'You start with Clouet, Jean, not Francis, the sixteenth-century French court painter. It's a portrait of Queen Claude, wife of Francis I.' (Stolen, Archie remembered, from the National Gallery of Scotland in 1988.) 'Your Elizabethan portrait is anonymous like most Elizabethan portraits.' (And until three months ago it hung above Baroness Brechin's bed.) 'That's a nice Gainsborough, late, you can tell from the brushstrokes on the trees, the near-Impressionist atmosphere.' (Stolen from the boot of Sir Hugh Lynton's car.)

Archie paused and considered the next painting.

'I love Modigliani and this is one of the finest I've ever seen.' *The* finest according to Mary Marchant, who owned the painting until it was stolen a few months ago, Archie thought.

'In your opinion, have I any fakes in this room?'

'I can't possibly say from this distance. I'd need to have a closer look.'

'Then you shall.'

Hakomoto went over to a small bookshelf which stood in the corner of the room and pulled out a leather-bound volume. Behind it was a button which he pressed, cutting off the alarm system; the infrared lights went off. Hakomoto put the book back, walked over to the Modigliani, took it from the wall and placed it on the easel which stood near the fireplace.

'Take your time, Mr Dashwood.'

Archie stared for a long time and eventually shook his head. 'It doesn't feel right to me. But I could be wrong. This isn't my period.'

'They say you have a wonderful eye.'

'I have an instinct, a nose. Modigliani is relatively easy to forge, so is Picasso. Your Picasso of Françoise Gilot over there is very fine and definitely not a fake, in my view.' (And belongs to the Manchester City Art Gallery and was stolen during renovations in 1992.) 'But these days one can never be absolutely sure. Forgers have become artists in their own right. De Hory fooled everyone, and van Maegeren before him. Even Tom Keating pulled the wool over a great many experts' eyes . . .'

'I do not like to be tricked, by anyone.' Hakomoto said.

'No one likes to be tricked, any more than they like to be robbed.'

Archie turned his head slowly and met Hakomoto's stare head on.

'You see the empty easel over there?' Hakomoto said. 'That is where I shall place the Titian, if it is a Titian. Let's see if it can hold its own in this distinguished company, shall we?'

He called for Akira and moments later the bodyguard returned carrying the Titian and placed it carefully on the easel. Archie and Hakomoto stared in silence, imbibing the powerful, rarified atmosphere of the painting.

'I could be wrong,' Archie mused. 'She's very fetching, very Titianesque.'

'That's not good enough,' Hakomoto snapped. 'There must be no doubt.'

Akira lifted the painting off the easel, ready to carry it back to the studio.

'Leave it where it is,' Hakomoto snapped in Japanese, and turning to Archie, he said, 'I wish to spend a little time with my new lady friend. I must find out if we get on, if this is a passing fancy or a lasting relationship. Only time will tell.'

'But I haven't finished. It needs further cleaning and retouching.'

'That can wait,' Hakomoto said with a wave of his hand. 'Mr Dashwood, you've been working very hard. Have a break. Enjoy the skiing.'

Minako was wearing her blue kimono.

'Mama looks so pretty,' Yuji said, kicking a white football against the door.

'Thank you, my sweet,' she whispered; she had been crying and her skin felt taut from the hot tears. Archie sat on the sofa reading. Akira was outside on the veranda watching the ski officials marking out the Olympic run by floodlight.

'What's the big occasion?' Archie said, glancing at his kimono.

'Hakomotosan likes traditional Japanese dress. He—' She broke off, tears welling in her eyes.

'Not much longer now,' Archie whispered.

'I will not let you down,' Minako murmured.

Mirako slipped into the upstairs drawing room to find Hakomoto and Sulgrave arguing.

'I have the provenance of the Modigliani, and of the Picasso,' Sulgrave was saying, holding a glass of brandy in his hands. 'Of course it's genuine. Dashwood is just causing trouble.'

'Why would he want to do that?' Hakomoto said coldly. 'I am most disturbed by what he has told me. I shall have to get a second opinion before we can complete our business.'

'The money was due as soon as the painting was cleaned,' Sulgrave said, getting to his feet.

'No! The money was due when the picture was cleaned and authenticated.'

'Look, Hakomotosan, Dashwood's got it wrong. What do you expect? He can't believe it's *the* Titian that's been missing for centuries. But then he doesn't know where the painting comes from. You know and I know the true provenance of this great work of art, a provenance more impeccable, more prestigious than any painting in your entire collection. Don't lose your nerve, Hakomotosan, I beg you.'

'Maybe,' Hakomoto said, reconsidering his position. Sulgrave could be very persuasive. 'All the same, I want a second opinion,' he said, and glanced across the room at Minako, who was sitting in the kneeling position of the Japanese woman, dressed in her blue kimono, her hands quietly folded in her lap.

'Why are you dressed like that?' Hakomoto said angrily. 'Go and change. I pay for you to buy clothes in Paris and you don't wear them.'

Chapter 29

It was a glorious day and the cold air went deep into Archie's lungs, invigorating his whole being, while rays of winter sun warmed his face. The powder snow was deep and untouched, waiting for him; he plunged in, exhilarated by the fresh powder, the rhythmic movement, the rhythmic breathing, flakes of snow flying in your face, the sense of conquest, of dominating the mountain. Better than sex, his army instructor used to say, on those gruelling training sessions before the army championships. Archie won the downhill three years running.

He could hear Akira behind, carving up the mountain with irritating ease. The Japanese thundered down, with the aggression of a downhill racer, but he had no style. It was late in the afternoon but Archie reckoned there was time for one last run. The chair lift stopped at 3.50 p.m.; it was 3.15 p.m. He could make it, just, and end his day on a high note, skiing alone through powder, the sun on his back, the world at his feet. But first he had to lose Akira.

They were just above the tree-line. A forest of pines stretched to the valley below. Archie took off into the trees; Akira followed. At first the trees were wide apart and the snow was soft and deep; but further into the forest the snow became wetter and the trees were packed close together. Pretty soon skiing was impossible. You had to walk, kick turn, slide, anything to get down. Suddenly there was a yell from Akira, who had fallen and lost his left ski. He was jabbing his pole into the deep snow, searching frantically. If you want to sort out the men from the boys, ski the forest, Archie thought.

'I won't wait, if you don't mind. Cheerio!'

Archie skied, jumped, pushed and pulled his way through the trees, until he got out of the forest on to a broad open slope with the chair lift in the distance. To his right, further down the valley, he could see Sapporo; to his left, coming out of the forest, the angry figure of Akira.

But Archie was far enough ahead to lose him and he whistled as he skied across the empty slope. Everyone had gone home but the chair lift was still moving and with a bit of luck Archie would catch it and get the last ride of the day to the top. The attendant seemed to be waiting for him, smiled and nodded and allowed him through. Great, Archie thought. I've made it.

The chair lift swept him up and he sat back and closed his eyes and felt the last rays of sunshine on his face. Akira would never catch him now. The chair lift stopped. At first Archie thought nothing of it; he waited but it didn't move. Ahead of him all the chairs were empty. He looked behind; there was no one. He could see right down to the start of the chair lift where the attendant stood talking to a man in a blue and white ski-suit; it was Akira. He was staring in Archie's direction. Any second now the lift would start again, Archie thought. But the lift didn't start. The attendant put on his skis, turned his back on Archie and followed Akira down the mountain.

It's very simple, Archie said to himself. They've left you here to die. The bulk of the restoration work is done, the picture is identified more or less, and anyway Dashwood knows too much. He must be rubbed out. And what better man to do it than Akira? For a hatchet-faced Japanese the man is surprisingly ingenious. A skiing accident, how dreadful. Dashwood freezes to death on a chair lift. Very neat. No one to blame. No witnesses, once the ski-lift attendant is paid off with a fat bribe.

The drop was fifty feet at least on to a steep hard slope; there was no way he wouldn't break a leg, or both, and it was doubtful he could survive the night, injured on the mountainside; hypothermia would kill him if the fall didn't. If the snow below had been soft, he might have risked it, but this was a *piste*, packed hard. His only chance was to get out of the chair and haul himself up the steel pole to the cable and abseil down the cable for thirty metres to the pylon.

Archie took off his skis and let them drop; they clattered on to the icy snow. Then he let go of his ski-sticks, hurling them on to the frozen surface like spears. By now it was almost dark and the temperature was dropping fast. He tried to get a grip on the smooth pole which joined the chair lift to the cable, but his gloved hands kept slipping. He took off his gloves, clipped them carefully to his ski-suit and gripped with bare hands. Jesus, it was cold. His skin stuck to the bar, but at least he could grip. His ski boots felt like ten-ton weights on the end of his legs. He hauled himself up a foot then slipped back; his boots wouldn't grip. His arms felt as if they were being torn from their sockets and he was reminded of those weeks of army training when his instructor had pushed him to the limits of endurance. Except this wasn't training. He was fighting for his life.

With one superhuman effort, standing on the back of the chair, Archie pulled himself up the smooth iron bar and grabbed the cable with both hands. He held on by his arms, his legs swinging free in the freezing air. The bloody boots! If only he could take them off, but he couldn't. He couldn't walk down the mountain in socks; he wouldn't have any feet left. The cable was cutting into his hands like a knife. He swung forward then backwards to gain momentum and with one almighty heave he pulled his legs up and wrapped them round the cable, hanging

226

like a monkey on a branch. He inched his way down the steel coil which ripped his ski-suit and sliced into his palms. If only he could reach his gloves, put them on, but he couldn't and he had to keep moving, inching his way further down towards the pylon. A pallid moon was just visible in a sky streaked with orange and vermilion from the setting sun. Archie prayed.

He clung to the steel girder of the pylon, his heart pounding, his breath shooting from his mouth in white spurts; he had made it. He thanked God in the silence of the night; the only sound was the rasping of his own breathing. He pushed his frozen, bleeding palms and fingers into his gloves, climbed down the pylon, and slithered and slipped down the hard-packed piste towards the village lights. Eventually he found a road. A car came slowly round the corner and slowed. Jesus, he thought. Akira again. He couldn't run, not in ski boots, and his fingers were useless. His whole body stiffened as the car door opened.

'Get in,' Madeleine said. An hour earlier she had received a desperate telephone call from Minako saying that Archie hadn't come back from skiing. Minako knew which slopes he was skiing on and for the last hour Madeleine and the French Head of Station, Serge Noailles, had been driving on the mountain roads, hoping against hope to find Archie.

Madeleine glanced at Archie's ashen face as Serge Noailles drove in silence to the ski chalet hired by the French Ambassador where they were both staying. In the valley below were the flickering lights of Sapporo. Archie cracked a smile when he saw Harry, downed three stiff brandies in succession, and he sat by the log fire while a Japanese doctor bandaged his damaged hands. When the doctor had left, Archie gave a blow-by-blow account of his last two weeks, culminating in a description of Akira's attempt to leave him for dead on the chair lift.

'I'm pulling you out,' Madeleine told him. 'Today they tried to kill you and they'll try again. I'm aborting this operation.'

'What about Minako?'

'Tomorrow morning when she takes her son to school I shall pick them both up and get her out of Japan. She kept to her part of the bargain and I shall keep to mine.'

Archie drained the last drop of brandy. 'Well, that's all very interesting but I'm going back. I want that Titian.'

Harry threw back his head and laughed his deep guttural laugh. 'She wouldn't believe me. I told her, he'll never pack it in, not now. But she said she could make you.'

'She can make me do many things,' Archie said, touching Madeleine's face with his bandaged hand, 'but not this. I want Hakomoto to remember me, Madeleine. I want to leave a few empty spaces on those walls.'

'We might open a bottle of champagne, don't you think?' the Earl of Sulgrave said to Seiji Hakomoto.

'Yes, I think we might.'

Akira was sent to fetch a bottle of vintage Krug. Dicky eased out the cork and filled two glasses.

'To us,' he said, raising his glass.

'To us!'

Minako slipped into the room.

'I am getting worried, Hakomotosan. Mr Dashwood is still not back and it's dark.'

'He's probably having a drink at the Imperial Hotel,' Hakomoto said. 'We must let the man enjoy himself occasionally.'

What have you done to him, Minako felt like screaming. She had been horrified to learn that Oliver Dashwood was none other than Archie Gibbs, best friend of Harrysan. Did he not realize, she had asked Madeleine, the danger was immense; and if he were caught, the retribution would be terrible? At least she had been able to warn Madeleine by telephone that Archie was missing; missing presumed dead, Minako thought.

The internal telephone rang. Minako answered it. She covered the receiver with her hand. Her face gave nothing away, but her eyes were smiling as she said, 'Mr Dashwood is at the gate.'

Moments later Archie walked into the villa followed by Harry Wardington, who threw out his arms and said, 'Dicky! Well, fancy meeting you here! It really is a small world, isn't it? Good evening, Mr Hakomoto. Once again I am the uninvited guest! I bet you're glad to see poor old Oliver again. There I was driving down the main road in a taxi and who should I find but our friend here. Can you believe he got stuck on the chair lift? Look at him! Clothes ripped. Fingers half-frozen. Blood all over his hands. I took him to the doctor and got him bandaged up, and I've packed a knapsack for him with spare bandages, dressings and antiseptic.'

'But Hakomotosan, you said—' Minako began, and then she met Hakomoto's furious stare and she stopped speaking, hung her head and took several small steps backwards.

'What he needs – what we both need – is a drink,' Harry went on.

'Of course,' Hakomoto said. 'Champagne? Whisky?'

'Champagne,' Harry said, 'to celebrate Oliver's safe return.'

'I was getting worried, Mr Dashwood. You ski too fast for Akira; he couldn't keep up. I was just about to send out a search party.'

'I'm sure you were,' Archie said, holding the glass of champagne between his bandaged hands.

'You got stuck on the chair lift, that's terrible. How did you get off?' Hakomoto asked.

'With great difficulty.'

Meanwhile, Harry was looking through the open sliding doors which led into the library.

'Dicky, she looks just like your mother-in-law,' he announced, staring at the Augustus John.

'Do you think so?' Dicky said vaguely. 'I don't see it myself. Anyway, my mother-in-law is where she's always been, above the fireplace in our drawing room.'

'I think we'd better get you back to Tokyo, Mr Dashwood, and get those hands properly looked at,' Hakomoto said. 'You won't be able to do any restoration work with those bandages. We'll leave first thing in the morning.'

'You can't possibly leave tomorrow,' Harry said, throwing up his hands. 'It's the opening of the Olympic trials and you're all invited to a Royal bash.'

Harry pulled out two large envelopes from his coat pocket and handed one to Seiji Hakomoto, one to Dicky Sulgrave.

'My old friend Prince Hito's giving a party. I told him my old pal Dicky Sulgrave was in town, staying with Seiji Hako-moto. Not *the* Seiji Hakomoto, Hitosan said. He's been longing to meet you. If you ask me he wants to get you on to his charity committee for disabled skiers. Anyway, these are the formal invites.'

'Mr Dashwood is not invited?' Hakomoto said, fingering the thick card.

'After my ordeal today I am not in a party mood,' Archie snapped.

'Akira can stay and look after you,' Hakomoto said drily.

'Akira was supposed to look after me skiing.'

'Great,' said Harry. 'So you're both coming?'

'We have no choice, Mr Wardington,' Hakomoto said, holding the thick gold-edged ivory engraved invitation embossed with the Imperial chrysanthemums. 'Our Royal Family may not have quite the same standing as the British Royal Family, but I assure you that no Japanese would ever ignore a Royal command.'

'Hitosan will be delighted. Well, if you'll excuse me, I promised to be back in time for dinner. He wants to talk about old times. I took him to his first cricket match. To Henley, Wimbledon, to the House of Commons. I even took him hunting. We killed a fox and he was blooded. See you all tomorrow.'

On his way out of the room, Harry lingered in front of the Augustus John and said to Dicky, 'I still think she looks the spitting image of your mother-in-law.'

Oliver Dashwood asked to be excused; he was not feeling well and wanted to sleep. Minako saw him down to his room and carried his knapsack.

As soon as they were alone, Hakomoto turned to Dicky and said, 'We'll take care of Dashwood in Tokyo. He's a cat with nine lives. Akira, come here!'

Akira stood, his head bowed, as Hakomoto ripped into him in a torrent of shrill Japanese. Akira replied in a low, contrite voice.

'What does he say?' Sulgrave asked impatiently.

'He says he left him hanging in the chair lift. It was too high to jump. The man was done for. If you ask me, we've under-estimated Mr Dashwood. He's surprisingly resilient.'

Downstairs in his room Archie was smiling as he emptied Harry's knapsack; here was everything he'd asked for and more – a wig, two craft knives with retractable blades, a stun grenade and an MR 9 phosphorus grenade.

Chapter 30

'So you see,' Prince Hito said to Harry the following evening in the Royal suite of the Imperial Hotel in Sapporo, 'the Oxford years were the best years of my life.'

The Prince was a short man. well-built, with a round, chubby face; he was sitting in a deep armchair drinking whisky; Harry was sipping a glass of vintage Laurent-Perrier rosé champagne.

'When I look back on those days,' the Prince went on, 'I was so free. I could walk down Broad Street and no one knew who I was. In Japan I can't move without a cameraman taking a picture, or a journalist asking me a question. My life is so boring, Harrysan! I'm forbidden by law to do a proper job so I'm stuck with charity work, and I'm always short of money. We're kept on a shoe-string by our Parliament. If only we had a proper civil list like your Royal Family.'

A courtier came in, bowed low and said a few words in Japanese.

'Time to go,' said the Prince, finishing his drink. 'Your friends are coming? Good, I'm hoping to get a nice fat donation for my charity from Seiji Hakomoto.'

The Prince got to his feet. He looked the epitome of an English gentleman in his Saville Row suit and Vincent's tie. 'Tell me, Harrysan, can you still get jam doughnuts in the market off the High Street?'

*

Minako bowed as Hakomoto and Dicky Sulgrave climbed into the black Nissan and disappeared down the drive into the full glare of the floodlights. She glanced at her watch. 5.50 p.m. At 6.30 p.m. the security guards had been told that Miss Setsu would leave the villa to collect her son Yuji, who was one of a thousand schoolchildren taking part in the torchlight procession.

Minako brought her car round to the front of the villa. She opened the boot briefly to check that everything was in place: Archie's restorer's bag in which he'd packed the stun grenade and the phosphorus grenades from Harry's knapsack and next to this modest arsenal her own small suitcase with a few essential clothes for herself and her son.

Mr Dashwood had complained of a severe headache and gone to bed. Akira stood in the sitting room of the main villa staring out of the panoramic window waiting for the torchlight procession and the fireworks.

At exactly 6 p.m. the chief engineer in the northern suburb of Sapporo switched off all public lighting with the exception of streetlights for traffic. Householders then turned off their lights in accordance with the 'Municipal Instructions'; dutifully the chief security guard switched off the floodlights at Hakomoto's villa. The house was lit by an eerie half moon, now and then eclipsed by cloud; it was bitterly cold and the night air was flecked with snow; stars flickered in the moody sky. Several security guards came on to the veranda holding cups of warm *sake* in their hands; they shouted to Akira to join them.

'Hakomotosan told me to stay inside and keep an eye on you and Mr Dashwood,' he said bitterly.

Minako came to him slowly, silently and put a hand on the back of his neck. He swivelled round, angrily.

'Don't you like it when I touch you, Akirasan?'

She put her cool palm against his cheek. 'You think I

don't like you, but I do. And when we're married you'll be surprised . . . Why don't you enjoy yourself tonight? I'll take care of Mr Dashwood. Go and have fun and we won't say a word to Hakomotosan. We'll ask the security guard to bleep you as soon as his car arrives at the outside gate. That way you'll have plenty of time to get back into the house.'

'One more mistake and I'm out on my ear.'

'There won't be a mistake,' she said, stroking his face.

He pulled her towards him roughly and kissed her hungrily on the mouth.

'I like a strong man,' she said, laughing and pulling away. 'Go along now, Akirasan. I'll watch you from the window.'

Akira joined the other security guards outside and soon he was laughing and drinking warm *sake*. The torchlight procession began and Minako watched the river of a thousand flames, pinpricks of nervous light, weaving down the mountain. Somewhere in the flickering mass was her son Yuji. Minako prayed for him and for her new life in France which she had been promised by Commissaire Husson. They would live in the Massif Central and one day Yuji would go to the local *lycée* and she would be happy and free from fear. For the first time in many, many years Minako was filled with hope. But first she must carry out her side of the bargain.

Carefully she opened the cabinet with the ceremonial daggers, removed an eighteenth-century stiletto, slipped it into her handbag and headed for the lift, where she punched in the code for the third floor underground. The door to the secret gallery stood open. The first room was pitch-black but Minako headed towards the second room and the torchbeam which darted in the blackness. Suddenly the torch went out.

'Archie,' she whispered.

A torchlight flashed in her eyes, blinding her.

'Sorry,' Archie said, 'I had to be sure.'

He was standing in front of the bookcase, searching frantically.

'It's here somewhere, a life of the Hideyoshi Toyotomi; interesting choice when you think about it, the shogun who unified Japan, attacked Korea, dreamt of conquering China, a megalomaniac, just like our host. Here it is!'

Clumsily with his bandaged hands Archie pulled out the thick, leather-bound volume and found a small red knob. 'There's the button. Press it!'

Minako pushed the knob with her long, elegant finger. The infrared beam cut out.

'Now, we'll start with the Modigliani,' Archie said, carefully lifting the painting off the wall. 'Take the hobby knife and cut as close as you can to the frame. Go on, hurry!'

Minako stared at Archie with her dark, frightened eyes before she pressed down on the razor-sharp blade. Archie noted with satisfaction that her hand was steady.

'Now the Gainsborough. Same again, Minako.'

'I'm sure Madeleine said —'

'Don't argue.'

Minako cut the Gainsborough neatly from the frame.

'Well done. Anyone would say you do this for a living. Now, the Elizabethan portrait and that's it.'

Once again Minako cut the canvas from its frame.

'Right, hang all three frames back on the wall. Now, roll up the three canvases together, picture on the outside so you don't compress the paint. Good. We'll take the Titian as it is. Now,' Archie said, flashing his torch across the walls, 'is there anything else that takes my fancy?'

'Archie, we must get out of here. Akira could —'

'Well, I never,' Archie said, beaming his torch on to an oil painting of haystacks in a summer landscape. 'That's the Monet stolen from the Tours museum and a big favourite with Madeleine. This *is* my lucky day.'

Moments later Minako had cut the Monet from its frame, rolled it with the other canvases and hung the empty frame back on the wall. Archie passed Minako the torch, lifted the Titian off the easel where Hakomoto had placed it, and with Minako lighting the way they closed the gallery door and hurried along the corridor to the lift.

Minako punched in the code to the ground floor. They hurried through the dark hall out of the front door; their breath showed white in the black night air.

'First the Titian,' Archie whispered, crouching in the shadows and watching as Minako opened the boot of her car and carefully laid the picture on top of her small suitcase. She closed the boot without fastening the catch. Suddenly she jumped; a muffled bang echoed through the mountains and a dazzling explosion of fireworks lit up the night sky, rockets screaming in different directions, a thousand petals of silver cascading through the black air. For a moment Minako and her car were floodlit by a blaze of light from the fireworks. A security guard glanced back from the veranda where he was standing, saw her and waved; she waved back.

Her mouth dry with fear, Minako whispered, 'Into the car.'

'Take these,' Archie said, handing her the roll of four canvases and his restorer's bag. 'Get in the car and keep the engine running.'

'Where are you going?'

'To rescue somebody's mother.'

'Not going, surely? The torchlight procession is just about to begin. It should be spectacular,' Harry said, clapping Dicky Sulgrave on the back.

'Mr Hakomoto is rather tired . . .' Dicky protested.

'But Prince Hito will be here any second. He's just gone down on to the veranda to fire the starting gun. I know he wanted to talk to you. Have something to eat, the food is delicious.' And Harry led Dicky to the buffet table groaning with dishes served in the most elaborate and imaginative way: pyamids of prawns, beetroot sculpted as roses, fillet of beef cut wafer-thin and coiled into shells, scallops planted like flowers at the base of magnificent ice sculptures.

Meanwhile, Seiji Hakomoto was standing impatiently by the door waiting for Dicky.

Harry came over to him smiling. 'I've just told Dicky you mustn't leave yet, Mr Hakomoto. The Prince is so looking forward to meeting you. Ah, here he is. Let me introduce you.' Harry took Hakomoto by the arm and led him over to the Prince.

Hakomoto and Sulgrave could not escape; the Prince was in full flight, telling his favourite skiing story. Harry helped himself to a piece of smoked salmon from the buffet and slipped out of the emergency exit.

Chapter 31

There was another loud bang as a rocket burst and the whole sky lit up with a shower of shimmering confetti which glittered slowly down through the blackness; this was followed by wave after wave of rockets streaking upwards, making a strange whinnying noise before they exploded into a thousand silver fragments.

Archie slipped into the dark sitting room and crouched down by the panoramic window from where he could see Akira and the security guards standing on the veranda sipping their sake, laughing and pointing to the sky.

But the next eruption caught Archie by surprise: a high-pitched scream ripped through the air followed by an explosion, and all at once a gigantic red rose filled the sky and for one beautiful moment the rose seemed fixed in the firmament, until it disintegrated into a myriad of flaming red particles. For a few seconds the sitting room was lit up and the samurai sword on its lacquer stand glinted in the flash of roselight. Archie dived behind a sofa. Darkness fell once more. Archie crept over to the Augustus John.

'I'm taking you home, old girl,' he said to Cordelia Sulgrave's mother. 'Hakomoto isn't your type.'

Once again he checked the ceiling for infrared lights; there were none. Archie moved forward, placed both hands on the frame and lifted it gently away from the wall.

All hell broke loose. The silence of the villa was shattered by a bellowing alarm and one second too late Archie saw the thin, black cable which wired the picture to the wall from behind. He raced to the door to meet Minako running into the villa.

'Archiesan, what's happened?' she cried above the searing noise.

'The Augustus John was wired from behind.'

'Please, get in the back of my car. Hide yourself under the rug. Hurry!'

She could see the guards were running along the veranda heading for the side entrance to the villa. By the time they arrived in the sitting room Minako was standing by the telephone with a receiver in one hand and a torch in the other.

'It's all right,' she said calmly to the chief security guard, putting her hand over the mouth of the receiver. 'I'm afraid I set off the alarm. I was trying to straighten the picture. I'm so sorry. Hello? Is that the police station? Thank you, this is Mr Hakomoto's villa, Miss Setsu speaking. I've set off the alarm. Yes, I can tell you the code. Water-fowl on lotus pond. Of course you must come and see for yourself. How long? Twenty minutes. Excellent. Once again I'm so very sorry.'

'Where's Mr Dashwood?' Akira said.

'I told you, he's not very well.'

'No one could sleep through this noise,' Akira said, putting his hands to his ears.

'The police are on their way,' Minako said to the chief security guard, 'meanwhile, can you turn off the alarm?'

'Yes, but I can't reset it. That has to be done by the security engineer. Here's his number. I daresay he'll know all about it by now. The alarm goes straight through to his switchboard.'

Minako dialled the security engineer, spoke for a few moments and hung up. 'He's on his way,' she said quietly.

The chief security guard put his hands to his ears. 'I can't think straight in this din. Come on, Tatsuo.' He nodded to his friend who was staring out of the window at another dazzling explosion in the sky. 'Let's switch off this racket and go back and enjoy the fireworks.'

The two guards came into the hall. Archie could see them clearly from where he was hiding behind a massive eighteenth-century travelling palanquin. He had decided against getting into Minako's car in case she needed help. A few feet away, standing long, straight and lethal in a huge blue and white china urn were the guards' iron-bound kendo staves.

Crouched in the darkness, Archie watched the two security guards fumbling with their torches, pulling out their different key chains and simultaneously inserting their keys in the Shorrock control panel to switch off the wailing alarm. It was textbook stuff, Archie had to admit: two men necessary to shut off an alarm, so if one guard was overpowered and forced to use his key the alarm would not be cut off. Hakomoto had thought of every-thing. It needed an army to invade this stronghold. What chance did they have, a woman and an unarmed man with bandaged hands? This was looking more and more like a suicide mission.

Akira was in no hurry to leave the sitting room. He stood by the panoramic window until the searing noise of the alarm stopped.

'Thank God for that,' he said to Minako. 'Hakomotosan's going to hit the roof when he hears what's happened. I wouldn't like to be in your shoes. Perhaps, if you're very nice to me . . .' and Akira let his hand drift down the side of her face to her neck and below to her small perfect breasts, 'I'll say it was my fault.'

'You're very kind,' Minako whispered. 'But if you will excuse me, Akirasan, I must go and collect my son.'

'I'll go and check on Mr Dashwood,' Akira said, reverting to his hard professional voice.

'Don't wake him up whatever you do. The poor man is not well. His hands are terribly painful.'

The sky lit up again with exploding rockets and whirling wheels and a million diamonds falling through the night air.

The chief guard and his colleague came back into the sitting room. 'That's it, then,' he said, the beam from his torch darting nervously about the room. 'The alarm's off until the engineer gets here. All we can do now is wait. I need a drink.'

'I'll join you in a minute,' Akira said, heading for the underground corridor. The guard went back outside while Minako hurried into the hall. From somewhere in the darkness, Archie whispered: 'Get in the car. Make sure the boot is open. Start the engine and wait for me.'

'Archiesan, we must go now! Akira is looking for you.'

'Do as I say!'

Akira stood in front of Oliver Dashwood's door, tapping lightly. There was no answer. He pushed open the door and saw, in the bed, a body sleeping, and resting on the pillow a mop of grey hair. Was it possible Dashwood had slept throughout the alarm? It was unnatural. But so was his stillness. There was no breathing. Akira came closer, and in disbelief hurled back the bedclothes, to see a wig on Yuji's white football and pillows stuffed beneath the bedclothes. He ran from the room.

Archie waited for the next flash of fireworks to give him enough light and with his bandaged hands he took the Augustus John gingerly off the wall. Suddenly the hair on the back of his neck bristled and he knew it was too late: he swivelled; a fierce flash of red light lit both the sky and the sitting room and in that brilliant moment Archie saw Akira standing in the entrance, clasping in both hands the lethal iron-bound kendo fighting staff. Archie kept his eyes trained on the Japanese as he dropped the painting to the ground.

Akira was breathing slowly, steadily, marshalling his concentration for the final act. The Englishman was a traitor, Minako too, but he would deal with her later. For the moment he was going to finish the job he had started yesterday on the ski-slope. Hakomotosan had told him to kill the Englishman. He had failed. This time he would succeed.

Another red flash burst across the sky and a red glow fell on Archie, who was crouching like a cat waiting to spring, every fibre of his body alert. Akira saw him, raised the staff and brought it down with all his might. Archie sprang back and the staff, slicing the air, missed his face by centimetres. Outside, the security guards were only a few metres away on the veranda, laughing and drinking.

There was another burst of fireworks and a green flash lit the room, and Akira's staff smashed a small table that stood between himself and Archie. In the dying rays of the green glow, on the table in front of the window, Archie saw the fifteenth-century samurai sword on its lacquer stand. The light faded and Archie lunged forward, did a body roll over the top of the table, grabbed the sword and tumbled to the ground the other side. He crawled under the table and unsheathed steel blade. Akira stumbled forward in the darkness, and, holding his staff tightly with both hands, he let out a high-pitched battle cry. Akira brought the iron-bound bamboo stave crashing down on to the table above Archie's head. Archie struggled to get a firm grip on the hilt of the sword with his bandaged hands. He knew he would only have one chance, one thrust.

Akira took a deep breath. The Englishman was on the ground. Where? Under the table? Yes! Of course! He shortened the grip on his staff, to lunge at him with the iron-bound end, break a few ribs, force the traitor out of his hole, and then kill him, slowly, blow by blow, paralysing him first, then destroying him. The Japanese dropped down on his haunches, and from this crouching position he strained his eyes to see in the dark.

Archie waited for Akira's face to appear; the samurai sword was balanced in his right hand. He dared not breathe. The darkness was total. Suddenly another massive explosion lit up the room and the two men stared at each other beneath the table, but only for a second, as Archie lunged forward and thrust the tip of the sword deep into Akira's left eye.

With a terrible cry Akira fell back, dropping his staff, desperately trying to drag the blade from his eye, cutting his hands to the bone on the razor-sharp edge. He rolled from side to side, blood gushing from his wound. Archie stumbled towards the door, tripping over the Augustus John. He grabbed the painting and glanced back at Akira. Blood was pouring from the side of his face and he lay motionless, his limbs sprawled on the red-stained floor.

Clutching the Augustus John in his bandaged hands, Archie walked out of the front door to Minako's car, laid the picture face down on the Titian so the frames touched but not the canvases, and climbed into the back seat where he crouched on the floor and covered himself with the blanket.

'I was so worried about you, Archiesan. I thought something must have happened. Any minute now the police will arrive.'

'I had to say goodbye to Akira.'

Minako forced herself to drive slowly down the drive towards the steel gates even though her whole body was cold with fear. Inside her bag was the stiletto. If they caught her then she would kill herself and die in the knowledge that her son, Yuji, would have a new life; Commissaire Husson had promised to take care of the boy whatever happened. He was with her now, safe from Hakomoto's vengeance. Minako stopped in front of the steel gates. The security guard came out of his booth.

'Where is your dog?' Minako said, smiling.

'Under the table. He doesn't like the fireworks. I should have locked him up.'

'I didn't think a Rottweiler was afraid of anything, but I must hurry. You see, my son was in the torchlight procession and I don't want him to catch cold.'

'He's a nice lad, your son. What's he called?'

'Yuji.' Minako's hands gripped the steering-wheel.

'My daughter's five. I wanted to ask your advice about schools. They say the primary school in north Sapporo is very good.'

Suddenly the Rottweiler was on his feet, standing in the entrance to the booth growling.

'What's wrong with you, then?' said the guard, untying the lead from the table-leg. The dog lunged forward and the guard had a job stopping him as he barked furiously, baring his pointed teeth and red gums.

'I can't think what's got into him,' the guard said, pulling hard on the lead. 'Stop it, you brute! Is this a nice way to greet Miss Setsu?'

'We'll talk about the school later,' Minako said. 'Forgive me, but I'm very late for my son.'

The guard dragged the dog back into the booth and pressed the red button to release the gates. They opened slowly; Minako watched the gap between them widen, inch by inch. Her foot hovered above the accelerator. Not yet, she told herself; the gap isn't wide enough for my car. A few more inches.

And then she heard the shouting and in her driver's mirror she saw the chief security guard running up the drive.

'What does *he* want?' the guard said, stepping out of his booth. At the same time the internal telephone started to ring.

'I'll leave you to sort things out,' Minako said with a smile, and she squeezed her car through the gap between the gates with barely a centimetre on either side.

'Let's move,' said Archie, throwing back the blanket as

Minako pressed hard on the accelerator and skidded down the icy dirt track towards the village. In the rear window Archie could see the guard running after them, the Rottweiler barking and straining at the leash.

'Slow down here,' Archie said as they entered the village and passed the local supermarket, 'we take a left,' and Minako turned into a side-street. Archie looked frantically down the empty road poorly lit by streetlamps. 'Don't tell me they're not here —'

A black Peugeot with French diplomatic plates slid round the corner. Harry jumped out and opened the boot.

'What took you so long?' Archie said. 'Hurry!'

At that moment a volley of rockets shot into the sky, and one magnificent multi-coloured explosion followed another until the whole sky was ablaze with shimmering crystals. Everyone stopped for a second to watch the breathtaking sight.

'That's the end of the fireworks, the grand finale,' Harry said. 'Let's get a move on.'

They transferred the Titian, the Augustus John and the roll of canvases into the boot of the Peugeot. Archie gave Harry Minako's suitcase but kept a bandaged grip on his own restorer's bag.

'That's it, let's go,' he called out, when a black Nissan slowly turned the corner and bore down on them, inexorably, headlights blazing.

'It's Hakomoto,' Minako cried in anguish.

The headlamps went out. For a moment there was absolute stillness as each person stood bathed in the brilliant blue moonlight. The car doors opened and Hakomoto stepped out, followed by the guard and the Rottweiler straining at his leash. Archie thought he saw the outline of Sulgrave's head in the back seat of the Nissan. He slid a hand into his restorer's bag and silently pulled out a canister of picture varnish.

'This is no way to repay my hospitality, Mr Dashwood,' Hakomoto said. 'And, Mr Wardington, I'm very shocked to find you involved with a common thief.'

'A very uncommon thief, in the business of recovering the property of Her Majesty the Queen.'

Hakomoto snorted with contempt and turned his gaze on Minako. 'As for you, you little bitch, I shall enjoy punishing you.'

Minako's fingers tightened round the stiletto knife which she'd taken from her handbag. Archie slipped a hand into his restorer's bag.

'Here, take this,' Archie whispered, and passed Harry a spray can of Rowney number 800 Artist's Clear Picture Varnish.

'Kill him!' the guard shouted to the Rottweiler, letting go of the lead. Archie grabbed the phosphorus grenade with his bandaged hand and grappled with the pin. The dog lunged forward, jaws apart, aiming for Archie's neck. Archie couldn't get a grip on the pin so he pushed his restorer's bag into the dog's face. Even so he was knocked over by the force of the brute as it wrestled with the bag, tearing at the fabric with his teeth. Somewhere above him Minako hovered like a butterfly, holding a gleaming blade. She caught the collar of the dog and plunged her stiletto deep into the Rottweiler's skull behind the ear. The jaws went slack and the dog rolled to one side.

Meanwhile, the guard had advanced on Harry, his hands and fingers stiff and pointed, in the classic karate position, ready for the kill. He shouted out some war cry in Japanese and lunged forward. Harry sprayed the canister of picture varnish into his eyes. The guard yelled out and reeled backwards.

Hakomoto stared furiously at the dead dog and the security guard staggering about, hands pressed to his eyes. A Toyota pick-up truck drew up and five more of Hakomoto's security guards scrambled out; from the other end of the village a police car, siren wailing, screeched towards them.

'Here,' Archie said, handing Harry the stun grenade, 'you have to take out the pin.'

'You don't say.'

Harry waited until the guards were bunched together before he threw it into their midst. The explosion flattened them all, even Hakomoto, who went sprawling on to the tarmac.

'The pin, Minako,' Archie said urgently, still holding out the phosphorus grenade in his bandaged hand, his thumb pressed on the safety lever. As Minako pulled at the pin, slowly and carefully, a police car skidded to a halt beside Hakomoto's Nissan and two policemen jumped out. Archie released the safety lever and hurled the grenade; a huge fireball exploded, and the night air was filled with a billowing cloud of dense white smoke.

'Into the car,' Archie shouted, and he dived into the Peugeot, followed by Minako and Harry. The driver, a member of the Deuxième Bureau and hand-picked by the Tokyo Head of Station, put his foot on the accelerator and the Peugeot hurtled through clouds of smoke out of the village and into the quiet countryside.

The schedule was tight, Archie reflected. At Hokkaido airport they were meeting Madeleine and Minako's son, Yuji; the French Head of Station had commandeered the Military Attaché's jet to fly them straight into Narita, where they would transfer on to the Air France flight to Paris. Archie glanced back at the village high above them and saw a distant cluster of twinkling lights; the power supply was back on, the firework display was over.

*

Hakomoto was still coughing when he walked into his sitting room. He was shaken and bruised from the blast of the grenades and his lungs burned and his eyes smarted from the phosphorus fumes. Dicky Sulgrave, who was looking out of the window, turned round.

'Why are you just standing there?' Dicky said, the anger grating in his voice. 'Call the airport. Stop them!'

'And have the Sapporo police in here, snooping around, asking questions? Dickysan, sometimes you are very stupid. At times like this you need to keep a cool head. I told the Chief Constable of Sapporo – he was inside the police car – I was the victim of an attempted robbery. My secretary, Miss Setsu, Akira my bodyguard, and my English restorer, Mr Dashwood were trying to steal my sword collection but my security guards caught them in the act. Unfortunately they got away but at least nothing was stolen. That's what I told the police.'

'And you think they'll believe you? Dashwood had stun grenades and God knows what else. The police won't let this drop; they'll be back.'

'Of course they'll be back,' Hakomoto said carefully. 'And they'll find nothing on my walls but superb examples of seven-teenth-century Japanese monochrome paintings which I have bequeathed in my will to the National Museum of Tokyo. By tomorrow morning every Western painting in this building will have disappeared.'

'What about him?' Dicky said, glancing at Akira's body lying in a pool of blood.

'I've found the perfect grave for such an incompetent fool. It so happens we're just laying the foundations to a new hotel on the other side of Sapporo. Akira will sink without trace.'

'And what about me?'

'You, Dickysan?'

'I kept my side of the bargain. I found the Titian; you lost it.'

'Was it a Titian, who knows?' Hakomoto said, and was convulsed in a fit of coughing.

Dicky stared at the floodlit slopes. So that was it, no money; the end of his dream. Furious thoughts crowded into his mind; and he could hear his wife laughing.

'It was Titian's finest painting,' Dicky said, swivelling round, 'if only you had the stomach for a fight!'

'I know when to cut my losses,' Hakomoto said evenly. 'Did you see the number plates on the getaway car?'

'I couldn't see anything in all that smoke.'

'I could, before they threw the grenades. It was a black Peugeot with French diplomatic plates.' Hakomoto paused and poured himself a stiff whisky. 'I am betrayed,' he went on, 'not once but twice, first by Minako, who must have plotted this little conspiracy with her English lover, but also by you.'

'Don't be such a bloody fool.'

'You betrayed me without knowing it. Commissaire Husson followed you all the way to Japan and you led her straight to me.'

Hakomoto took a large gulp of whisky, banged his empty glass on the lacquer table and said to Dicky, 'Get out.'

As Dicky left the room, Hakomoto called out to his guards to take Akira's body away. Wearily he walked into his library and faced the empty wall where the Augustus John had hung only that morning.

'One,' he said out loud.

He took the lift down to the third floor, punched in the code and turned on the lights to his secret gallery.

'Two,' he said, as he saw the empty frame which had once held the Monet of the haystacks. He walked into the second room.

'Three, four, five,' he said, registering the empty frames of the Gainsborough, the Elizabethan portrait and the Modigliani. Finally he turned his gaze to the easel.

'And, of course, six.'

Chapter 32

Air France flight 601 from Tokyo landed at Charles de Gaulle airport on schedule at 6 a.m. and the first person to disembark was Commissaire Husson. Her assistant Pierre Lamartine was there to meet her with two official Citroëns, a blue Renault van and a police car.

'Congratulations,' Lamartine said.

'Thank you.'

At Narita airport Serge Noailles, the Tokyo Head of Station, had neatly bypassed Japanese customs by including the paintings in the diplomatic baggage of the outgoing French Military Attaché.

Now, on the tarmac of Charles de Gaulle, Madeleine watched as the priceless luggage was loaded into the dark-blue van from the Quai d'Orsay. She gave Lamartine precise instructions: only the Monet was staying in France; the other paintings would be leaving for London later that day with Mr Gibbs and Mr Wardington. She would like to see the Titian before it left the country, so would he please take it to her office under the strictest security.

Madeleine went over to Minako and Yuji, who stood huddled on the tarmac, and led them over to a woman police-officer standing in front of a white Citroën.

'Inspector Mathieu will take you to a safe house in the Massif Central and stay with you for a few days to make sure you have everything you need. After the Christmas holidays your son has a place in the local school and there is a job for you at the university of Clermont Ferrand. I shall come and see you

251

in a month or so. The police will give you round-the-clock protection for as long as we think it necessary. Off you go, and good luck.'

Madeleine kissed Minako on both cheeks. The child got into the car first. Minako lingered, staring at Harry, who stepped forward and hugged her.

'You're all right now,' he whispered.

'Don't forget me, Harrysan.'

She was crying. He took her face in his hands and wiped away a tear from her white cheek. 'Of course I won't forget you. We'll spend New Year together and you can show me round the Massif Central,' he said tenderly, and she smiled and climbed into the police car. Moments later they were gone.

Madeleine turned to Lamartine. 'Will you take Mr Wardington and Mr Gibbs to the St James et Albany and see they're comfortable. I'll see you all later in my office.'

'But, Commissaire Husson,' Archie said, 'you and I are in the middle of important discussions. We can't break off now.'

Madeleine hesitated then invited Archie to follow her into the waiting police car.

'And what exactly were we discussing that couldn't wait?' she murmured.

'A holiday. You and me alone without the mobile phone.'

'Only if you shave off your beard.'

The drive into Paris seemed interminable, as Madeleine and Archie sat demurely in the back of the police Citroën. Being back in France, out of immediate danger, released their pent-up longing for each other, and the moment they arrived at Madeleine's flat and were inside the ridiculously small lift, they kissed, urgently. But again they had to wait, standing awkwardly in the entrance hall as the police driver delivered the luggage. Eventually he left, shutting the door behind him. For a moment Madeleine and Archie stared at each other, searching for something in the other's face. Madeleine led Archie into her bedroom, took his bandaged hands and kissed them.

'You'll have to undress me,' he said.

'I shall enjoy that.' She pushed him back on to the bed and started with his top button. She kissed his chest with a hundred small kisses, her lips brushing against his hair. With his bandaged hands he fumbled at the zip of her dress.

'I'll do it,' she said, and stood up and peeled off her black suit. Naked, she lay on top of him, sighing with pleasure at the sensual contrast of their bodies, her soft breasts pressing against his hard muscle. The tips of her fingers roamed over his chest and stomach and thighs, feeling the contours of his athletic body. She slithered down his torso, kissing him every inch of the way. Archie closed his eyes and drifted into a stratosphere of pure pleasure, until he could stand it no longer; in one abrupt movement he rolled Madeleine over and pushed himself into her, looking down at her beautiful face; she was smiling.

They showered and dressed, and while Madeleine made telephone calls Archie went to the barber. By lunchtime he felt a new man, walking arm in arm with Madeleine down the Avenue Victor Hugo. The beard was gone, his hair had been washed and cut, his clothes were clean, so were the bandages on his hands. It felt so good to be back in Paris, even though the skies were grey and he could feel rain spitting through the damp air.

Archie had forgotten about Christmas but in Paris the shop windows were filled with festive decorations and he realized with a shock that it was already 20 December. For the first time in weeks Archie thought of his parents, his self-educated father with a passion for Gothic architecture who had spent twenty years in local government and was now retired, living in Winchester in the shadow of the cathedral and planning a book on tombstone effigies in British churches; and his mother, a history teacher and specialist on Roman Britain. They had scraped and saved for their son, giving him everything, and he loved them. He would buy them presents right here in Paris; a Hermès tie for his father and for his mother the latest Dior scent. He turned to Madeleine. 'What do you want for Christmas?'

'I don't want to think about Christmas,' she laughed. 'Our job isn't finished. I've booked you and Harry on the five fifteen to London. Hewitt will meet you at Heathrow. He can't wait to see the Titian. Nor can I.'

Early that afternoon Commissaire Husson walked briskly into her office wearing her smartest Chanel suit, followed by Archie. Lamartine sat behind his desk.

'Where is it?' Madeleine said, glancing round the room.

'Madame le Commissaire. I contacted the President's office and suggested this painting be taken into safe custody.'

'You did *what?*'

'A painting by Titian of Marie Stuart, Queen of France, is part of the patrimony of this country. I'm happy to say the President's office agreed.'

Archie's instinct was to leap forward and throttle the desk-bound bastard; but he hadn't survived Japan to stumble at the last fence and be hauled into a French jail for assaulting a police officer. Instead, between gritted teeth, he said, 'Where is the Titian?'

'Safe.'

Madeleine eyed Lamartine coolly. Part of her was not surprised. She had never really trusted him, and now he had betrayed her, hoping, no doubt, for spectacular promotion. But she was a match for him, as he was about to find out.

'You will tell me exactly where it is,' Madeleine ordered.

'It's where it should be. At the Louvre.'

'Those were not my instructions, Pierre. You're in breach of your duty as a police officer and, make no mistake, there will be a disciplinary enquiry at the highest level.'

'We shall see,' Lamartine said, almost in a whisper.

'How dare you!' Madeleine replied, her black eyes flashing.

It was mid-afternoon before she tracked down the Titian in the Louvre laboratories where, for the past four hours, it had been in the safe custody of Professor Barre. He did not seem particularly surprised to see her, or her colleague Mr Gibbs.

'I must congratulate you,' Professor Barre said to Archie. 'You've carried out a very thorough surface clean with no damage to the paint. For a man of your inexperience I find that quite remarkable.'

For several long minutes Madeleine stood in wonder in front of the painting before turning to the Professor. 'I'm sorry to tell you —' she began.

'I know, I know,' the Professor interrupted. 'The painting isn't ours to keep. But I have basked in the genius of Titian, enjoying the exquisite company of this beautiful woman for several hours. I am eternally grateful to you.'

'The painting is the property of Her Majesty the Queen, stolen from the Royal Baggage Train in October,' Madeleine explained. 'The traces of sixteenth-century pigment which you found at the time will match the paint on this canvas. Mr Gibbs and Mr Wardington here, whose father is Director of the Royal Collection, will take the painting back to London tonight. My deputy, Lamartine, was not in possession of all the facts. He overreached himself. I apologize.'

'On the contrary, please tell him I am eternally grateful. The Queen is very fortunate. Perhaps at some future date she will send us the picture on loan. Mr Wardington, please mention this to your father. France would like to pay its respects to Marie Stuart.'

That evening Madeleine gave an exclusive interview to the

art correspondent of *Le Monde*. She was economical with the truth but it made a good enough story and hit the headlines of the paper the next morning; more important, it made a second double-cross from the President's office impossible.

At Heathrow, Archie and Harry were met on the tarmac by Chief Inspector Hewitt. They drove straight to Windsor, where Detective Inspector Burns and Sir William Wardington were waiting. Archie placed the Titian on an easel in the middle of the Print Room.

'I have to sit down,' Sir William said. 'The emotion is too much for me. This painting is exquisite!'

Harry smiled at his father's rapture; he was standing by the lattice window looking down on the deer which moved slowly across the Great Park. The trees were black skeletons against a grey sky. It was good to be home: he liked the bleakness of an English winter.

Archie told the story of the Titian from beginning to end.

When he had finished, Sir William said, 'Do you really think it's possible Dicky Sulgrave's an art thief? I find the idea incredible. The man is one of us!'

'He's a crook,' Archie said emphatically, 'but the difficulty is proving it. As far as the Titian's concerned, he's bound to argue that he first clapped eyes on it in Japan and that he was invited to Hakomoto's villa in Hokkaido to give his expert opinion.'

'What about the Augustus John?' Harry said. 'He can't say he'd never seen his mother-in-law before.'

'No. But what he can say is that he stole from his wife because he needed the money, and hope she won't press charges. She hates him; the question is, how much? And anyway, the forgery of one painting is a minor charge given the extent of his criminal activity.'

'And Flora?' Sir Williams said. 'You think he – '

'Killed her. Yes,' said Archie, 'but again we can't prove it.'

'You mean he'll get away scot-free?' Sir William said desperately, looking first at Archie then Hewitt.

'Not bloody likely,' said Hewitt. 'This man is the Blond Maniac, and he's going down, if it's the last conviction I get. Maybe we can't prove he nicked those other blondes, and he's hardly likely to confess to murdering the girl, but if you ask me, once he's under the spotlight he'll crack. I don't agree with Archie; stealing to order and forgery isn't a bad start. We know for a fact he cheated his wife, took her Augustus John and replaced it with a fake. The original painting was recovered in Japan in the house of his client, Seiji Hakomoto. Let's see his lordship wriggle out of that one.'

'And Hakomoto?' Harry said. 'What about him?'

'Of course it's up to the Japanese,' Hewitt said, 'but with Archie as the chief witness for the prosecution they can put together a pretty good case. Ex-Oliver Dashwood can tell them all about the secret gallery, and what's more he personally walked away with five stolen paintings. That's pretty hard evidence. Of course, Hakomoto's bound to say he bought the paintings in good faith, but then he has to explain where he got them and how much he paid for them, and that won't be so easy.'

'Can we really count on the Japanese to prosecute?' Harry said, 'They're famous for brushing this sort of thing under the carpet.'

'Look,' said Hewitt. 'If the Japanese police let Hakomoto off the hook they'll have all hell to pay from the French, who want his head on a plate. They know now that a hefty percentage of Impressionist pictures stolen from French museums ended up in Hakomoto's secret collection. What's more, they're convinced he's the man behind the royal hijacking, responsible for the death of two of their gendarmes.'

'As far as the Queen's concerned,' Harry said jauntily, 'it's a double whammy. She's recovered a painting she never knew she had.'

'You're absolutely right,' Sir William said, 'and it seems to me we owe a huge debt to Commissaire Husson. I shall recommend her for an award. You too, Archie. Don't you agree, Detective Inspector?'

'Whatever you say, sir,' Burns said, glaring at Archie.

'There's still one unsolved mystery,' Sir William went on. 'Why was the Titian hidden behind the Honthorst in the first place?'

'I'm sure Flora knew,' Archie said. 'She was such a fanatic about research.'

'We've been through all her personal papers with a fine-toothed comb. There's nothing,' Burns said flatly.

At 6 p.m. the meeting broke up and everyone went in a different direction – Sir William to his grace-and-favour flat in the Windsor cloisters, Harry to his London flat and Burns to Scotland Yard. Archie stayed behind in the Print Room. It was a starless night and the Keep was floodlit. He savoured the winter stillness and sat at Flora's desk, remembering her. It made him sick to think that Sulgrave, who had killed her, might get away with it. And even if he was convicted for theft and forgery, what would he get? A fine? The man was a murderer and should be sent down for life.

He wandered next door into the reference library with its two thousand volumes and without thinking picked out a book on Venetian painters and took it back to Flora's desk. Veronese had never moved him, Tintoretto neither until he'd been bowled over by his massive crucifixion in Scuola Grande di San Rocco in Venice. He thumbed through the book; Carpaccio, Bellini, Titian, what a galaxy of stars, he thought. He lifted the book to close it when a small plastic folder fell on to the desk. Inside was a letter on brittle brown paper, obviously several centuries old, written in a neat italic hand in Latin. With it, scribbled in pencil on a lined sheet of paper, was a rough translation in English in what Archie recognized at once to be Flora's handwriting. Archie went over to the internal telephone and called Sir William Wardington.

Sir William hurried back to the Print Room where he put on a pair of white gauze gloves and spread the fragile paper on the green baize table. He didn't refer to the rough translation, nor did he need a Latin dictionary. He translated the text without effort.

'I, John Cameron of Scottas in Knoydart, Clerk of the Closet to his late Majesty Charles Stuart, anointed King of Scotland, England and Ireland am ordered by my Lord Steward at the Palace of Holyroodhouse to do away with and destroy by fire this painted image of her late Catholic Majesty Mary Stuart Queen of Scotland, and rightful Queen of England and Ireland, this burning to be achieved by nightfall this day before the arrival of my Lord of Argyle and the Lords Commissioners charged to recognize, record and confiscate all personal effects of his late Majesty the King.

'To protect the sacred memory of Mary Queen of France and Queen of Scotland so treacherously slain by the excommunicant bastard Elizabeth, usurper of the throne of England and Ireland, I hide this image behind that of his Grace of Buckingham. I pray to God that this my stratagem and endeavour will preserve the beauteous image of the Martyr Queen, Grandmother of the Martyr King, Charles.

'John Cameron of Scottas in Knoydart, S. J. Twelfth day of March 1649.

'Fascinating,' Sir William said, straightening up, his whole face elated. 'See the signature, that is most significant. Cameron was a member of the Society of Jesus – a Jesuit priest. We know there were several disguised priests in Charles I's household in

Scotland and England, probably brought in by his wife, Queen Henrietta Maria, who was a practising Catholic. All the same, this good man, Father Cameron, was running a terrible risk hiding this portrait. Many of the Scots were violently anti-Catholic, particularly in Edinburgh where they fell under the spell of John Knox. Father Cameron could have gone to the stake on two counts, for disobeying the orders of the Lords Commissioners, and for being a Catholic priest. What a debt we owe to this man!'

Sir William picked up Flora's rough translation. 'If only she'd trusted me,' he murmured.

In Chief Inspector Paul Hewitt's office at Scotland Yard the telephone rang for the fifth time in less than five minutes. Edgar took the call.

'It's *The Times*,' he said, covering the receiver.

'Give them the usual spiel,' said Hewitt.

'Yes, that's right, we have had a big haul of stolen art, including a Titian belonging to the Queen. Found in Japan, that is correct. No details have been released yet, I'm afraid. No, I can't tell you any more. Yes, the owners have been told. Yes, yes, including the Queen. They're all delighted. Wouldn't you be?'

All except for Cordelia Sulgrave, who had said nothing when Hewitt broke the news to her on the telephone. Hewitt then asked if it would be convenient for him to call.

'Come at seven this evening,' she had said. 'And bring Mr Gibbs.'

Hewitt was leaving his office when he was summoned upstairs to see the Chief Commissioner. He found Sir George Nayland sitting behind his desk on the fifteenth floor of Scotland Yard with a signed photograph of the Queen on the wall.

'Well done, Hewitt. Your department has taken a hammering recently, and this will stop a lot of people talking.'

'Oh?' said Hewitt. 'And what are they saying?'

Eager Edgar was sitting in the chair next to him, his hat on his knees, under strict orders from Hewitt to say nothing.

'Mickey Mouse organization, that sort of thing.'

Hewitt leant forward and spoke with feeling. 'Give us the tools to do the job, sir. What we need is a state-of-the-art optical computer so we can build up an international register of stolen art. At the moment we rely on private enterprise like *Trace* magazine and the Art Loss Register. We need a database that's exclusive to police forces throughout Britain and until we get it we're working with our hands tied behind our backs, sir.'

'I'll do what I can, Hewitt.'

They took the lift down to the seventh floor. Edgar said, 'That was quite a little speech, Chief. I was most impressed. And I thought you didn't give a toss.'

'We're the flavour of the month, thanks to Gibbs. If we want something, now's the time to ask for it.'

'All the same, you could have knocked me down with a feather.'

'Where did you find it?' Cordelia Sulgrave said, pouring herself a large whisky and staring at the Augustus John portrait of her mother. Hewitt was standing by the window in her elegant drawing room overlooking the garden, watching a thrush hop between patches of snow. Nelson lay contentedly in front of the crackling fire.

'Japan,' Hewitt answered.

'Really? I'll get the other one, I stuck it in the loo, and we can compare the two.'

She walked unsteadily out of the room and came back with

the fake. At that moment a key turned in the lock and Dicky Sulgrave came into the drawing room, unwinding a silk scarf from around his neck; there were flecks of snow on his cashmere coat.

'Darling,' said Cordelia, 'you'll never believe this but Mummy turned up in Japan of all places!'

'How extraordinary,' Dicky said. Nelson was on his feet growling.

'What is that dog doing here? I won't have him in this flat, Cordelia, you know that.'

'This morning when I left Yattendon he looked at me so sadly. I just couldn't leave you behind, could I?' she said, patting the dog's head.

'Good evening, Chief Inspector,' Dicky said, collecting himself. He shook hands first with Hewitt, then with Edgar and finally with Archie. He even managed a smile as he ordered himself to stay calm, lie, bluff it out; they had no hard evidence. But he felt the palms of his hands go cold.

There was something familiar about Gibbs, Dicky thought as he scrutinized Archie's face. Hewitt laid out the Augustus John from Japan and laid it beside the fake.

'It's a remarkbly good copy,' the Earl conceded. 'It would fool most people.'

Cordelia said nothing, which surprised Archie since she was normally so outspoken. He watched her as she went over to a drinks cupboard to get another bottle of whisky; she left the door ajar then turned round to Nelson, who had been padding behind her.

'Do your stuff, then,' she said.

The dog stared at the cupboard, wagging its tail, then it sauntered forward and with its nose closed the door.

'You can close all sorts of doors, can't you, my pettikins? Front doors and back doors, even a car door although you couldn't quite slam it shut, could you? But the heavy door to my safe, on those easy-peasy hinges, that was no problem, was it? You gave it just the tiniest shove. Who's the cleverest dog in the whole wide world?' And Cordelia crouched in front of the labrador and pressed her nose against his.

Dicky turned away in disgust and stood at the window with his back to them all, staring at the snowflakes drifting down. What was it about Gibbs? His voice. Where had he heard that voice?

'Lord Sulgrave,' said Hewitt, 'this painting was found in the Japanese home of a friend of yours, Seiji Hakomoto.'

Dicky swivelled round. So the British police had been comparing notes with the French; or had the Japanese girl talked? Or Wardington perhaps? Harry had recognized the Augustus John, damn him. They were putting two and two together, tightening the net. Careful what you say.

'I know Mr Hakomoto,' Dicky admitted.

'He had this painting on his wall in his villa in Hokkaido and you were staying with him.'

'Did he? I'm afraid I don't remember.'

'Harry Wardington remembers,' Hewitt said. Dicky went sheet-white. That's enough, Hewitt decided; keep the rest for later. The man is scared witless; let him stew and the first cracks will appear.

'You know, Chief Inspector,' Cordelia drawled, 'my husband is right. This copy would fool most people, and I'm wondering if it didn't fool me.'

'I don't follow you, Lady Sulgrave,' Hewitt said cautiously.

'Now that I see them side by side I'm not sure any more. Perhaps we've been living with a copy for all these years. Perhaps the painting was swapped years ago, before I was born. Who knows? I couldn't possibly cross my heart and hope to die, that this,' and she pointed to the fake, 'was not the painting which hung on my drawing-room wall. Oh dear, does that complicate things?'

It blows the whole case against Sulgrave out of the water, Archie thought. What in God's name is she playing at?

'That's not what you said to me last time we met,' Archie said curtly. 'You were one hundred per cent sure this was a fake.'

'Was I? Then I've changed my mind, Mr Gibbs. A woman's prerogative.'

Right, thought Hewitt, the gloves are off. We can all play silly buggers if we want to.

'It's not just a matter of the Augustus John, Lady Sulgrave. Seiji Hakomoto was receiving large quantities of stolen paintings, many of them from this country. I must warn you, Lord Sulgrave, I shall be conducting a detailed enquiry into your business affairs on suspicion of conspiracy to handle stolen art.'

'You may find it rather difficult to get a court order, Chief Inspector,' Dicky said evenly. 'It seems to me your evidence is wholly circumstantial.'

'I don't think so.'

'Really, Chief Inspector, you're barking up the wrong tree,' Dicky said with a brittle laugh, racking his brains as to what, if any, incriminating evidence he kept in his office. The police would find nothing, he decided with immense relief; everything to do with Hakomoto was in the Banque Weber in Switzerland. All the same, his palms felt like ice and the nausea was rising in his throat. Keep calm, he told himself; ride out the storm, you're in the eye of the hurricane. He glanced at Cordelia and felt the usual loathing. At the same time, he was puzzled; why had she saved him? What did she want?

Dicky walked over to the drawing-room window, breathed deeply and pulled back the curtain. Millions of tiny white flakes were tumbling through the night air, settling on the garden in a soft white blanket; he felt soothed by the silent snow and turned round. His eye fell on Archie. Why did he find this man so disturbing? His voice was familiar, so was his smile. In a moment of blinding clarity he realized this man was Oliver Dashwood. Dicky's jaw dropped.

'Is anything the matter?' Cordelia said.

'Nothing at all,' Dicky said, turning back to the falling snow.

Chapter 33

The invitation lay on Archie's desk, unmistakably large, headed with the Royal Arms, edged in gold and printed in sweeping italic.

THE LORD CHAMBERLAIN IS COMMANDED
TO INVITE
MAJOR ARCHIBALD GIBBS
TO ATTEND THE UNVEILING BY
HER MAJESTY
OF THE RECENTLY DISCOVERED TITIAN PORTRAIT
OF MARY STUART, QUEEN OF FRANCE AND LATER
QUEEN OF SCOTS, IN THE QUEEN'S GALLERY
AT BUCKINGHAM PALACE
ON 30 JANUARY AT 6.30 p.m.

Harry Wardington rang Archie's doorbell at 6 p.m. and told his friend to get a move on.

'You look disgustingly healthy,' Harry said, eyeing Archie's Caribbean suntan.

'How was New Year?' Archie countered, taking a brush to his dark suit.

'I couldn't believe how much French Yuji had learnt in a couple of weeks. And Minako was smiling from morning till night. She can't believe she's free; and the village people are so kind to her, and no one cares if she married Yuji's father or not.'

'Wedding bells?'

'Will you get a move on? We're late.'

The Queen's Gallery was housed in a wing of Buckingham

266

Palace. The taxi took the direct route down Constitution Hill. As it swung round the side of the Palace by the tall iron railings a large crowd of press had gathered. As soon as Archie got out of the taxi, cameras flashed.

'Give us a smile, Archie,' someone yelled out.

'Is it true you're getting a knighthood?' another voice shouted.

At the entrance to the Queen's Gallery they were stopped by a member of the Palace staff dressed in the Royal livery who discreetly ticked their names off on a printed list; so did Detective Inspector Burns, who stood behind holding his copy of the guest list. Archie savoured the moment.

The art world was there in force, Archie thought as he entered the large, nondescript rooms and noticed Neil Mac-Gregor, Director of the National Gallery, talking to Nick Serota, head of the Tate. Lord Rothschild, patron and collector, was paying court to Lady Annunziata Asquith, 'the thinking man's dream' according to the gossip columnists, an art dealer and one of the most beautiful women in London with luminous blue eyes and an exquisite figure. Archie spotted several top art dealers; Johnny van Haeften was laughing with his old friend Michael Goedhuis, both Hollanders who had never learnt Dutch; Julian Agnew was locked in earnest conversation with Anthony Spink. Chief Inspector Hewitt was, for once, a guest – Archie had wangled him an invitation – and he was talking to Alan Bradford, the top picture restorer in England, who'd dropped everything at Sir William's request and spent the last three weeks working day and night on the Titian. Bradford had done a magnificent job and Archie told him so.

The painting, which hung in the middle of the main wall, was hidden by a dark-blue velvet curtain. An equerry dressed in the navy blue and white full-dress uniform of the 17/21 Lancers called Archie over.

'Major Gibbs, you are part of the group to be introduced to the Queen. There is no formality or receiving line but you, Commissaire Husson and Mr Wardington should stand in the group to the left of the Titian. Her Majesty will enter through the side door, followed by her Private Secretary and members of the Royal Household including Sir William Wardington, who will say a few words before the Queen unveils the painting.'

Madeleine arrived with the French Ambassador. Archie noticed at once that she had cut her hair, and the short black dress with padded shoulders was new, probably Yves Saint Laurent, cut low to show off her deep suntan.

A hush fell as the Queen entered the Gallery followed by the French Ambassador and a troupe of courtiers. Madeleine was brought over to be formally presented; she curtsied.

'Commissaire Husson,' said the Queen. 'Once again please accept my thanks for all that you have done, and I'm so pleased the President of France has allowed you to become a member of the Royal Victorian Order.'

'Thank you, Your Majesty. But without Major Gibbs we should not have succeeded.'

'Major Gibbs,' the Queen said, turning to Archie, 'we're greatly in your debt.'

The introductions over, Sir William asked the Queen's permission to make a short speech.

'Your Majesty, Your Excellency, Commissioner, Ladies and Gentlemen, in a few moments Her Majesty will unveil the latest addition to the Royal Collection. I use the word "addition" advisedly because we have not acquired this portrait; it has been ours all along, part of the Royal Collection for over three hundred years but we didn't know of its existence. It was the best-kept secret in Britain.

'As you will see in a moment, it is a portrait of outstanding beauty by that master of the human face, Titian. His subject?

Mary Stuart, Queen of France, Queen of Scots and claimant to the thrones of England and Ireland. Titian painted this portrait in 1560 when Mary was Queen of France, the eighteen-year-old wife of Francis II. When Mary became Queen of Scots and left France for Scotland she took the portrait with her to Holyroodhouse, where it remained after her death. It came by descent to King Charles I, and was catalogued along with the rest of his magnificent collection in 1635, and indeed it was recognized at once as a masterpiece. We have letters to that effect. But after the death of King Charles I the picture disappeared. It is not recorded in the dispersion of the King's collection organized by Cromwell. All the same, it vanished, and until today we did not know why or how.'

A ripple of excitement ran through the Gallery. People edged forward to be closer to Sir William, and to hear his every word.

'In fact it didn't vanish at all. It stayed right where it was, in Holyroodhouse, but was carefully placed behind a portrait of the Duke of Buckingham by Geritt van Honthorst. Why? At the time, and remember these were the months following the death of King Charles I, a wave of anti-Catholic feeling spread throughout England and Scotland. The Lords Commissioners ordered Catholic effigies to be burnt left, right and centre. The Puritans destroyed paintings and statues in churches and public buildings throughout the country. It was a sort of cultural revolution. This painting was at the top of their list to be destroyed. And the man who saved it was John Cameron of Scottas in Knoydart, Clerk of the Closet to King Charles in Scotland. He was a Catholic and a Jesuit, and instead of obeying his instructions to burn the picture he hid it in the most ingenious place, inside a deep seventeenth-century frame, behind another canvas.

'As I am sure you all know, the Honthorst, and more important the Titian, was stolen from the Royal Baggage Train on its way to Paris. Two French gendarmes died in this vicious attack and we all hope it won't be long before those responsible are brought to justice. Meanwhile, thanks to the magnificent efforts of the French police under the direction of Commissaire Husson, who is with us this evening, and to Major Gibbs, the security co-ordinator, the painting has been recovered. In recognition of their outstanding services Her Majesty will be making both of them companions of the Royal Victorian Order.'

There was a general round of applause; only Burns didn't clap.

Sir William went on, 'To commemorate the discovery of this great work, Her Majesty has graciously agreed to lend the picture to the National Gallery for one year, and for a further year to the Louvre. And now, Your Majesty, we should all be honoured if you would unveil the portrait.'

The Queen pulled on the tassel and the dark-blue velvet curtain fell away. There was a gasp of admiration; Titian's Mary Stuart, Queen of France and of Scots, radiated a powerful, sensuous beauty. People crowded forward to get a closer look at the burnished gold hair, the ivory skin and the enigmatic smile. This was Flora's moment of triumph, Archie thought sadly.

Brusquely a side door swung open and an army of footmen in Buckingham Palace livery swept into the Queen's Gallery carrying large circular silver trays with glasses of wine, champagne and spirits. The party had begun.

That evening the French Ambassador gave a dinner at the Embassy in Madeleine's honour. Archie sat on her right.

'We've got to nail Sulgrave,' he muttered, stirring his black coffee, 'and the place to do it is Paris. I'm coming with you on the early flight to pay a little visit to the Baroness von Arnim.'

*

Lotti von Arnim had been riding in the Bois de Boulogne and looked large and handsome in her well-cut jacket, jodhpurs, and black leather riding boots. Still holding a crop, she received Archie and Madeleine in her drawing room in Avenue Foch, where the yellow lacquered walls were hung with aggressive paintings by Beuys.

'I've nothing else to add to my initial statement,' she said, smiling. 'I'm so sorry I can't help.'

'If you have no objection, I should like to interview your staff,' Madeleine said.

For a moment the Baroness looked anxious, then she smiled, tapping the crop lightly in the palm of her hand.

'Please, feel free. Would you like to use the library?'

Surrounded by leather-bound sets of Goethe and Schiller, Madeleine summoned the cook, a large, smiling woman from Provence who lived in a bed-sitting room by the kitchen. Madeleine explained she was interested in the evening of 10 October last year. The cook thumbed through her old diary and shook her head, muttering that she wore ear plugs at night and a bomb could go off and she wouldn't hear a thing. The chauffeur, smartly dressed in a black uniform, lived out, in a flat in Nanterre. He remembered driving the Baroness and the Earl of Sulgrave to the British Embassy for the opening, and then he'd been dismissed.

Alone with Madeleine in the Baroness's library, Archie brought a clenched fist down on to the desk. 'The answer is here, in this house. Who else can we talk to?'

'Only the daily, but she doesn't live in.'

'Let's see her.'

Jeanne, who wore a neat white apron and cap, told them the 10th of October was her mother's birthday and she'd taken the day off and driven out to Versailles with her where they'd eaten

271

a very expensive lunch. It was a pity Suzanne couldn't join them, but she was doing something for Madame la Baronne.

'Suzanne?' Archie said.

'The Baroness's maid, Suzanne Mott. She got the sack last week. I'm surprised she stayed as long as she did; they didn't get on.'

Suzanne Mott lived in a tenement block near the Porte de St Cloud. At 7 p.m. Madeleine and Archie drove up in an unmarked police car. Suzanne was the other side of fifty, with an angular but kind face; she looked carefully at Madeleine's identity card before allowing her into the small, neat flat.

Yes, she remembered the evening of 10 October very well. Madame la Baronne had made a dreadful fuss about the state of her dress for the party at the British Embassy, saying it hadn't been cleaned properly, and she got the lining caught in the zip and, as usual, Suzanne was blamed. Madame la Baronne had a house guest, an English aristocrat whom she called 'Milord'. He was very charming and that evening he escorted the Baroness to the party. They didn't stay out very late; in fact, Suzanne saw them come home, it must have been about 11 p.m.; she was in the kitchen at the time making a cup of Ovaltine. On the video security machine she saw the couple kissing. They went into the Baroness's bedroom and shut the door.

The Ovaltine didn't work; Suzanne still couldn't sleep, hardly surprising after all those dreadful things the Baroness had said. At 1 a.m. she went back to the kitchen to get herself a glass of cold Evian from the fridge. This time on the security camera she caught sight of Milord leaving the flat.

'We've got him,' Archie murmured as they walked back to the police car. 'What's more we've got him on videotape.'

The following morning Madeleine and Archie called on the Baroness with a search warrant and took the tape from the video security camera. Madeleine told the Baroness she would be charged with misleading the police, which could lead to a prison sentence; however, if she co-operated they might find ways to mitigate the sentence, even drop the charge altogether, depending on how helpful she was. The Baroness crumbled; there were tears followed by a stiff whisky as she explained that Dicky had asked her, as a favour, to tell the police they'd spent the night together. He had said it was all to do with an attempted theft inside the exhibition tent which had nothing to do with him, of course, but all the same he didn't want to be pestered by a lot of questions. So, she had agreed to help him out. Her statement was very nearly true; they had spent part of the night together, making love, then he'd gone back to his room. He said he wanted to read. She thought it was a little unromantic, but she put it down to English eccentricity. He left her bed just before 1 a.m. She slept soundly until the next morning.

'Thank you, Baroness von Arnim,' Madeleine said. 'I shall be calling on you as a witness. You will not leave the country without telling my office.'

'Dicky wouldn't hurt a fly,' the Baroness said, blowing her nose. 'What's he supposed to have done?'

'You'll find out soon enough,' Madeleine said.

As soon as Madeleine and Archie had left, the Baroness reached for the telephone.

Dicky was in Scotland, at Redgorton. He'd been out walking on the moors and felt exhilarated by the clear, February air, the wind biting into his face, the moody clouds scudding across the sky. The house stood magnificent on a hill above the Tay. From a distance you'd never know it was a hotel. Only when you got closer did you see the dreadful signs, Car Park, and Entrance, and Keep Off the Grass.

As he walked through a side door into his small flat, the telephone was ringing. It was Lotti von Armin who told him about her interview with Commissaire Husson; Dicky put the

273

telephone down, stunned. Those bastards were out for his blood, but they hadn't got him yet. He could see his way out of this unholy mess. He would tell the police the following: all right, so he'd lied about Flora. She had begged to see him and they had met up after dinner that night when he told her once again the affair was over. She'd cried and thrown herself into his arms and said she couldn't live without him; it was the same, desperate language of that unfinished letter he'd been shown by the police. She refused to go back to her hotel so he'd left her on the bridge, weeping. He would have come clean and explained all this at the enquiry, but he was completely thrown by the news that Flora was dead; he was the last person to see her alive and he knew that he would be suspected of killing her; so he lied. And the Titian? He'd never seen it before Japan. Hakomoto wanted an expert opinion and called him in. This was his story and he would stick to it. If he kept his nerve he'd get off; they didn't have the evidence to convict him.

Dicky reached for the malt whisky and changed his mind; he felt like vodka.

'Darling, you look as white as a sheet,' said Cordelia, coming into the small sitting room, taking off the scarf around her head.

'Where's the bloody vodka?' Dicky said irritably, searching the drinks tray. Nelson padded softly into the room, saw Dicky and growled.

'In the game freezer,' Cordelia said, smiling at the dog, 'where else?'

Of course, Dicky thought, that's where she keeps it, the old soak. He hurried out of the room, down a passage to a steel door. He pulled back the handle and the door swung smoothly on its hinges. Dicky stepped inside the small, freezing room. You couldn't open the door from the inside, so he reminded himself to be careful and keep the door open wide. He turned on the light and ducked beneath rows of lamb, beef, pheasant

Painted Lady

and carcasses of venison. Nothing was his any more, he cursed; he even had to share the game freezer with the blasted hotel.

Cordelia stood at the far end of the passage stroking the labrador. They'd been for a long walk by the glen and Nelson had chased a rabbit down a hole and was covered in mud. Cordelia crouched beside him. 'Do your stuff,' she whispered to the dog, who padded forward towards the open door and with wet and muddy nose pushed, and pushed again and the door swung shut. Nelson turned his head slowly and looked at her.

'Good boy,' Cordelia whispered. Back in the flat she gave the dog a biscuit. It was off season, Cordelia thought, and the hotel was down to a skeleton staff; with luck it would be a long time before anyone found Dicky.

An hour or so later the Countess of Sulgrave went up to the front desk of Redgorton Castle Hotel and asked the receptionist if anyone had seen her husband, explaining that he'd gone out for a walk on the moors and said he would be back for lunch but he hadn't come home. Later that afternoon she went out looking for him herself; by nightfall she called the police who, at first light the next morning, carried out a helicopter search but found nothing.

The next day Chief Inspector Hewitt, accompanied by a member of the local police, arrived at Redgorton Castle shortly after 2 p.m. He found Cordelia Sulgrave chain-smoking and drinking whisky.

'I've got a warrant issued in England for your husband's arrest,' Hewitt said. 'The French police are charging him with the murder of Flora Fenton.'

Her eyes widened at the word 'murder'. 'Perhaps he's done a bunk,' she said. 'I wouldn't put it past him.'

At 2.15 p.m. Constable McLean from Redgorton village opened the game freezer and found the frozen body of the Earl

275

of Sulgrave. There were no suspicious fingerprints on the outside of the door but forensic experts found traces of mud and saliva which matched those of the labrador, Nelson. In her statement, Cordelia Sulgrave said she'd come back from a walk with her dog, opened her front door and let the dog in, then caught sight of the gardener and gone out again to ask him about cutting back the roses. The dog must have been alone in the house for a good ten minutes. By the time she came inside, there was no sign of her husband.

Hakomoto was sitting cross-legged in the sitting room of his Tokyo house, staring out at his Zen garden. The gravel, raked into sweeping lines, seemed to flow like water either side of the boulders; he would ride this spirit of eternity, back to his Samurai past, and forward into the next world. Beside him on the floor was the ceremonial sword which had been defiled by the Englishman.

That morning an unexpected visitor had called at his house, Serge Noailles, the French Head of Station, who told him that the Earl of Sulgrave had been charged with the murder of Flora Fenton.

'Why are you telling me this?' Hakomoto had said.

'We thought you ought to know.'

Sulgrave was a man of straw and Hakomoto felt sure it was only a matter of time before the flabby, weak-minded Earl told the police everything. His own position was not good. The French police were pressing the Swiss for a court order to freeze his account at the Banque Weber in Geneva, and sequester his works of art which he kept in the bank vault. Several of the crates contained stolen pictures.

It would be foolish to hope against hope, Seiji Hakomoto

276

thought. He prided himself on being a man who was not afraid of his own fate, whatever it might be. What he did fear was the sort of humiliation suffered by his father who had been refused the right to die in dignity.

Hakomoto opened his kimono, baring his white chest, and reached for the sword.

The coroner of the Minako-ku district in Tokyo had never seen a death by ritual suicide and he was impressed by the depth of the incisions and the violent tearing of the flesh. It reminded him of Japanese painting; once begun there was no going back.

As Madeleine pointed out, it could have been a very different story if Hakomoto had known that Dicky was already dead.

It was the ides of March and gusts of wind whipped up sodden dead leaves in the gardens of London. Madeleine and Archie walked arm in arm across Kensington Gardens, past the Albert Memorial still boxed in scaffolding, exchanging information, buffeted by a blustery wind.

Archie told Madeleine about his trip to Birmingham the day before, to see Flora's father, John Fenton. They had spent a couple of hours together in the local pub and Archie had given him the official version of events.

'Accidental death, that's too good for him,' Fenton had said, wiping away a tear.

'Even so, it was a slow death.'

'May he rot in hell.'

For her part Madeleine told Archie the case would be kept open for the sake of the families of the dead gendarmes. Personally she doubted they would ever catch the Russian assassins.

Archie stopped walking and took her face in his hands. 'If

you and I got married . . .' He paused when he saw the alarm flashing though Madeleine's eyes, then finished his sentence. 'It would be a disaster.'

Relief spread across Madeleine's face.

'You career women are the kiss of death. It's all work and no play.'

Madeleine smiled her beautiful smile. 'I do love you, Archie.'

Archie had to see Cordelia Sulgrave one more time, to establish in his own mind, beyond a shadow of doubt, that what he thought had happened, had happened. He telephoned her.

She seemed glad to hear from him and immediately invited him round to the flat in Rutland Gate that evening at 6.30. As soon as Archie walked into the drawing room he realized something was different. Cordelia wasn't drinking. 'I'm on the wagon,' she said, inhaling on her cigarette. 'I thought I'd start a new life and all of that.'

'You look ten years younger already,' Archie said.

'I hear you've got a gong. Congratulations.'

'Thank you. About your husband's death —'

'They were going to arrest him for murder, as I'm sure you knew. Did he do it?'

'Yes.'

Cordelia blew a smoke ring. 'Rough justice, you might say.'

'You might, if you thought it was an accident.'

'Mr Gibbs, I don't like your tone.'

'You always said you'd kill him.'

'*Façon de parler*, Mr Gibbs. Anyway, Nelson got there first.'

Nelson padded softly across the room and rested his head in Archie's lap.